CU00341264

PERIL

JOSS STIRLING

FROST WOLF

For Lucy

And with thanks to the Peril Super-Team who gave me such helpful feedback:
Alexandra Aramburo, Tamara Ashton, Alejandra Barranco, Tia Barton, Charisse Baxter, Emma Bilson, Helen Blakemore, Emily Bown, Sammy Bredesen, Narda Calles, Amy Carroll, Vicki Cawley, Ellie Chapman, Katarzyna Chmaj, Lexie Chorlton, Alana Collins, Maddy Cozens, Rachel Cruz, Melissa Curtis, Rachel Denton, Rachael Doig, Catherine Evans, Jess Evans, Maud Grefte, Valeria Guerrero, Lisa Guest, Stephanie Gurman, Siobhan Hayes, Rosa Hernandez, Jodie Hicks, Mia Hoddell, Georgia House, Sarah Beth James, Nina Jansen, Ria Jones, Roisin Kelly, Dani King, Kata Kosztyi, Melisa Kumas, Rachel Langford, Laura Laszlo, Kirsty Ledger, Steph Lott, Chloe Madge, Estefi Mari, Ciara McGhie, Patricia Medina, Lilly Moore, Hannah Muir, Nina Mueller, Jime Murga, Andrea Navarete, Robin Newman, Sophie Nicholson, Megan Ord, Beth Paffey, Sarah Peters, Ana Maria Pirlea, Gracie Price, Greete Ratsep, Natalya Red, Alice Shaw, Nelly Silver, Katja Stout, Sarah Suttling, Helen Toovey, Molly Tunley, Giselle Turner, An-Sofie Valeemput, Andrea Valeri, Chelsea Van Gompel, Rheeba Van Niekerk, Marinka Van Wingerden, Emily Yates.

PROLOGUE

'There are gifts you do not want. Mine has marked me out to be hunted.

Now I am the last of my kind.

Because I see peril.'

Meri Marlowe, in her diary

MOUNT VERNON, *Washington D.C., fourteen years earlier*

THE LAST DAY Meri Marlowe saw her parents alive was spent at George Washington's home. The four-year-old Meri didn't know why they were there waiting in the heat to look at a bunch of old stuff. The big white house with the red roof lay at the end of the drive. Worse, it was also at the end of a slow moving line of people all wanting to enter. The day was humid and the queue snaked out into the sunshine. She had already decided the visit wasn't going to be worth it, even with the promise of an ice cream. Theo had managed to get out of coming by saying he had to catch up on his reading. Meri wished she had stayed behind with him because he would've allowed her to watch cartoons.

'Mom, do we have to?' Meri asked in a low voice, tugging at the hem of her mother's checked blouse.

Her mother brushed the top of Meri's head, moving her baseball cap to shade her eyes. 'Darling, you know this is your father's highlight of the tour. He came here at your age and he wants to share it with you. It'll be fun. Mount Vernon, George Washington's house. You know who George Washington was?'

Meri scanned the dusty ground for inspiration. Her teacher at kindergarten had talked about him the week before. 'He cut down a tree. A cherry tree.' It had seemed a terrible waste to her. Real cherries were red and sticky and tasted much nicer than cherry-flavoured candy. Mom had bought them some just yesterday and had taught her to spit out the stones. She'd managed to launch one and it hit Theo but he hadn't minded. He was good that way.

Her mother laughed. 'Yes, George Washington did cut down a tree—among other things.'

More facts tumbled out now Meri had got going. 'His face is on money too.' Meri was quite proud she could remember that. 'And he has funny hair.'

The lady in the queue behind them smiled at her mother. 'Isn't she a darling? They say the most direct things at that age.'

'How true.' Her mom knelt beside Meri and took out a dollar bill. 'He only has funny hair because it was fashionable when he lived. That was a long time ago.' Her long brown locks dangled around Meri, making a little sweet-smelling cave.

'I like your hair better.' Meri batted it, making it sway

like the bead curtain over their back door at home in California.

'Pleased to hear that, munchkin.'

A shadow fell over them. 'Two ice creams as ordered, ladies.' Dad held out the cones. 'You'd better be quick. They're already melting.'

By the time Meri had eaten hers, they were at the front of the line. Her mom wiped Meri's fingers with a wet tissue, ending up with a quick swipe of her mouth before Meri could duck. The lovely taste of strawberry was now spoiled with lemony soap.

'I don't know about you but I'm dying out here. Let's go inside.' Dad led them to a building where they could get out of the sun. An old lady sat on a low stage at the end doing some spinning like a witch from a fairytale. Meri couldn't decide if that meant she was a goodie or a baddie—it went both ways in the stories.

'Who's that?' she whispered.

'That's Martha Washington—well, someone pretending to be her,' said Dad. 'She's here to tell you about the house. Go on—you can ask her questions.' He pushed Meri gently forward.

Meri went and sat with the other children on the benches at the front while her parents took seats several rows behind. Martha was wearing a long flowery dress with a white collar and she had a puffy cap on her head. She seemed quite skilled at spinning, managing to talk and work the wheel at the same time, which Meri found much more interesting than what she was saying. As Martha's hands moved, Meri noticed that there was a glowing spiky line around her wrist. It was very pretty, a little like the cutout of a snowflake Meri had made last Christmas. It glowed faintly like the imprint you saw on your eyelids after staring at the

sun by mistake. Looking closer, Meri noticed that the edge
of a similar design was peeking out of the collar. Did that
mean the snowflakes went all the way from wrist to neck? If
so, that was awesome! They were such a pretty colour, somewhere between blue and green, but she had never been able
to describe it properly to anyone else as only she and her
parents saw that shade. Not even Theo or any of her friends.
They were colour-blind but Mom said it was rude to
mention it. Were skin patterns the fashion when Mr and
Mrs Washington were alive, like the funny hair? Did that
come before or after the dinosaurs? Meri sucked the end of
her ponytail. Things were very confusing.

Were any of the other grownups dressed in the skin
snowflakes, Meri wondered, taking a quick look around the
room. A guide wearing a short-sleeved shirt had just entered
with his tour party. He had the glowy squiggles but his were
a different shape, sort of all swirly like the ice-cream she'd
eaten. They lit up his face with the same special colour. Her
mom had told her the colour was called peril, but Meri
wasn't to mention it to her kindergarten teacher even
though it was all over the classroom, especially at the
painting table. And if she forgot and talked about it, Mom
told Meri she should say peril was all make-believe and that
she didn't really see it. That was confusing too as Mom
usually said not to lie.

'Now, do any of you children have any questions for me?'
asked the lady-pretending-to-be-Martha.

The four children either side of Meri were struck dumb
by being put on the spot. Meri wanted to raise her hand to
please the lady but didn't know what to ask.

'How about you, dear? You seem as though you have a
question.' Martha was looking directly at her.

'Me?' Meri wriggled in her seat.

Martha nodded.

'I...um....' She wasn't going to mention the colour but she did wonder about the pretty pictures, 'why have you got snowflakes on you?'

Martha's expression went from a kindly smile to the round-eyed shock. Meri knew that face: her parents made it when she blurted out something she shouldn't in front of strangers. Most of the adults behind her, however, laughed indulgently. The freckle-faced boy next to her elbowed her in the ribs.

'They're not snowflakes, silly. They're flowers.'

After the briefest moment of gaping like a stranded fish, Martha gathered her wits. She jumped to her feet, yarn flying like one of Spider Man's webs. Searching frantically for the guide in the audience, she pointed at Meri.

'Jim, she can see them!'

But her parents were already either side of Meri and pulling her away. Dad lifted her into his arms and ran from the room.

'Hey, stop them!' The guide with the squiggles was running after them. The marks were blazing much brighter from his skin now even though they were out in the sunshine. Martha had pushed aside her spinning wheel and was chasing them, her white cap flapping like wings either side of her ears, peril-coloured light distorting her features so she now looked like a bird with a hooked beak. More people were joining the pursuit—the unsmiling man from the ticket office, a lady gardener with a wicked pair of shears. She was talking into a black thing on her shoulder. It was like the illustration in Meri's fairy-tale book of the people chasing the little Gingerbread Man.

'They want to eat us,' Meri sobbed.

The crowd outside didn't know how to react, making way for them as Dad bundled his family past.

'Does the little one need a doctor?' asked a woman, grabbing Dad's sleeve. 'I'm a nurse.'

'Keep back. They're terrorists!' shouted the guide, which immediately made the crowds run screaming from the three of them. Chaos ensued as children were gathered up, picnics abandoned, and shelter sought in house and outbuildings.

Paying no heed to Keep Off notices, Dad charged straight across a flowerbed and through a bush.

'Quickly, Naia! Why didn't we see?' panted her dad, sweat pouring from his brow.

Meri knew she'd done something bad—so bad her parents weren't even telling her off. She screwed up her face to hold in the tears. The gardens jolted by, a blur of hedges and summer flowers.

Dad next ignored a No Entry sign and ran right past the front of the big house, wide expanse of river to his left. Meri's hat jolted off. Not even missing a step, her mom snatched up the fallen cap and crammed it back on Meri's head, hiding her face from the pursuers.

'Where can we go, Blake? They'll have staked out the parking lot by now.'

Meri's dad had his really scared face on—the one he wore the time when Meri ran in front of a car. He glanced up at a signpost. 'Call Theo at the hotel. Tell him to look for Meri in the Pioneer Farm. That's where we're going.'

More jogging. Meri was feeling sick now. She heard her mother gabble out a message to their best friend, sprinkled with words like 'disaster', 'enemies' and 'immediately'.

'What did I do wrong, Daddy?' Meri sobbed as he

sprinted down a woodland path, feet skidding on the leaf mould.

'Nothing, darling. This is not your fault.' Her father hid her face against his chest as they took a shortcut through some trees. His shoes clonked on a wooden walkway and they entered into a stuffy, hay-scented barn. 'I just didn't expect today...stupid risk. It's our fault—not yours.'

But she knew that was a lie. She must've done something very bad.

'No, Blake, we can't leave her here!' protested her mom.

Panic bloomed, hot and ugly in Meri's tummy. 'I'll be good, I promise, Mommy. Don't leave me.'

'Hide under there.' Dad dumped her in a deep drift of hay near a tethered horse, a real big one that smelt horrible. Would it tread on her? Meri was sure it would. 'Don't move till Theo fetches you, got that? It's really important you do exactly what I say.'

Meri whimpered.

'You mustn't come out for anyone else, OK, darling? Not a peep, not a squeak.' He brushed a tear from her cheek.

'Please, Blake,' moaned her mom.

'What else do you suggest, Naia?' He sounded furious but Meri could tell he was mostly terrified. 'We can't draw them away fast enough if we're carrying her. We have to make them think she's somewhere else. We don't know how many Perilous there are hunting us.'

Mom looked so pale in the dim light of the barn. 'You're right, you're right, I know it but I just can't!'

Dad gripped Mom's shoulders and gave her a little shake. 'Then we all die. At least this way we all have a chance at living.'

Mom sank to her knees on the hay and gathered Meri into her arms. 'Be brave, Meri. Do as your Dad said and wait for Theo. Remember, precious, we love you more than anything.'

Dad ran to the door, picking up an ancient rake. 'Naia, they're coming!'

'We love you, sweetheart, so much!'

'We're doing this for her. You've got to leave her. Into the woods. Here, cradle this sack and make it look like we still have her. Put the hat on it.'

Meri felt her mother's hot fingers pull from hers. 'Mommy!'

'If you love us, you'll be quiet,' warned Dad.

Meri zipped up her lips, not even whimpering as more hay was piled on her head.

'Be safe, little one.'

Prickly and hot under the stalks, Meri listened so hard it felt like her ears were humming. There was the sound of footsteps running away, then silence. The horse shifted its hooves in the heat. Then came the babble of many people approaching, all speaking a foreign language. The barn echoed with too many feet on the planks. Mingled with that racket, Meri heard distant pops, two then another two in quick succession. A terrible dread filled her, though she wasn't sure why. Somehow she just knew that she wouldn't see her parents again.

WIMBLEDON, *London, before the flood.*

'DON'T BE SHY, Kel. Go outside and find Ade.'

Kel looked up through his fringe of fair curls at his father, a mile of denim clad leg at this angle. 'I don't want to.' Last thing he wished to do was let go of Dad's hand and join the children playing in the paddling pool in the back garden. There were three of them, all strangers.

His dad crouched beside him and brushed the hair out of Kel's eyes. 'This is the day we told you about. You're going to live with Ade now in this house. He's your prince and you're to be his bodyguard when you're trained. Right now we want you to be friends.'

Kel bit his thumbnail. 'He's a prince—like in the stories?'

'Yes, but a real one, not storybook. A secret one. Bad people want to kill him—the Teans, remember what I told you about them?'

Kel nodded solemnly. He had had nightmares the last few weeks about the Teans—burnings, whips, bloodied fangs and demon-eyes.

'Ade will need people around him when he's grown up, people he can trust absolutely. You put him first from now on, OK?'

It was dawning on Kel that Dad was saying goodbye. 'What about you and Jenny?'

His father smiled, but it was a little strained at the corners where normally he had deep dimples. 'We've got our jobs too but we'll see you whenever we get holiday. And Ade will visit his family from time to time so we'll be there, guarding our people.' He reached out and tugged the cords on Kel's blue hoodie. 'We've been in service to Ade's family for as long as our family can remember. It's what we Douglases do. It's what your mother gave her life for.'

Kel looked down at his bare toes wriggling in his sandals. The loss of his mother was raw. She had been killed by Teans while on a job in America a few months ago. Kel kept waking up and thinking she was still alive. Remembering she wasn't was almost as bad as when he had first heard the news.

His dad squeezed Kel's shoulder. 'I started with the king at your age so I know what it's like. You're going to be confused for a while, a little lost, but then you'll make friends and you'll get a new second family here. You'll fit in.'

Kel's lip wobbled dangerously. It had been drummed into him that Douglases didn't cry so he mustn't let his parents down. 'But I don't think I'm going to make a good guard, Dad,' he whispered.

His father curved his mouth, not quite smiling. 'We all think that but with the right training, you'll do great. It's in the genes. Go on, Kel, make a start as I've taught you: no hesitation, be brave. Make your mother proud.'

Swallowing back tears, Kel took a step out into the sunshine. The boys in the pool broke off squirting each other with water pistols to watch the stranger approach.

Kel raised a hand. 'Hi.' He wished he had better first words but that was all he could think of saying.

Behind him he heard a woman talking to his father. 'Commander Rill, thanks so much for bringing Kelvin today. Your family can always be relied on.'

'We heard there was a need and we could provide,' his dad said gruffly. 'And since we lost Marina.... I can't look after him and do my job—not like before.'

'I understand. I'm so sorry.'

'Kel's mother died doing what she believed in. We both knew that what happens to Ade and his family is the difference between survival and extinction for us. You can't ask too much when you look at it like that.'

'True. We'll make sure Kel's treated well, trained thoroughly. I'll look after him as if he were my own. My son, Swanny, will keep the younger boys in check; he'll make sure Kel feels at home.'

'Thanks, Sandy. Much appreciated. He's still grieving—

we all are. I'm going to miss him like crazy. He's a really lovely boy, our pride and joy, but every parent probably would say that. I know this is right for him.'

Reluctantly, Kel took a few more steps towards the boys. One with black curly hair and dark skin came to meet him across the lawn, body beaded with water from the pool like an otter emerging from the sea. He had friendly cartoon turtles on his swimming trunks. 'Are you my new guard?'

'That's what my dad said.'

'Brill. I'm Ade.' He chucked Kel a water pistol. 'You're on my side then. We're the reds; those guys are the blues. Direct hit on the front and you're out. On back or side, you survive but sit out for ten. Got it?'

'Yep. Is this loaded?' Kel was relieved to see it was a pump action like one he'd used before at a friend's house. He glanced back and saw that his dad was still there, watching him. He tried to hold it like he knew what he was doing.

'It's full. Ready?'

Kel returned Ade's smile, liking the mischief in the prince's eyes. He decided that maybe, just maybe, this wasn't going to be so bad. 'I'm ready.'

1

W *imbledon, London, after the flood*

GAZING out at the storm-damaged trees of the common, Meredith Marlowe toyed with the punnet of cherries sitting on the sink to drain. She couldn't eat one without thinking of that day at Mount Vernon. The chill still lingered, like the aftereffects of a dip in a cold sea. She shook herself back to the present.

'They're not in season, you know, Theo.' Cherries were a bitter sweet luxury to her, the pleasure always marred by the hard stone of remembering in the middle.

Theo Woolf looked up from the Arts Section of the newspaper. Thirty-something with straw blond hair, a spike earring and sparkling blue eyes, he appeared nothing like anyone's idea of a staid guardian for a seventeen-year-old orphan. 'But I know how much you love them.'

'What about global warming?' She took a couple and sat

down opposite him at the breakfast table. 'Did you consider that, Mr Eco-warrior?'

'One punnet of Spanish cherries is not going to be single-handedly to blame for that.'

She rolled her eyes.

'If it would make you feel better, I'll cycle to work rather than take the car. That should even it up.'

'You always cycle. We don't have a car anymore.' They'd got rid of it last month when Theo couldn't keep up the payments.

'Ah yes, but imagine I was going to call a taxi but decided not to.'

'I'm not sure you can measure your carbon footprint that way.'

He smiled, turned the page of the paper, and spread out an article which he read with renewed concentration. He punctuated his reading with groans.

'What's wrong?' Meri poured herself some apple juice, admiring the deep golden green in the glass. Ordinary things were filled with so many beautiful colours if you just looked.

'They cut the grant to the North-East community singers. Bloody Birmingham mafia. Guess who will be ringing me up first thing this morning?' Theo ran a small office in a lottery funded charity that supported grass-roots organisations building community links for the influx of refugees. 'The politicians just don't get how music helps integrate the newcomers—from rock choirs to opera, it all plays a part.'

'You always claim you're the richest person you know, being in charge of a budget of five million pounds.'

'But don't forget I always add that I'm working for the smallest salary, barely enough to pay the rent on our little flat.' Since much of central and south London had been lost to flooding or accessible only by boat, the outskirts had become even more sought after. They could only afford such a nice address because the landlord, a retired opera singer who lived downstairs, was an old friend of Theo's.

Meri tried not to worry about their precarious financial situation. 'Can't you squeeze something out of your budget for the singers?'

'I'll have to refuse as I've already allocated it this year.'

'I'm sure you'll find a very diplomatic way of saying "no". You always do to me when I want something.'

He whisked her over the head with the sports section. 'Cheeky. This is the respect I get from my almost eighteen-year-old foster daughter. Which reminds me, on my desk I have tickets for the Hammersmith Odeon on Saturday. Tee Park is playing.'

'Oh wow, that's great!'

'I had to pull serious strings to get them and I thought we could make it your birthday treat. Is there anyone you want to bring?'

Meri had once calculated that Theo's real income was double its paper amount if you included all the freebies he got as part of his job. 'No one.'

'Come on, you've been at that school for a few months now. There must be some friends in the wings.' He sipped his black coffee and winced. Meri knew that he really wanted sugar but had decided to give up as it had become so expensive recently.

'Oh yeah, you know me and my vast social circle.'

'You don't want to be always hanging out with me and my mates at your age.'

She stirred her cereal, drowning a couple of freeze-dried berries. 'I like your friends.'

'But none of us are under thirty. You should be social-ising with people your own age.'

Meri had a sudden, unwelcome thought. 'Am I cramping your style, Theo?' Her guardian had been catapulted at twenty-five from footloose student lodger doing a Masters in Arts Administration into the role of carer for a trauma-tised four-year-old. That entailed having to move every few years to make sure she was safe, as well as training her to say nothing about herself until she was old enough to know the importance of keeping her secret. He didn't know the exact nature of the danger she faced but he said he under-stood enough to believe her parents hadn't been exag-gerating.

'No, Meri, you are not cramping my style.' Theo smirked at the thought. 'The ladies love a lone dad with a cute little girl. And when they find out I'm a foster parent, they all think I'm a saint.'

'I'm way past being cute. And you're not a saint.'

'I agree about the sainthood thing but you don't do too bad at being cute. Now I get sympathy for having taken on a teenager—it's regarded as a tougher job than river dredging.'

She smiled. 'I bet you milk it for all it's worth.'

'You know me so well.'

They fell into a companionable silence. Meri finished her cereal and apple juice as she glanced through the head-lines—mass movements of climate refugees, reports on cities being lost to flooding or desertification, resource wars. There was lots of news from America but not the sort she wanted, not the 'missing persons found' kind. Her birthday was coming and her parents were going to be absent again.

'Theo, I've been wondering about that day a lot recently. Why do you think they left me?'

From his pained expression, he knew exactly what she meant. 'They didn't leave, not willingly.'

'You think they were murdered.' He had always told her this. Only something as terrible as that would keep her parents from claiming her, he had said. They had been completely devoted to their daughter. 'But there were no bodies.'

'There's a river right by Mount Vernon, Meri. And there was the fake terrorist alert. All the staff involved in the chase just vanished. It wouldn't be hard to dump two bodies there and still get away. I suppose I could pretend and let you hope that they'll turn up one day but I think false hope the cruelest kind. I promised myself I'd never lie to you.'

They hadn't been just bodies; they'd been Mommy and Daddy.

Not something that she could dwell on and keep her sanity. Theo had always been straight-talking so Meri forced herself past the mention of bodies. 'So what was it that killed them?'

'My best guess is they got tangled up in some organised crime hit. Your mother said on the phone that they were in trouble with old enemies.'

'The Perilous.'

'Sounds like a gang tag to me—pretentious, meant to strike fear in the other person. I looked them up but there's nothing on the Internet but then, Wiki doesn't know everything.'

If it had been a gang, it had been the oddest one she'd ever heard of: an actress, guides and gardeners, hardly the stuff of the mafia. She had often wondered if her memories were confused with dreams of that last outing and it hadn't really happened like that. The glowing skin didn't seem likely, more like a hallucination stirred up by a fever. It had become hazy and surreal in the details, swirling in the colour only she could see. 'And you think I'm still in danger?'

Theo sighed. 'We're going to do this now, are we? Really? You have to catch your bus in ten minutes and I'm supposed to be out of the house already.'

Meri nodded, rearranging the saucer of butter, pot of parsley, and the jar of organic honey Theo liked on his toast so as to make a more pleasing still life.

'OK, cards on the table. I don't know that you're *not* in danger, which isn't exactly the same thing. It's been years, fourteen years to be exact. If there was some crime vendetta going on, it might all now be history. I promised your parents I would save you so you could live a long and happy life. Maybe it's time you started to do the living part of that.' He got up and picked up his messenger bag. 'So the Theo advice of the day is go out and live a little. Make some friends, take some risks, but not too many, mind.' He grimaced. 'Do as I say and not as I did as a teenager.'

'I'm not sure I know how to make friends,' Meri confessed.

'Just be your usual sardonic self. It'll scare a few feeble types away but that should whittle the list down to a couple of good mates who like a wise-cracking know-it-all. That's all you need in my experience.'

'Gee, thanks, Theo. Your confidence in my charm is so reassuring.'

'There, you'll do fine. It's still early in the new school year; you can make a fresh start. See how you get on today.'

MERI REMEMBERED Theo's advice only after she took her usual seat in the bus half way down on the lower deck with the old age pensioners, not upstairs with the others going to her school. That wasn't the new start she meant to make.

'Excuse me.' With a smile to the birdlike lady with the frizzy grey hair who sat next to her each morning, Meri squeezed past and headed up to the top deck. The bus swung round a corner and she almost went flying. A hand reached up and steadied her from behind.

'Thanks.' She glanced round and smiled at a tall, dark guy she'd seen in the common room. She remembered he had a big name—Adetokunbo according to the register, but everyone called him Ade, to rhyme with daddy. It suited him as he was a big guy with a big presence.

'Any time, Mouse.' Ade smiled brightly. Already sporting a close-clipped beard and moustache around his chin and mouth, he was one of those guys who looked too old for school.

She winced at the nickname. Following Ade's lead, her year had started calling her Mouse Marlowe after she had got the reputation for creeping in and out of class without talking to anyone. Old habits died hard. She was only herself when with Theo. However, her guardian was right: she didn't want to be that mouse anymore. It was past time for a change. Reaching the top deck she looked for a place to sit down. There were two double seats near the front free so she slid into the one by the forward-facing window. The comp-punk girl across the aisle reached over and tapped Meri's shoulder, her multiple piercings glinting like a row of little ear-fortifications.

'You don't want to do that,' she said with a kindly shake of her head. Like many of her computer-mad set, she wore a data-stick among the earrings. Funny to think of all those terabytes of information acting as jewellery.

'Sorry? What?'

'You're in Ade's seat,' said a new voice behind her. Ade stood in the aisle, flanked by his two mates, Kel and Lee, she thought they were called. It was Lee who had spoken.

'We have allotted seats now?' Meri didn't like being spoken to in that tone. 'And I thought this was public transport.'

'I suggest you find another seat down the back,' said Lee. He had an angular pale face, fly-away brown hair and grey-green eyes which were currently narrowed at her. He reminded her of the old Hollywood actors cast in the 2010s vampire series that they were always repeating on TV. Hollywood itself had gone, of course, lost to wildfires a few years ago. New Hollywood in Colorado had moved on to making endless disaster movies which meant chisel-jawed actors rather than the fey vampire types were getting the cream of the jobs. 'Go on: move.'

That damn well settled it. Meri folded her arms and stayed put.

Ade put a hand on his friend's arm. 'Lee, it doesn't matter. We'll sit behind.'

Meri wasn't going to let it go so easily. 'So, Lee, you got a memo from the mayor, saying that the front row was reserved for your friend here? Somehow I was missed off the distribution. You're going to be busy, chucking out all those little kids who like making bus noises and pretending to drive. Their mums and dads must love you spoiling their day.'

Ade shook his head at Lee and sat down behind her. Lee slid in next to him which left the other seat at the front to the third of the trio, the blond one who had been silent so far. He sat, his jean-clad thigh squeezing her into the corner as he had to spread his legs to fit. She recognized him from lessons, partly because she'd spent rather too long looking at him across the classroom when she thought she could get away with it. Kel was a gifted artist. Meri had a shrewd suspicion, though, that the exchange with his two companions wasn't what Theo had meant about making friends, unless most friendships began with pissing off the people involved.

Ade tweaked a lock of her straggling brown hair hanging over the back. 'I've never heard you string two words together before. What happened to Mouse?'

'She never existed.' Meri tucked her chin lower, feeling awkward now she had won that small battle. Really these boys were too full of themselves if everyone else had bowed out of their way for weeks on the top deck. It was disconcerting, though, to be crammed so close to guys whom she had just mocked. She could feel the warmth coming off the body of the one next to her, the scent of the soap he must've used that morning, so different from the old lady talc smell downstairs. There was something so intensely there about her neighbour, like she was sitting in the full beam of a car headlight.

'She shouldn't talk to you like that, Ade,' muttered Lee.

'Why not? I'm not her boss. You need to lighten up, Lee, or people will think we're dicks.'

Meri couldn't resist. Ade had left himself wide open. 'Too late for that.'

The guy next to her started to laugh but turned it into a cough.

'Bitch,' said Lee.

Back for Round Two. 'Ouch. Looks like someone's got a bad case of PMT.' She turned to face Lee. 'That's Permanent Male Twitness, if you were wondering, far more trouble than the female monthly sort.' What had got into her? She must have a death wish.

Lee told her crudely where she could get off.

'That's enough, Lee. Apologize to Mouse.' Ade ordered it in such a tone of authority that Lee muttered something that might have included the word 'sorry'.

Meri shrugged and pretended to be only interested in the view from the window. The bus journey wasn't long but there was so much traffic it was often quicker to go on foot. She measured their progress by a guy in a tracksuit with a collie dog. Yep: quicker to walk as long as you knew where the emergency shelters were. As the minutes passed after the little spat with Lee she found her attention drawn back to the boy beside her. In contrast to the stormy energy whirling off Count Twit behind, Kel seemed to radiate a kind of lightness. That was a stupid idea, Meri decided. Probably just an association with his honey blond hair that seemed to go every which way like it didn't need to obey gravity. She studied his reflection and decided he had an unusual but nice face. Maybe not as drop dead gorgeous as his friends but there was a strength to the jaw line and aquiline nose. What colour were his eyes? The reflection didn't give a definitive answer. Not that it mattered. After today she wouldn't make the mistake of sitting up front again.

'What's your name? Not really Mouse, I guess?'

He was speaking to her. Oh crap, he hadn't caught her watching him, had he? That would be so lowering to admit. 'Meredith Marlowe.'

'Nice to meet you, Meredith. I'm Kel Douglas. Actually Kelvin, but I'll never forgive my parents for that.'

She almost added her friends called her Meri but was brought up short by the thought she didn't have any. 'Oh. Um, nice to meet you too.'

'We have Art together this term.'

'I know.'

He waited but she didn't expand on her comment. 'Not much of a talker then?'

'No.' She had been once but she'd learned to shut up.

'Anyway, nice finally to meet you.'

'And you.'

It was an oddly formal conversation, the kind you might have with a chance met stranger, not someone you saw around school each and every day. Meri kicked herself wondering if there was something she could say that would make her seem more normal. 'So, er, do you like Art?'

'She speaks.' Kel turned to her and grinned. The power of that smile was enough to knock her off her feet if she hadn't already been sitting down. OK, that was a little hyperbolic but his smile was just amazing. 'Yes. I like making things. Ceramics mostly. You?'

'Painting. I like painting.' Thankfully the bus was drawing close to their stop and the students were beginning to gather in the aisle.

'See you later then. In Art.'

'Yes.' She waited for him to leave with his two friends before following. 'Awkward,' she whispered.

KEL WATCHED the girl in the art room from his corner by the potter's wheel. She'd pushed her glasses to the top of her head and was lost in contemplation of her canvas. It was an amazing abstract of tiny dots with such minuscule colour differences in the blue spectrum. It was hard to see how she could paint it, but when you stood at a distance as he was you could see the overall effect of the sweep, like pixels becoming a photo. It was reminiscent of the curling wave in the Hokusai print, governed by the principles of the Fibonacci sequence of perfect proportion. She had a sketch next to her easel with the spiral marked out. He liked that. His own simple white pots all aspired to those same clean lines, nature when it was under control, not like the world outside that humans had mucked up.

Kel cut the piece he had just made from the wheel with the wire. He hadn't thought much about Meredith Marlowe before. She had kept in the background, always dressed in muted colours and usually hid herself behind that pair of thick black-rimmed glasses too big for her small face. It wasn't until she laid into Lee with her snarky comments that his interest had been sparked. Geez, his friend annoyed him sometimes, completely overdoing the privilege thing. Since being appointed to Ade's personal guard last month, Lee seemed to have forgotten the other vital part of their role was to be subtle and draw unwelcome attention away from the prince in their midst. Ade was going to have to have a word with him.

'Kel, that's lovely.' The art teacher, Miss Hardcastle, came to stand at his shoulder. 'I don't know how you get it so even. It looks almost as if a machine made it.'

'Does it? Oh.' That wasn't the effect he wanted at all. He wanted it pure, not inhuman.

'No, no, that's not a criticism; it's great. And they always come out of the kiln so much whiter than the other pieces we put in. I don't understand that either.'

That was all part of being him. His hands could lightly bleach things if he concentrated hard, a channelling of his natural UV energy. All his kind absorbed it from the environment and could release it back when they learned control. 'I must have the magic touch, I guess.'

The teacher laughed. 'You can say that again. OK, so into the kiln with this one. You're doing really well on your A level pieces. Make sure you keep your art book up to date with your notes and observations.'

Inspired by a famous British potter who had a show at the New Tate in Alexandra Palace, Kel was making a wall display of his pure white pots on shelving made from drift-wood. 'I'll do some now.'

'Then I'll leave you to it.'

The teacher walked off to talk to Meredith. Her face was less appreciative as she contemplated the girl's canvas. Kel could hear her complaining that she couldn't see what Meredith was trying to achieve, nor understand her influences. From happy concentration, Meredith had turned to sullen listener. Kel eavesdropped as he washed his hands at the sink.

'What are you going to say in your project write-up about your inspiration, Meredith? I'm not sure the examiners will see the point of lots of dots of the same colour on the canvas.'

'They're not the same colour.' Meredith had bundled her brown hair up in a scarf to keep it out of the way. Strands were beginning to escape as she grew more upset, her movements jerky.

'As near as makes no difference. It's making my eyes cross. What school of art are you following?'

'I'm not. I'm just painting something I can see in my head.'

'But that's not good enough to get an A level. Look, why don't you have a think about the other pieces the students are doing and study their write-ups? Kel's doing a really interesting ceramics project, for example. I can see that you've got a vision here but I just don't think the execution is doing it justice.'

Miss Hardcastle was wrong. It was brilliantly done, technically flawless. Why couldn't she see it?

'OK, Miss.' Meredith put her brush down and wiped off her fingers on a rag. 'What should I do with this?'

Why wasn't she fighting her corner? Kel wondered. The snarky girl on the bus had vanished.

'You've got time to start again. Paint over it if you want. Good canvases are expensive.'

Meredith looked away and out of the window to the rooftops of the flats opposite the school, looking a little lost and a lot damaged by the criticism. Kel's heart ached for her. 'Can I take it home?'

'If you like. Will your parents be able to stump up for a new canvas? The school budget is cut to the bone and you know what strict controls there are on resources these days.'

Meredith swallowed hard. 'I'll ask my guardian.'

'Sorry, yes, er, parent or guardian I meant to say.' The teacher patted Meredith awkwardly on the arm. 'Don't worry about making mistakes. You're here to learn. If I had my way, we'd have an endless line of supplies to play with but governments cutbacks mean I just don't have that luxury. They're rationed like everything else.'

A siren wailed in the street outside and immediately shutters scrolled down over all the windows. The solar-powered lights flickered on.

'Looks like another storm front, people,' announced Miss Hardcastle, checking her watch. 'But it's also the end of the lesson. You can stay here during break if you wish. I'm off to have a lovely cup of coffee-sub in the staff shelter.' She grimaced. 'To think I took real coffee beans for granted when I was your age. See you next lesson.'

Kel finished packing up, all the while keeping an eye on Meredith. Her stance was so telling; it was almost as if he could hear her thoughts as she stood in front of her canvas. She was devastated by the teacher's verdict, particularly because she'd been so proud of it until that moment. Suddenly she took up a fat brush and dipped it in the darkest shade of blue on her palette. He knew what she was going to do before she did it.

Vaulting a table he got to her side just in time to seize her wrist. 'Don't.'

Her sea green eyes were glittering with fury. He hadn't noticed their colour until that moment; they fairly snapped with energy. 'Why not? You heard her: it's rubbish.'

'It's not rubbish. It's beautiful.' He didn't let go of her wrist, though he could feel her straining to get free.

'That doesn't matter. Theo can't afford another canvas.'

'Who's Theo?'

'My guardian.' Mind made up, she moved to deface her picture again, jerking against his hold.

'Look, Meredith, I like it. I'll buy it off you.'

That surprised her. She let him take the brush from her fingers. 'With what?'

'Money. What else do you think? Not my body. I have my pride,' he teased. And he also had his wage as Ade's guard to draw on.

'Funny guy, huh?' Disarmed of paintbrush, he allowed her to wriggle her wrist free of his grip.

He leaned a little closer, wanting to make her smile again. 'You mocking the value of my skills in that area?'

She blushed and looked away. He guessed that meant she didn't do the flirting thing but he was pleasantly surprised when she came up fighting. 'I've no idea what you're worth on the open market, Kel, but I'll take payment for the painting. In cash.'

He grinned. 'OK. How much?'

She named a sum that was the exact amount of a new canvas. He came back with an offer double the amount.

Meredith shook her head at him. 'I don't think you've grasped the concept of this bargaining thing. You're supposed to undercut my price, not suggest more.'

God, she was cute when she got all serious with him. He doubled his amount again.

She held her hand up. 'Stop, stop, you crazy guy! OK, I'll accept that first price. And I'll trust you're good for it so you can take this today if you want.' She turned back to look at it, sliding her glasses over her eyes. 'I don't want to see it again.'

The storm arrived just as expected, five minutes after the siren. Rain drummed down on the roof making it difficult to hear what anyone was saying. The roads and playground outside would soon be awash, storm drains struggling to cope.

Kel picked up the canvas and took it over to the potter's wheel that was unofficially his part of the art room. He didn't trust her alone with the picture. 'I'll wait until this passes. Don't want my new painting to get wet.'

She pretended not to care, occupying herself with clean-up, putting brushes in white spirit. 'Suit yourself.'

'And it really is very good. I don't know why the teacher couldn't see it. A perfect curve.'

She bit her bottom lip shyly. 'You think?'

'I think.'

Picking up her bag, she turned to go. 'I'm Meri, by the way.'

'Come again?'

She wrinkled her nose. 'That's not a statement about my frame of mind, but my preferred name. M E R I. Meredith sounds too old somehow.'

'Meri.' He tested it out. The nickname didn't really suit the quiet, sarcastic girl before him but he'd go with it if she liked. 'See you around, Meri.'

WITH THE PLAYING FIELDS A QUAGMIRE, afternoon sport was moved inside. Most of the sixth form preferred to slope off as it wasn't compulsory, but Kel enjoyed the chance to exercise. He wondered what Meri would do. She so looked the sloping off sort. When he didn't see her among the girls playing basketball, he decided he had called that right.

Ade lined up his bat against the stumps in the nets. 'Sock it to me.'

Kel took a run up and span the ball. Ade managed to connect but it went off at an odd angle. Ade swore.

'You'd've been caught behind if this was a real game,' said Kel, collecting the cricket ball and rubbing it on his tracksuit bottoms.

Ade's dark eyes glared at him through the wire mesh of his helmet. 'Again.'

The second ball went straight past him and took out the middle stump.

'Bloody hell, Kel, can't you let a guy warm up?'

'I thought you said, and I quote, "sock it to me"?'

'I kind of meant ease me in gently. We all know you county level players far outclass the rest of us.'

'OK, I'll bowl underarm next time.'

'Hah, hah.'

'Anyway, I was thinking about giving up the county next season.'

'What? Why?'

'My duties take up too much time.'

'Kel, I'm your friend, not a prison. When they brought

you to be with me, I don't think they meant you to take it so seriously.'

Kel rotated his arm in preparation for the next ball. 'Why not? You know what you mean to our people.'

'Yeah, like there are hundreds of people just queuing up to assassinate me. The last Tean attack was what? A decade ago?'

It had been fourteen. Kel even knew how many days had passed as it was the attack in which his mother had died. 'Doesn't mean they're still not out there. You know that's why you and your cousins are spread out all over the globe.'

'So one or two of us might survive come hell or high water. Yeah I get it. The high water bit is no longer so funny since sea levels started going mad.'

Kel bowled an easy ball, allowing Ade to make a connection with a satisfying crack. 'Better?'

'Yeah.'

'You going to have a word with Lee about this morning?'

'Already did.'

'His job has gone to his head.'

'Can't think why. Guarding a guy who may or may not one day be ruler of a scattered people—I'm using ruler in the loosest sense here as I bet none of you will take the least notice of my directions—it's hardly something to boast about.'

'Lee thinks it is. He thinks our civilization is superior and therefore to be preserved at all costs'

'He always put too much store by tradition.'

'It's what's kept us together over the millennia.'

'So no pressure then.'

A whistle blew and the sports teacher shouted from the other end of the gym. 'Are you two old women going to stand there gassing all day or are you actually going to, you know, PLAY SOME CRICKET?'

'See the grovelling respect I get,' said Ade sourly.

'Yes, your highness,' murmured Kel, taking another run at him.

Later, in the locker rooms, Kel stood under the hot shower meditatively rubbing soap into his skin. Still nothing to see. Funny to think that hidden under there were his tribal markings, bred into their race over the millennia of artificial selection. He already knew what they were likely to be. His dad was a spiral, his mum had been a leaf, but spiral usually came out dominant in the male line. Soon the marks would start to show when he was in combat or in a highly emotional state, visible only to others like him. It was the real mark of adulthood for their kind and he couldn't wait for his turn to come.

Tying a towel round his waist he padded out barefoot to join Ade on the bench. Ade's markings had, of course, come through very young. He'd been only thirteen when the turtle-backed markings of the ruling house had become apparent. His family always did things early. The average for the flare-out was between eighteen and twenty.

Kel pulled on a shirt. 'I bought a painting today.'

Ade looked up. 'You serious?'

'Yeah, from the mouse girl. The teacher had told her it was crap so she was going to destroy it.'

Ade rubbed his short hair dry. 'And is it crap?'

'Why would I buy a crap painting?'

'It didn't escape me that the mouse is not totally without her good points.'

'What? Sarcasm and bag lady clothes?' That was unfair. Her clothes were perfectly acceptable, just very dull and calculated to hide everything about her figure.

'OK, so it's not crap. Why did you buy it?'

'Because it is brilliant, so subtle. I'll show you later. The funny thing, the teacher really couldn't see it. The colour definition went totally over her head. Sure, it's on the edge of what ordinary people can perceive but I could see it clearly. Must be ironic that it's the art teacher with the poorest eyesight in that class. I'm sure there are plenty of others who would've got it.'

Ade turned that over in his mind for a moment. 'You know that sight is one of our markers?'

'That's what I was beginning to wonder. Do you think the mouse might be one of the lost ones?' That was the name they gave to people born outside their community, perhaps on the rare occasions when someone married out or had a child with a person who didn't carry the same genetic code that gave them their distinctive characteristics. Occasionally a kid would emerge who knew nothing about their way of life.

'Sounds like you should find out more. If her markings come through and she doesn't know what that means, she's going to be very confused and the doctors very interested, thinking she's hallucinating—that's until they turn a UV lamp on her and go wild with speculation. I can't count how many hours we've spent changing official records to hide these lapses in our security.'

'There are no markings. I saw her arms as she was wearing short-sleeves.'

'Still, they might come through any day now. Worth checking.'

'I think she's separated from her birth parents. She mentioned a guardian.'

'Then get close to her and find out as much as you can.

They might be on our database. I'll run her name tonight to see what we might already know.'

'And if she is?'

'Then we cross that bridge when we come to it. She could just have exceptional UV vision. It's not unknown, though usually only very young kids tend to have the skill for a few years. That helps because we can easily pretend what they see is childish make-believe. They come to think that too when the ability fades.'

'And yet she wears glasses.' Kel frowned. 'Not when painting though, so that means she's what, short sighted?'

'You figure it out. Consider it part of your bodyguard duties. Now let's get that picture of yours—I'd like to see what you're seeing—and head back to headquarters. We've got training tonight.'

'Yes, sir.'

Ade punched him lightly in the stomach. 'Don't call me "sir".'

Kel knew exactly how to wind up his best friend. 'No, sir. I won't call you "sir", sir.'

'I'll get you redeployed to my cousin in Greenland if you don't cut that out.'

Ade would never do that to him. 'I hear and obey,...sir.'

Ade laced up his shoes. 'Are princes still allowed to order summary executions, I wonder?'

2

Meri squashed the garlic through the press and scraped off the white residue into the frying pan. It sizzled, quickly going brown at the edges. She divided and conquered it with a wooden spoon, humming a song under her breath.

The front door banged and a few seconds later Theo entered the kitchen. He dropped his shiny black cycle helmet on the table. It lay there like an upside-down beetle.

'Smells good. What are you cooking?'

'Veggie lasagne.'

'My favourite. I think I've just died and gone to heaven.' He kissed the top of her head, using that move to steal a carrot off the side.

'You will go to heaven with no lasagne if you keep that up.' She mock threatened him with the spoon.

He chuckled and opened the fridge. 'Apple juice?'

'Please.'

'I thought the stove was broken.'

'Not broken, Theo. You just hadn't read the manual.'

'I'm a bloke: we like to muddle through.'

'Well, I'm a girl and I find reading the instructions helps sort out tricky little details, like how to cancel the delayed timer you'd programmed by mistake.'

'Smarty pants.' He poured her a glass, taking a beer for himself. 'Do you remember the days when we used to think orange juice was boring?'

'Not really. I think I was too young when everything started changing. I don't remember the before.'

'Yeah, before the carbon tax sent prices soaring. Best thing they ever did though. Put a true price on saving the world.' Theo placed her glass within reach. 'So, how was your day? You didn't get caught in that storm, did you?'

Meri grimaced, remembering. 'No. I was in Art.'

'A couple of Tube stations went underwater again.' He went out into the hall to collect the post she'd left on the mat, then sat down with his beer to look through the envelopes. 'I think they're going to have to give up on the Northern Line entirely. It's costing a fortune to keep pumping it out.'

'Anyone hurt?'

'No. It was evacuated well in advance. We're getting all too used to this situation. It's bizarre how you can adapt even to the weirdest things. It's hard to remember what life was like before the flood.'

Meri stirred the onions and garlic mixture. Almost ready for the red lentils. The pile of little pulses reminded her of her pixelated picture. Maybe that had been her inspiration? She cooked with them often enough. Would Miss Hardcastle accept that as an explanation? 'I did more on my painting today.'

'That sounds fun.'

'It wasn't really. Miss thought it was rubbish.'

'What! But you're a brilliant artist!' Theo banged down

the beer bottle and froth bubbled out. 'Right: I'm ringing the school. That teacher is an idiot.'

Meri should've guessed this would be his response. 'It's OK. She kinda had a point. You see I was painting without wearing my glasses.'

'Oh.' Theo drew a circle in the spillage before mopping it up with a cloth. 'I thought we agreed.'

'Yes, but I can't help how I see. I was doing what you suggested: living a little. It feels so strange painting with all the colours dulled down to nothing.'

'That's not how the rest of us perceive it. What you see with them on is what the rest of us see all the time.'

Meri poured the lentils, a tiny avalanche, into the frying pan. 'I know.'

'Those lenses cut out the UV, making your sight more normal.'

Meri closed her eyes for a moment. 'Maybe I don't want normal. It's hard to explain to you but colours to me are so... so alive. It's like every single one has an entire rainbow of potential in it. And then there are shades you can't even see that I lack the words to describe. Peril is such a pretty colour, like blue but not blue. Oh, I don't know how to say this.'

Theo held the stem of the bottle to his lips. 'You make me wish I could see that way. I'm trying to imagine. It's like describing music to someone who is deaf from birth: I can get the vibrations but not the full experience.'

'That's it exactly.' She flashed him a grin. 'You are such a cool guardian, Theo.'

'Why thank you.' He raised the beer in a toast. 'And you are a very cool foster daughter. So what did you do when your teacher said it was, you know?'

'She didn't actually say it was rubbish. I'm just paraphrasing her words.'

'Pleased to hear it. Crappy teaching method if she had.'

'She told me to start again and paint over it if I couldn't afford another canvas.'

'Ah.' Theo put down the beer and shuffled the letters. Quite a few of them were bills.

'But it's OK. A boy in my class bought it off me instead so I'll get the money for a new canvas. He said he liked it. In fact, he said he could see what I was trying to do.'

Theo looked up, intrigued. 'Do you think he really could?'

'What?'

'See it. Because if he did, then that's really interesting.'

'You mean, he might be like me?'

'It's possible. Or he could just be saying that to chat you up. If so, I must commend him on his tactics because, from that soppy smile on your face, I'd say he was succeeding.'

'Oh, stop it!' Meri added the vegetables and stock to the pan, turning that over in her mind. She wasn't sure if she wanted Kel to have done it because he liked her rather than because he appreciated her art. The best outcome would be if it had been both.

Theo opened a bill and grimaced. 'Anything else happen today?'

'I took your advice and exhibited my charming self to some of the guys on the bus this morning. You're right: it quickly weeds out the feeble types.' Not that Lee was feeble, but he wasn't friend material either.

'Good on you, girl. Ah, a letter for Miss Meredith Marlowe no less.' He handed over the white envelope. The weight of the paper was a sort rarely seen in modern London. The king probably had a stack tucked away in the attics of Buckingham Palace but few others did. 'Looks like it took a couple of decades reaching you. Love the touch of the wax seal—never seen that before.'

'What fun. Who on earth would be writing to me? I feel like Harry Potter. Will you take over stirring while I open it? Wouldn't want to get tomatoes all over my first proper letter.'

They switched places. Meri slid her fingers under the flap, broke the seal and pulled out the folded insert.

'So is it Hogwarts?'

'Sadly not.' She read it slowly because at first it didn't make sense.

Dear Miss Marlowe,

I was instructed by my late clients, Dr Blake Marlowe, and Mrs Naia Marlowe, that in the event of our firm not hearing anything from them for seven years, I was to presume they were deceased and wind up their affairs. This was done seven years ago and the money held in trust for you until such time as you reach eighteen. Your guardian was informed of these proceedings.

Meri's delight in receiving a letter vanished. 'Theo, did you know about this?' She waved it at him.

'Know what?'

'That Messrs Rivers, Brook and Linton of,' she checked the address, 'Charterhouse Square, have decided my parents are dead?'

Theo turned down the biogas flame and put a lid on the pan. 'Yes. The money is with a firm of investment managers and doing quite nicely considering the fluctuations in the stock exchange.'

'When were you going to tell me?'

'When you turned eighteen. Looks like they beat me to it

by a few days. It's not a huge amount but it's a nest egg, something to help with college fees in a few years when you've done your time in the ecological service.'

Meri grimaced at the unwelcome reminder. All eighteen to twenty-year-olds had to serve two years of national service unless they were going into one of the protected professions, like medicine, army or the police. Jobs usually revolved around the coast or big rivers, building flood defences. Theo had tried to tell her it would be fun, a seaside adventure, but he hadn't had to do it when he was growing up so wasn't speaking from experience. Of course he hadn't: it was her generation who had got landed with the environmental bill. Meri returned to her letter.

Part of our instructions was to send a message to you in two instalments. Your parents specified this unusual procedure because they did not want to put all the information in one place and would only allow a single physical copy of each. Following their instructions, I request that you collect the first in person and sign for it in front of witnesses. I have arranged for the second to be sent on to me by courier from our office in New York. I will notify you when it arrives so that you can return to receive it, again this must be in person.

'They have some messages for me and want me to go to them,' Meri explained. 'Bit over the top, isn't it? Two messages in separate places?'

Theo shrugged. 'I'd agree if it wasn't for the issue of Blake and Naia's disappearance. We've been keeping a low profile for years but who knows if anyone is watching?'

The old-fashioned seal on the outside of the envelope made sense now. Digital communications were notoriously hackable; pen and paper had made a comeback for really private matters. She couldn't imagine any spy who might have planned to steam open the envelope being equipped to replace a very distinctive seal. Still, it seemed a very fragile thing to carry such an important message.

'He's left me a number to call. I might have to miss school.'

'Every cloud has a silver lining.' Theo got out the lasagne dish and tipped in the first layer of mix. 'Have to say I think you should go soon or I'll burst with curiosity. If they can see you tomorrow, I've a lunch meeting at the Barbican and can go with you. Would you like that?'

'Thank you. Yes, I would.'

Between them, they finished layering the lentils, pasta and cheese and put it in the oven.

Theo stretched his lanky arms over his head. 'We've got forty-five minutes. Want to go for a run?'

Meri had successfully ducked organised sport at school so thought it a bit much her guardian had put her on the spot. 'Tragically, I'm not sure there's time.'

'Meri, whose New Year's Resolution was it not to be such an exercise shirker?'

'You're not going to let me forget that.' Theo had pinned her unwise pledge to the fridge back in January and got her to sign it. 'OK, a short one.'

'Just think how much nicer that lasagne will taste.'

'Yeah, yeah.'

'It will.'

'I'm going, I'm going.' Meri picked up the letter and took it into her bedroom to get changed. She tucked it into *Jane Eyre* on the nightstand. A message from her parents. It sounded a little creepy, voices from beyond the grave. But maybe, finally, she'd get some answers to the many questions that surrounded her. There had been no relatives to ask, just Theo who had known little more than she did. He was right though: she had to go tomorrow or she wouldn't be able to relax.

ONE OF THE quickest ways to get to Charterhouse Square from Wimbledon was to use the Thames bus service. Since the river had burst its banks five years ago in the last great flood of that year, many of the old routes had disappeared and Londoners had gone back to the water. Some bridges were in the process of being replaced by cable cars and the one at Putney was still under construction. Theo and Meri joined the queue to get on the next boat.

'Nervous?' Theo asked. He was looking unusually smart having got out his one suit and accessorised it with a thin tie. He looked a little like a throwback to the 1960s. All he needed was a Liverpudlian accent and a guitar and he'd make his fortune as a tribute band singer.

'Yes. Very.'

The conductor issued them with life jackets as they boarded. The tidal Thames had become a wild river since it overwhelmed its embankment. The mayor had ordered new safety procedures after a fatal shipwreck on one of the old bridge piers last year. Only expert pilots were now allowed to command a vessel, much to the disgust of the unregulated river cab companies that had flourished for a few years before being put out of business.

Meri chose a seat near the lifeboats. Theo, more used to this mode of travel, sat next to her and got out his newspaper to do the crossword. That left her to watch the scenery pass without the distraction of conversation. From the jiggle of his leg, she could tell that Theo was nervous too and was using the puzzle as a means of stopping himself saying anything he would later regret. They had no idea what was going to be in that message so there was little point speculating. Meri got out her pocket sketchbook, her usual way of turning nerves into something more productive.

Their river bus passed the floating village of Chelsea. She tried a quick sketch of horizontal lines of the boats and the fairground feel of the strings of flags threaded between the boats, many of them fluttering with peril between the ordinary oranges, reds and blues. That was odd. You didn't normally see so much of the colour in one place. When the big houses of Chelsea had gone under, poorer folk had moved in, mooring houseboats and rafts together to make a precarious slum. The squatters had broken in to the upper floors of the tallest houses where they were still above the surface, using them for storage and, if pressed for space, for living quarters. Washing lines and makeshift power cables looped between the buildings. The mayor had said many times he considered it an eyesore. A few landlords who had owned the ground under the water had tried to levy a rent but that had got nowhere. The slum remained. People had to live somewhere with so much housing lost.

Rounding another bend, the old Houses of Parliament appeared. Meri turned a page in her sketchbook, pleased to see Big Ben was still standing despite its foundations being submerged. A big friendly circle for the face, gothic turrets like squirrel ears pricked to alert position. Squatters had moved into the top floors of the parliament building but it had to be fairly grim living there with no power and the lower floors flooded. The MPs had moved away completely, taking over the Central Library building in Birmingham. People in the regions had complained for decades that they hated being ruled from Westminster and now, thanks to the changing climate, they weren't.

Looking towards the other side of the river, Meri couldn't see anything she felt like sketching. How sad it was that so many historic sites on the South Bank were entirely gone. The water had encroached much further that way due to the low-lying ground. The once vibrant cultural heart of London and several key railway stations had all been inundated; the London Eye had been disassembled and put in storage until a new embankment could be constructed on the shoreline. She missed the carnival feel the Eye had brought to this part of London. The upper floors and flat top of the National Theatre remained, now a favourite mooring spot for boats. One enterprising business advertised scuba diving in the flooded ruins but how much anyone would see in the murky Thames was debatable.

The bus pulled into the north shore. Tucking the sketchpad back in her bag, Meri followed Theo up the gangplank as they got out at the stop near St Paul's. They walked the rest of the way to Charterhouse Square, her quick steps keeping up easily with his more bouncy stride. They were used to striding in sync. The financial district held on just to the east of this area thanks to the expensive flood defences the bankers had built around the tower blocks and Liverpool Street Station. Rich financiers were still able to zip into town on Crossrail from their mansions in the Home Counties, carrying on making money like it was still the 2010s. People in Wapping had claimed the defences had diverted the river to make the flooding worse in the East End but, as the financiers had rehoused the mayor in a swanky new office right in their midst, those complaints had gone unanswered.

'I went on the protest march about that,' Theo

commented, pointing to the huge new dike, an ugly
construction of concrete blocks like the old Berlin wall
dividing the climate haves and have-nots. 'The police used
water cannons on us. You have to love the irony.'

Turning into Charterhouse Square was to walk into one
of the few places that had escaped change. The luxury flats
and offices and the ancient school buildings still occupied
their old places. The plane trees of the square looked a little
battered by storms but were still standing, hand-shaped
leaves fluttering like an enthusiastic audience in rapturous
applause. Electric cars on charge lined the curbs. Messrs
Rivers, Brook and Linton even had a brass plaque on the red
brick walls beside their black front door. Theo rang the bell
and the lock buzzed.

He pushed the heavy door open. 'Ready?'

Vulturelike foreboding flapped wings in Meri's chest. 'I
suppose I have to be.'

A cool foyer greeted them with pale yellow tiles and a
black cage lift like something out of a retro-detective series.
They eventually managed the complicated opening and
closing of the two layers of lift-doors in the right order, then
Meri selected the second floor.

'It's only two floors. We could've used the stairs,'
she said.

'And missed this?'

They smiled at each other. Sometimes, Meri thought,
they acted more like best mates than guardian and ward.

With a creak and a groan of ancient machinery they rose
slowly up the building. When they opened the cage on the
correct level, they were confronted by yet another door.

'I can see why my parents chose these people for their
secrets. No modern fishbowl digi-cubicals, no sign of
anyone. I feel like I've travelled back in time,' mused Meri.

'Maybe if we're lucky they'll charge old fashioned prices.' Theo pressed another buzzer.

'You mean, we have to pay?'

'Meri, these are lawyers. The seas may rise, the ice may melt, but we still have to pay them just to breathe in our company.'

'But can we afford it?'

'I guess we can take this as a charge on your inheritance. Is that OK?'

Meri nodded. Of course Theo shouldn't bear the costs of her parents' choice of messenger. He'd already sacrificed so much to accommodate her.

'Miss Marlowe? And this must be Mr Woolf?' The woman who opened the door was a slim grey-suited individual who looked like she did not know what a smile was, let alone allow something so unsophisticated on her face.

'Yeah, that's us, darlin',' said Theo a little too cheerfully.

'Please come in and take a seat. Mr Rivers will see you momentarily.' The lady disappeared down a corridor with a tap-tap of her high stilettos.

'*Darlin*'?' whispered Meri. 'Since when have you been so "cor, blimey, guv?"'

Theo winked at Meri. 'She liked it. A bit of the old Cockney charm. But did Miss Fancy Pants mean he'd see us soon or that he'd see us for a moment only? Oh, the danger of unclear grammar!'

'Contain yourself, Theo Woolf; you're not to get us chucked out of here for being an annoying syntactical know-it-all.'

They had been left in a brightly lit waiting room. An elegant bow window dominated the longest side. An Art Deco fireplace held up by sinuous robed ladies graced the wall opposite the reception desk. A delicate arrangement of twig and single flower sat on a low coffee table between the butter-coloured leather armchairs. Meri found the atmosphere both intimidating and beautiful. She looked down at her jeans and canvas plimsols and realized she had made the wrong selection of outfit.

'So who's going to come through that door, do you think? Professor Dumbledore?' teased Theo, trying to lighten the atmosphere.

'He's dead, remember?'

'Aargh, plot spoiler!'

'I was thinking it's more likely to be Hercule Poirot.' She'd loved the re-runs of that ancient detective programme.

'I wish. You know what, I think I saw a version that they filmed round here.' Theo wandered to the window. 'Yes, I recognize that building over there.'

'We could do with a Belgian sleuth to work out why all this cloak-and-dagger stuff is necessary.'

'Let's see what the message says first. It might become obvious.'

'This way please.' Miss Fancy Pants was back and waiting to usher them into the senior partner's room.

'Don't you find it odd they don't use any tech at all?' Meri whispered to Theo. She had noticed there was no computer at the desk, just a large appointment diary. 'This would be a comp-punk's idea of hell.'

Theo, by contrast, was in heaven. 'They promise absolute confidentiality. I guess that means they're so retro they're cutting edge, going back to pre-buggable, pre-digital methods of working. They probably have a filing clerk and typists! This is so adorable.' One of his favourite things to do was watch old spy series set in offices before the 1980s, an era where the top technology was an electric typewriter and they had to dial numbers on huge desktop phones. He collected such memorabilia if it came up dirt cheap in junk shops or online auctions. 'I wasn't joking about the Dumbledore thing. I bet they'd use owls to deliver their letters if they could be trained to do so.'

'Wouldn't anyone?'

The lady knocked lightly on an open door. 'Mr Rivers, your guests are here.'

They stepped into the book-lined room with a white-haired gentleman sitting behind a desk writing with an ink pen.

'Pinch me: we've suddenly walked into a Dickens' mini-series,' whispered Theo.

Meri bit her lip to stop a giggle. Nerves were making them both misbehave.

Not noticing, or perhaps magisterially ignoring, their laughter, Mr Rivers stood up and came around the desk to greet them. His hair gave the wrong indication of his age; he was actually much younger than it suggested, no more than forty. He had a fragile air, like a manuscript that should only be handled wearing cotton gloves. 'Miss Marlowe, delighted to meet you at long last. Please accept very belated condolences on the loss of your parents.'

She shook his hand. His palm was very dry and a little warm. 'Um, thanks.'

'Mr Woolf? Thank you for accompanying your ward today. Would you mind acting as one of our witnesses?'

'My pleasure, guv.'

'Shall we get right to it?' Mr Rivers was looking at her, Meri realized.

'Er, OK.'

Mr Rivers rang a little bell on his desk. The receptionist returned with a dull grey metal cashbox. The lawyer dug in his breast pocket and drew out the key. 'Here. This is yours.' He passed it to Meri.

She took the key and gripped it hard, letting the cuts in the metal bite into her skin.

'Now if you would sign that you have received it? The message is in the box, which we have held for you in our storage facility, and that is the only key kept here to open it. Even I haven't seen the contents since putting them inside fourteen years ago but I can assure you no one has had access to it during that time.'

'Right, thanks.' Meri took the ink pen he offered her and signed the document lying ready on the desk.

'Mr Woolf?'

Theo signed beneath her, then the receptionist added her signature.

'My instructions were to allow you to read this in a private room. I have set aside the office next door for this purpose. Your parents also suggested that you leave the box here for safe keeping once you have had time to absorb the contents.'

Meri remembered the conversation with Theo about costs. 'Will that be expensive?'

Theo looked away, his cheeks a little flushed. Oh. Maybe she shouldn't have been so crass as to raise the issue of money?

Mr Rivers shook his head, the smile in his eyes betraying his amusement. 'No, Miss Marlowe. It has all been taken care of long ago.'

'OK then.' Meri picked up the box. 'Theo, will you wait for me?'

Theo dropped his Cockney chappie act, expression deadly serious. 'You don't want me in there with you, Meri?'

Did she? It would be easy to cling to him as she had

always done but, if the secrecy surrounding this message was any indicator, the information might put him in danger. 'I think I'd better follow my parents' instructions until we know what we're dealing with.'

'Mr Woolf, you can wait in reception and Sophia will bring you coffee' suggested Mr Rivers.

'If that's what you want?' Theo held her gaze for a moment.

'It is.' Meri clutched the box to her chest and went through the door into the empty office. Mr Rivers shut the door behind her. Theo was going to hate that—being kept on the outside of a secret: he was a terrible gossip, truth be told.

She placed the box in the centre of the bare desk. There was nothing special about it. You could probably get another just like it at any bank or storage facility. She fitted the key in the lock, turned it and paused, not quite ready yet to lift the lid. This gave her time to notice that, though it was quiet in here, she could hear the sounds of people working in the rooms beyond, a faint click-click-click that she finally identified as typewriters at work, the low ringtone of a phone, and the murmur of voices. They probably saw hundreds of clients with family secrets. That was what they did here. Rather than lawyers, they should advertise their firm as secret keepers.

She opened the box. A single sheet of white paper lay inside, folded and sealed with red wax. She broke the seal and spread it out flat.

Darling girl,

If you are reading this, it means that our enemies have caught us. We are so sorry that we couldn't prevent this. Even if we weren't there for all those milestones in your life—the first day at school, the first crush, the first kiss, and waving you off to Prom with that boy I would've intimidated as he waited for you on the doorstep—please believe that we were with you in our hearts. You are the most precious thing to us both and we love you forever and always.

Meredith blinked away tears. Would they mind that she hadn't yet got near most of those milestones being so afraid to mix with others? They had imagined an ordinary high school experience for her and she had spent the years in seclusion.

It would have been foolish of us not to consider that disaster could strike anytime and this is why we have prepared these messages for you. Please do not tell anyone what is contained in these letters. You are the last of our kind, the last full blooded one of us. You may meet those with one parent from our people, or a grandparent, but the genetic inheritance gets diluted with every step away from the source and powers weaken. Because you are special, the knowledge of who and what you are is too dangerous to share with anyone, even your most trusted friend. They would also be put at risk or, what may be worse, be tempted to betray you. It is far better to prevent that situation arising by keeping this to yourself.

In this letter we will tell you what you are. In the second, we will tell you about the Perilous. Do not be anxious: they should know nothing about you as there is no child of your name registered where you were born. We lived off record as much as possible, thanks to some sympathizers, and people like Theo, whom we encouraged to think that we were part of a US government witness protection programme. But if our enemies do hear that you've survived, please do not underestimate their ruthlessness. Cut all ties and run—run as hard and far as you can. Above all else, you have to survive.

Meredith rubbed the bridge of her nose. Who were these Perilous? The criminals who assassinated her parents? Why did her father and mother have to be so guarded about telling her all this? Clearly she needed the information right now if her enemies were as dangerous as claimed, not wait for Episode Two like some cliffhanger in a drama serial.

We may never have had a chance to explain to you that your ability to see differently is not actually something strange, nor is it unnatural. It was an ability common among our kind for generations beyond count. We left instructions with Theo that you should keep your ability quiet and should act as if you had normal vision as far as possible, not because you should be ashamed of it but because it would put you in danger to reveal it.

Your ability evolved through genetic variance. Our ancestors once lived in an isolated community, a large island nation. At some point in their history a genetic mutation was introduced resulting in children with four rather than three cone receptors in the eye. The fourth cone gives you the ability to see into the ultraviolet spectrum, somewhat like a bird. Each cone cell contains a tiny oil deposit that acts like a filter on the lens and this makes you better at differentiating colours and in effect seeing them as brighter than they are to ordinary people.

So that was why she saw differently! If only her parents had still been with her to explain, she could've avoided so much embarrassment and confusion.

It is an amazing privilege to see as you do and comes with other abilities which you'll understand as you grow into them. Use them wisely.

Finally, we should explain why we said you were the last of our kind. We mentioned that this ability developed among the population of a large island nation. Just as Darwin observed different beak formations among finches living on neighbouring islands, we developed differently from those peoples closest to us. It spelled disaster as difference is always punished. We have been relentlessly hunted and persecuted to the point that we are close to extinction.

This genocide has been a secret tragedy of the last few centuries. We don't know where we originated—our archeologists think it might have been in the Mediterranean— but our forebears borrowed a myth that summed up our plight. In exile we called ourselves the people from Atlantis, after the fabled land wiped out by a giant wave. In our case this wave of destruction has been our fellow islanders, the ones we call the Perilous. We have always hoped that more of us survive in hidden pockets but at the time of writing we believe the three of us are the last alive.

And now we too might be gone. As the last of a lost civilization, you are the bearer of our hope that one element of us will survive into the future, mixed in with the population at large. Keep yourself safe and keep our secret.

Love

Dad and Mom

Meri refolded the letter and put it back in the box. On second thought, she spread it out and took a photo of the contents with her phone so she could read it at home. There was too much to take in now. She locked it back inside the box and pressed the key to her lips. So her parents' death wasn't the result of some kind of mafia-style vendetta as Theo thought, but a bizarre centuries old struggle for survival. Why did a simple difference in the anatomy of the eye mean so much hatred was poured upon their kind? She didn't understand people who could act like that. It was racism, pure and simple.

There came a knock on the door. Theo put his head round the edge. 'Everything OK?'

She would have to say something or he would burst with curiosity. 'Fine. I mean, sort of fine as it is a kind of farewell note from my parents explaining that my vision is, you know, naturally different?' Some things weren't to be spoken aloud even in the office of professional secret keepers. 'Oh, and they thanked you for looking after me.'

Theo smiled sadly. 'Oh, OK then. That's kind of them. So, no earth shattering revelations?'

She tucked the box under her arm. 'No, Theo, I'm not the heir to a fortune somewhere or an alien beamed in like Super Man.'

He stepped back as Meri left the room. 'I think he arrived on a spaceship.'

'Whatever: beamed, crash-landed, neither was in my past.'

'Good to know. What are you going to do with that?' He pointed to the box.

'Leave it here as Mr Rivers suggested.'

'And did your parents say if you still need to hide?'

'Yes, and yes.'

'Why?'

'It's complicated and I haven't got the whole story. But they were clear that we're to carry on as we always have. You've done a good job so far.'

Theo took the hint. 'Fine, Miss Mystery, keep your

secrets. You missed something yourself though: they served real coffee!'

'What's that like?' She didn't think for one minute that he'd stopped trying to wheedle the entire contents of the message out of her but he'd given up for now.

'Real coffee? Nectar of the caffeinated gods.'

They said their farewells to the receptionist and Meri handed over the box for safe-keeping.

'Mr Rivers is seeing another client but he said he would be in touch when the second package arrives,' said the receptionist.

'Thank you.'

Theo leaned against her desk. 'Don't forget, Sophia love: concert at the Barbican next week if you like.'

The receptionist shuffled her neat pile of papers. 'I like.'

'Good. I'll meet you here at six-thirty.'

Meri waited until they reached the lift before whispering. 'Theo, really!'

He shrugged. 'She's hot.'

'She doesn't smile.'

'That's the challenge.'

Meri shook her head. 'I don't want to know.'

'And she has a supply of real coffee.'

'Mercenary or what?'

Theo chuckled. 'I liked her with or without the coffee.'

Meri tried to imagine what the uptight lady saw in her trendy guardian with his ear-spike and artsy clothes. A walk on the wild side maybe? The ingredients that went into attraction were always a puzzle. 'I'd better get to school. Try not to pick up any more dates between now and this evening.'

Theo's blue eyes' twinkled. 'One at a time, Meri, that's my rule. See you later at home.'

3

Under instructions to discover more about his classmate, Kel found Meri sitting on her own in a corner of the cafeteria. She was ignoring her meal and gazing at her phone as if it contained the secret to the universe.

'Hi. Missed you on the bus this morning.' He put his tray next to hers.

She stuffed the mobile in her pocket. 'I had a doctor's appointment.'

'Everything OK?'

'Yep.'

'Right. So, Meri, what are you going to do in Art this afternoon?' Digging in his jeans' pocket, he handed over the money. 'Now you can get yourself a new canvas.'

'You're a life-saver.' She tucked it away without counting. 'I guess I'll have another go at my painting, make up some influence guff to keep Miss happy.'

He stuck a straw in his carton of raspberry and pear juice. 'Tell her it's after the school of nineteenth century Japanese artists.'

'Sounds classy but what do you mean?'

Getting out his phone, he called up a picture of the Hokusai print. 'Seen that before?'

'Well, yes, I guess.' She took the phone from him to get a closer look.

'I've got reproductions of these on my bedroom wall. I was thinking yesterday that it's the same curve as yours, though yours was abstract. Tell her it is a reinterpretation and keep the colours a little more defined: that should keep her off your back.'

She touched the little image lightly with her fingertip. 'I love it.'

He felt a strong urge to tidy back the lock of hair that had dropped forward and was playing over the screen. There always seemed to be something slightly wayward, heading for out of control, about Meri. 'We could, you know, go see some more of his work if you like? I think they have some originals at the British Museum.' Did that sound lame, or what?

Meri didn't seem to notice his cringeworthy play for a date. 'They do? Then yes, I'd like that.'

'How about Saturday—if you're not already busy?'

She hummed noncommittally.

'Or Sunday?' Kel worried he sounded too eager. He wasn't doing this solely because Ade had asked him to get to know her but it was a fuzzy line he was walking.

'No, Saturday is fine. It's just that it's my birthday.'

'You must've made plans already.'

'Only for the evening. I'm going to see Tee Park at the Hammersmith Odeon.'

'Hey, so am I!'

'I think half the sixth form are from the gossip I've picked up.' She handed back the phone. 'Would you like to upgrade to a VIP ticket? Theo gets them as freebies with his job.'

Kel had to make a quick calculation. He was supposed to be going with Ade but if he passed the ticket on to Lee, he could get the night off from bodyguard duty. Ade would back him if he thought it would further his agenda to get to know the mystery girl. 'Thanks. That would be great.'

'Only downside is you'll have to spend the night with Theo and his friends.' She had a sweet little smile now as if this really wasn't much of a downside.

'I think I'd enjoy that.'

'Don't say I didn't warn you.'

'I'm intrigued.'

'I don't want to scare you off.'

'So this must be your eighteenth?'

'Well, duh.'

He grinned. 'Cool. Mine was a few weeks ago. I didn't get to go on a date for that though.'

'This is a date?' She pretended interest in her yoghurt, stirring in the strawberry that had reached the surface.

'Do you want it to be?' He had a sudden ego-puncturing notion that the attraction was all one-sided.

'Why not?' She pushed the tray from her and squared her shoulders as she faced him. 'Yes, thank you. I'd like to go out with you on my birthday, Kel.'

They chatted some more about their subjects, moving from their rather stilted exchanges to something more relaxed. Meri owned up to needing practice at small talk, admitting she had spent many years being very shy and barely talking to people outside her home. Now she dropped her guard a little, he learned that she was studying English and History as well as Art.

'You see I believe in preparing myself thoroughly for unemployment,' she joked.

'What about Art college?'

She wrinkled her nose. 'Don't think I'm good enough.'

'Of course you are.'

'Jury's definitely still out on that. Are you going to apply?'

'After eco-service? I think so. Part-time as I've got another job.'

'Which college?'

'Depends where Ade wants to go.'

'Are you, like, attached to him by an umbilical cord?'

'Exactly. We're like brothers, from different mothers.' He grinned.

'What about the rest of your family?'

How to explain that his people were in hiding and that he had been separated from his family for many years now, living in the community that gathered around Ade. 'Mum died when I was little so it's just my dad and an older sister. They've both got jobs that mean they spend a lot of time abroad.'

'Oh? Where?'

'They travel a lot.' He had to say something that wasn't quite so vague. 'My sister is coming back for Christmas though.' He'd not seen Jenny since Easter. She was one of Ade's cousins' bodyguards and living in Amsterdam.

'How much older?'

'Three years.'

'That's nice. I'd've liked a brother or sister but I suppose I got lucky with Theo.'

'What happened to your parents?'

She stuffed a wrapper into the empty yoghurt pot. 'They

disappeared—dead—something.' She got up. 'Sorry: I guess it's a difficult subject for me. See you later.'

Putting the tray on the clearing trolley, she hurried out.

Of course, it's a difficult subject, you idiot. Having lost his own mother Kel knew what it felt like to have that wound probed. He thumped his forehead. He had been doing so well until he had pushed just that little too hard. Ade may want the information as quickly as possible but Kel had to move at Meri's pace, not his employer's. With a sigh, he moved his tray to join his friends on their table in the centre of the cafeteria.

'How's that going?' Ade asked, nodding towards the door through which Meri had exited.

'Fine. We're going out together on Saturday and I'm meeting her guardian. He might know more about her origins if I ask the right questions.'

'Saturday?' Ade's eyebrow winged up. 'But...?'

'Yeah, I know, the concert. Lee, will you take my ticket?'

Lee groaned. He was more a soul music fan than Tee Park's brand of urban fusion that had become popular over the last decade. 'You'll owe me.'

'I'll be there too but as a VIP thanks to Meri's guardian.'

'You get VIP treatment and I get to sweat it out in the mosh pit with Ade throwing himself about like a demented meerkat.' Lee shook his head at the unfairness of life.

'Is he rich, this guardian guy?' Ade asked.

'No, he's got some job that gets him the tickets.'

'Interesting.' Ade entered the new information into his phone file on Meredith Marlowe. 'And how long have you been calling Mouse "Meri"?'

'Since she asked me to yesterday. I don't think she likes being called "mouse". We should stop.'

'But it suits her.'

'Only if you think mice are sarcastic critters with a sharp bite.'

'Well, now you come to mention it.... Anyway, good work.'

Kel rubbed his throat, feeling distinctly uncomfortable. 'It's not exactly work.'

Ade caught something in his friend's expression that set off alarm bells. 'Kel, it is. Don't forget that. If she's not one of us, then you can't be friends with her; she can't get too close.'

He knew that. Of course he knew that. 'It's just a date to a museum and concert. We're hardly shopping for rings.'

'The fact that you even had that thought kinda worries me.' Ade glanced over at Lee. 'Perhaps I should get you to find out more about her.'

'Him?' Kel snorted. 'After Busgate, I think she's rather taken against him.'

'She doesn't have to like me to answer a few questions,' said Lee.

'Look, no, that's not fair.' Kel couldn't bear the thought of Lee scaring the life out of her. 'Leave it with me. I like her— but just as a friend, I promise. I won't mess up and I'll get the answers without anyone getting hurt.'

'We'll see. I'm pulling you off this case the moment you get too involved, understood?' said Ade in his 'I'm the boss' voice.

By the time Kel reached the Art room, Meri had found a book on Japanese prints on the resources shelf and had it opened strategically next to the blank canvas she had purchased from Miss Hardcastle.

'New approach, Meredith?' asked the teacher.

Meri shrugged. 'Kel was really helpful. Pointed me in the direction of this guy.'

'Hokusai. One of my favourites. I always find his prints talk to a modern sensibility even though he was working in the nineteenth century.'

'I was going to do a collage of the tidal wave in my art book before I start the painting, echoing the shape but made up of tiny pictures of all the climate deniers.'

Miss Hardcastle pursued her lips. 'This isn't Citizenship, Meredith.'

'No, but art can be political. You told us that.'

Volleyed that one right back at you, Miss H, thought Kel as he put on his apron.

With a sniff the teacher stalked off. 'I'll leave you to it then.'

Making it look casual, Kel wandered over to Meri's side of the room. 'Starting over?'

'Hmm-hmm. I know now what I want to do with that.' She glared through her glasses at the canvas as if it had personally affronted her. 'I'm not sure Miss will approve. She doesn't like me.'

Kel flicked through the book of prints. 'She's always nice to me.'

'I don't know what I've done but I get this disapproving vibe off her. Can you spread some of your nice guyness in my direction so she doesn't get all shirty about my project again?'

Kel perched on the edge of the table. 'You think I'm a nice guy?'

'Aren't you?' Meri lifted the glasses to the top of her head, a nervous habit he'd noticed. She was always taking them on and off as if she couldn't decide if she needed them or not.

'I must be if you think so.' He stole the glasses off her head and put them on. They made barely any difference to his vision, just dulled the colours around him a little. Maybe they were tinted? 'What's your prescription?'

'It's just minus point five,' she said quickly, taking them back.

'Maybe you don't need them then?'

'You're an optician now?'

'Fair point.' He held up his hands. 'So, am I a nice guy or not?'

'Not when you're stealing my glasses. But I've decided that, on balance, you must be because you came to my rescue yesterday.' Hands on hips, she pursed her lips; he guessed she was doing battle with the canvas in her imagination. 'I think I'll go for a view of Mount Fuji. It's in almost all his pictures, have you noticed that? I want to get the heat of the volcano and the coolness of the shape on the horizon all in one abstract: do you think I can do it?'

Looking at her earnest face, Kel had to restrain himself. He would liked to have moved closer to stand behind her, arms casually wrapped around her, her head nestled under his chin as they chatted through her ideas, but that kind of behaviour was frowned on in the classroom. Kel ushered away his inappropriate thoughts. *Just friends, remember.* 'If your tidal wave was anything to go by, then yes. There's a lot of clever stuff going on in there.' He tapped her forehead. 'My friends think your last attempt is great. We've put it up in the clubroom.'

'Clubroom? You have a clubroom?'

'Yeah, where I live with the guys.'

'Of course you do, your family is abroad,' she murmured, piecing his life story together. 'Are you refugees? Is it like a hostel?'

'Some of us are, but it's a stretch to call Ade's place a hostel. You should come round and see the picture. I'll make sure we've picked up our socks.'

'Gross. How many guys in your house?'

'About sixteen.' Ade's court was one of the larger ones as he was first in line.

'Oh my God, it must be a health hazard in there: sixteen boys' worth of dirty underwear!'

'We fumigate from time to time and chase the rats out on Sundays.' In fact Ade ran the house like a military camp so no one left anything lying around.

Meri wrinkled her brow. 'You...you're teasing me?'

'What do you think? Do I smell that bad to you?'

She took a sniff before she realized what she was doing. Her blush was worthy of a Turner sunset. 'No, you smell, um, nice.'

'I'm a nice guy who smells nice: I'd better quit while I'm ahead.' Pleased with that encounter, Kel returned to his potter's wheel and settled down to work. He caught Meri's eye across the classroom and winked. So cute the way she blushed.

How could you be so stupid? Meri asked her reflection in the girls' toilets. *You actually sniffed him! Did you leave all your common sense at home this morning?* She splashed her face, wishing she could wash away the memory so easily.

The comp-punk girl from the bus, who also happened to be in her Art class, strolled in and stood at the next sink. Throwing her bag on the floor, she took out a lipgloss and touched up her dark red lips. Meri wasn't wearing her glasses so the effect was more clown smile than the vampiric cool that the girl was aiming for, one of the reasons Meri rarely wore any makeup herself as she couldn't take herself seriously with it on.

The girl noticed her watching. 'Hi. Systems running OK?'

Meri had heard that comp-punks had their own jargon and this was easy enough to translate. 'Fine. You?' Meri searched her memory for a name—Sadie Rush. She'd been the one to drop the hint about not sitting in the seats on the bus. A decade ago, comp-punks had taken over from geeks as the poster boys and girls for computer obsessives. Sadie and her friends still had the geek skills but had also developed their own music and sub-culture.

'Just rebooting.' Sadie waved the lipstick. 'So, you and Kel seem very friendly recently?'

'You noticed that?'

Sadie laughed. 'Of course. Nothing much better to do when Art gets boring than gather some data.' She plucked at the run in her fishnet tights, not bothered that it had reached all the way up under her imitation leather skirt.

'He's been really nice to me because, news flash, Miss Hardcastle has turned out not to be my greatest fan.'

Sadie rolled her eyes. 'God, yes, she can be bitchy. I think she prefers the guys, you know—sees us as competition?'

'So it's not personal?'

'Not in the sense you are the only one. She told me my sketch was "gauche" and the kind of thing you'd expect from a GCSE student.'

'Ouch.'

Sadie got out a brush and began back-combing her fountain of black hair. It crackled with static. With Meri's vision, the black had such depth and texture, shades of almost navy blue, she could have looked at it for hours.

'Something wrong?' asked Sadie.

Caught girl-watching, so embarrassing. 'You've lovely hair.' Meri felt rather envious of the easy-in-her-skin exuberance of Sadie.

'Oh, thanks. I was thinking of getting it highlighted.' She tucked a strand behind her ear.

'But you don't need to! It's got so many different colours in it already.'

Sadie grimaced. 'Crow black as my brother tells me.'

'You take fashion tips from your brother?'

Sadie brandished the brush at the mirror, eyes meeting Meri's in the reflection. 'You know, you're right. He still wears brown socks with navy shoes so he can talk. Why haven't we ever chatted before?'

Meri shrugged. 'I'm shy, I guess.'

'So am I—no really, I am. With boys that is. This may be the twenty-first century but I seem stuck back in the 1950s. I've been meaning to ask Lee Irving out for weeks now and never got up the courage.'

She liked Count Twit? 'Yeah, that would take courage.'

'The word is he digs comp-punks but I'm not sure that's right. Getting mixed signals from him. Hey! As you've got an in with his crowd with Kel, could you, you know, put in a good word for me if you get a chance?'

Meri laughed at the absurdity of that idea. 'You saw what happened yesterday on the bus. I couldn't exactly say a character recommendation from me would be helpful.'

'But you were so cool! We all said so when you got off the bus. We'd kinda got into the habit of making way for the three of them and finally someone stood up to that crap. We were high-fiving you, but just quietly and invisibly so they didn't see.'

'How brave.'

'I know.' When Sadie smiled she showed her slightly gappy teeth, a friendly feature, Meri decided. 'It's not that we're scared of them so much as in awe. Kel's definitely the most approachable of the three.'

'Yes, he is.' This time when her eyes met Sadie's, they shared a smile of agreement.

'Do you want to go to Crazy Beanz after school, you know, hang out and have a chat?' Sadie asked. 'Some of us comp-punks go there most days.'

'I'd like that. As long as I don't have to have my eyebrow pierced first or something.'

'Nah, that's only for the second meet-up. See you at the gate then.'

After Sadie left, Meri nodded at her reflection. Not bad: two friends in two days and one was a dating-boyfriend kind of friend. It seemed that as soon as one person reached out to you, others would follow. Theo had been right: there had been potential friends waiting in the wings.

KEL WOKE up on Saturday with a low fever. He'd stripped off his T-shirt during the night and all the covers but still he felt too warm. He rolled out of bed, stumbled over the guitar he'd left on the floor and then stubbed his toe on the desk. This sucked: he was supposed to be seeing Meri today and he really didn't want to cry off.

A shower: maybe he'd feel better after one?

He bumped into Lee in the corridor outside the bathroom. Both wearing towels round their waist, they looked like members of some Pacific island tribe. Lee's jaguar markings were slightly visible in the afterglow of his early morning jog.

'You feeling OK? You're looking a little rough. Late night?' asked Lee.

Kel shook his head. 'No. I think I'm coming down with something.'

'I'll get you some paracetamol.'

'Thanks.' Lee could be a pillock at times but he was always the first to offer a helping hand when someone was in trouble.

After a shower and a couple of tablets, Kel began to think he could manage the day. If only his skin would stop dry-itching. He had wanted to look good for Meri; if this went on he was going to be a blotchy mess.

Ade joined them in the sunny breakfast corner of the kitchen. 'You look like shit, man.'

'Thanks.'

'Feeling hot? Itchy?'

'Yeah.'

Ade and Lee exchanged a glance.

'Wow. This could be it. Our late developer might finally show his spots.' Lee grinned.

'Hardly late. But I really could do without this right now.'

'Oh yeah, today's the big date, isn't it?' Ade got out his phone. 'You should be fine as long as you don't strip down to a T-shirt. Markings sometimes take months to come through after the first fever but, if she is one of us, we don't want her to see you in blaze-out mode.'

'That'd scare her off for sure.' From his chirpy tone, Lee was thoroughly enjoying Kel's dilemma.

Ade elbowed Lee. 'Look, Kel, you need to read this. It was everything I could find on Theo Woolf, Meri's guardian.'

'Thanks.' Sticking to plain toast and black tea, Kel read through the notes. 'They've moved around a lot.'

'Yeah—some time abroad, then Durham, Nottingham, St Ives, now London. He's been working his way up the arts funding ladder. People seem to like him from the chat online.'

'Any chance he's one of us?'

'No sign of that. Parents, grandparents, all very middle of the road, traceable in their local area for years, no hint of difference from those around them. Theo is the only one with the wanderlust but he's never made contact with any of our communities in the various places he's lived.'

'And he's no relation to Meri?'

'None at all, which is the oddest thing about this. He can't be much more than twenty years older than her but he seems to have been her guardian since she was four. How many parents would leave guardianship to a man that age?'

'There was a lot of disruption around the time of the great floods in the UK—loss of life and some public records being ruined. Maybe it was something to do with that. Definitely something to ask about.'

'Try to be subtle, OK? We don't want to tip him off.'

'Yes, I get it.'

Ade poured a second bowl of cereal. 'It would be so great to find another girl out there. We don't have enough.'

'If our people stopped birth selecting in favour of boys, then our population wouldn't have become so out of balance. I know your uncle outlawed the practice but I think it still goes on in some countries. We can't carry on turning a blind eye.'

'And even if it doesn't, the time lag means that the imbalance will linger while our generation grows up. It's a crying shame,' said Lee, surprisingly weighing in on Kel's side of the argument. 'What?' He must have seen their expressions. 'Hey, I'm no misogynist. I can do the maths. If we want to hook up inside our own community we need a bigger pool of talent.'

'So tastefully put, Lee. Maybe we should transfer you from protection to the diplomatic service?' said Ade wryly. 'Kel, we'll keep an eye on you tonight from a distance. If the fever gets worse, call it off. Some guys have a strange time with their skin change.'

'Like you did.' Kel's spirits rose a little as he remembered his friend's embarrassment. 'I seem to remember you hallucinating in Geography one day, telling the teacher he was an alien and that he had antennae sprouting from his ears.'

Ade grimaced. 'It was tufts of hair and I still think Mr Bristow was very weird.'

'Teachers generally are, otherwise they wouldn't put themselves through the torture of teaching people like us.'

'By the way, I put in our applications for eco-service.' Ade gestured to the three of them.

'So early?' Kel didn't like the reminder of what lay around the corner. A wasted couple of years when he'd much prefer to be getting on with his studies.

'Yeah. Have to do that or we might get split up. I volunteered us for the new embankment works so we can stay in London and carry on living here.'

That didn't sound too bad. Some eco-service teams spent the year in old army barracks or under canvas in the wilds of the countryside. 'I'm all for that. But maybe, you know, you could have asked us first?' The balance between friend and prince was a tricky one to get right and in Kel's opinion Ade was getting more authoritarian with each passing year.

'Sorry, man. I wasn't thinking.' But Kel noticed that Ade didn't offer to withdraw the applications.

Lee inspected the pristine cuffs of his white shirt. Unlike Kel and Ade, he always dressed as if he were hoping for a fashion shoot rather than school lessons. 'I hope you can swing us an office job?'

'Nah, I said you wanted to shift mud with your bare hands.' Ade sliced an apple into quarters and shared it with his friends. 'I can't control where they post us within the team. We'll just have to take what they hand out.'

Kel wondered where Meri would apply. Eco-service was supposed to be a gender neutral lottery, though girls tended to be given the lightest duties. Maybe it was something they could discuss today? If she was one of them, he would suggest she also ask for the same posting.

'As the embankment is a competitive entry project, we're all going to have to put together a personal statement saying why we are just the right guys for the job,' continued Ade. 'We have to send them in next week so don't leave it to the last minute. I'll read them over and check we're saying the right kind of things.'

'Yes, sir.' Lee took his plate to the dishwasher.

Ade quirked an eyebrow at Kel. 'That wasn't an ironic "sir" was it?'

'Nope. You are coming over all masterful this morning, *sir*.'

Ade pointed at him with a slice of apple. 'Now that was ironic.'

'Always is, *sir*.'

Ade chuckled and pushed back his chair. 'Go sweet talk the mystery girl and just don't let your markings flame out.'

'And how exactly am I supposed to stop that happening?'

'It helps if there's no kissing or fighting.'

Kel frowned. 'That's OK then. The way I'm feeling, I'll be lucky if I get through the day without passing out. The chances of me making a move on her are little to none.'

Ade thumped him on the back. 'Best to keep it that way.'

4

K el waited in the pillared entrance to the British Museum. Despite feeling like death warmed up, a smile lit up his face as he saw Meri running up the white steps towards him, hair bobbing in a ponytail. She was wearing a clingy cream top, short black skirt and leggings. Hoop earrings completed the outfit. She always dressed in an understated way, no garish colours, but it felt just right to him. A nice figure, he noted. She kept that hidden at school, like she did her sassy personality. The transformation reminded him of a moth that had broken free of its chrysalis

'Hi there.' Hesitating, he moved forward to kiss her cheek. The protocol for meeting her out of school was a bit hazy. 'Happy birthday.'

'Sorry I'm late. I forgot they'd closed Tottenham Court Road to pump out the Northern Line.' She was a little out of breath. She must've run from Oxford Circus.

'That's fine. I wasn't waiting long.' He reached for her hand. It felt just right settled in his. 'It's given me time to find out where the Japanese prints are on display.'

The galleries were busy with tourists and there was so much to see Kel found it a little overwhelming in his mildly fevered state. He decided his time was better spent studying Meri as she pored over the Hokusai prints. Her lashes were long and curled slightly, framing her sea-green eyes. She wasn't the kind of beauty that got noticed at school, but he found himself drawn more and more to her. She did little to disguise her reaction to things when she was like this: happiness, curiosity, delight, all passed in succession across face. The impression was like he was watching someone experience the world for the first time, which was odd considering she was only a few weeks younger and presumably with her travel she'd had the chance to see as much, if not more, than him.

'I'm pleased I had this idea,' he said. 'You seem happy here.'

'I am.' She looked up at him shyly.

'I don't remember you smiling so much at school.'

'I don't—didn't. I decided last week I needed to emerge from my shell.'

'That explains it.'

'Explains what?'

'The appearance of Mighty Mouse on the bus and the fact that you've started talking to me and other people. I saw you hanging out with Sadie and the comp-punks.'

She shrugged. 'They're a nice bunch, friendly once you dig through the jargon. I guess I just reached a point where I couldn't be scared any longer.'

He took her hand for a comforting squeeze and led her on to the Greek gallery. 'What were you scared of?'

She wrinkled her nose, evidently perplexed by herself. 'I don't know really. Losing my parents when I was little probably did that to me. It was so sudden, I always think I'm going to lose everything in a blink of an eye.'

He brushed the back of her hand with his thumb. 'That's probably natural after an early bereavement.'

'I suppose so.' She had gone quiet. This was painful territory for her, he understood that.

'I only lost one parent—my mum—but it was still completely gutting. I can't imagine what it was like suddenly to have no one. So how did you end up with your guardian?'

'Theo's a family friend. I don't have any relatives so he took me on.'

'Sounds a great guy. So...er, you get on OK?' Dammit, not now! Kel's temperature was soaring just when she was beginning to open up to him.

'Oh, yes, we do. You'll see for yourself very soon.'

'Er, yeah, whatever.' A ripple of fiery itching spread up his arm from where he clasped her hand. He let go abruptly. 'Sorry—gotta sit for a moment. I had a big night last night and am feeling fragile today.'

'Oh, OK.' She followed him with a wounded look on her face. He led her to the cafe in the glass-roofed atrium, wondering if he would survive the next ten minutes without throwing up in front of her.

'Get me some water, would you?' He thrust a swipe card at her. He was a hair away from fainting. 'Buy yourself something while you're there.'

'Fine.' Leaving her bag with him, she took a place in the queue, a sniffy little toss of her ponytail telling him his brusque manner wasn't appreciated.

Kel rested his head on the table. Shit. He'd imagined such a different day and now all he wanted was to be in bed —alone.

Meri selected an elderflower for herself from the display of glass bottles and fizzy water for Kel. Not that he deserved it if he had been partying all night and got wasted. Clearly he hadn't been anticipating much from his date with her if he had thought that good preparation. She glanced over. He had his head buried in his arms, shutting out her and the rest of the world. How romantic.

'Happy eighteenth, Meri,' she murmured. This was one to tell the grandkids: that she spent her coming of age and first date with an hungover hunk of a guy who looked like he was going to throw up on her shoes. She sent a quick text to Sadie.

It's not going well. Help!

What's up?

Kel's hungover. I'm in nurse mode looking after him.

What a beachball. Dump him in trash and take me to the gig.

Would've been a better idea but I promised the VIP ticket to him. I can't back out unless he does.

Poor you! He doesn't deserve you.

Cheered that her new friend totally understood her perspective on her first date, Meri paid for the drinks and carried them carefully back to the table, glass bottles rolling precariously on the tray. She unscrewed the cap and passed the water to him, bumping against his forearm to get his attention.

'Here you go, party-animal.'

He looked up, cheeks flushed, eyes glittery. 'Hey, you've got weird sparkles around your hair.' He reached out to bat the imaginary sparks away.

'Crap, this isn't a hangover, is it? You're really ill.' She felt his forehead, regretting now she'd been so quick to bad-mouth him to Sadie. 'You're burning up, Kel.'

He gulped some water, washing down a pill as he did so. 'I'll be fine. Just wussy man flu.'

'Kel, this isn't man flu. You're running a temperature. You should be in bed, not traipsing around a museum with me.' She took out her phone. 'What's Ade's number? I'll tell him I'm bringing you home.'

He pushed the phone back to the table top. 'Stop—really, just stop. I'll be fine. It's not flu, not catching. I've got... malaria. Flares up from time to time.'

'Oh. Why didn't you say so? It's nothing to be ashamed of.' Since mosquitoes had started flourishing in the warmer climate of England in the last few decades, it wasn't unheard of for Thames valley people to get malaria. 'But that takes like three days, doesn't it?'

'I'll be fine. Look, it's a boring topic, just give me a moment for the paracetamol to kick in and I'll be fighting fit again. Let's change the subject.'

Meri wasn't sure what was a safe topic with someone who really didn't look well enough to hold up their end of the conversation. 'Anyway, um, those prints were really great; thanks for suggesting I came.'

He rubbed his eyes as if the sparkles were still bothering his vision. 'I'm glad.'

'You...you thinking of Art College then?'

'Yeah. Why don't you tell me your plans while I just drink my water?'

'Plans?' She laughed softly. 'I've never been really what you'd call a long term thinker. Theo and I have moved around a lot.'

'Why've you done that?'

'Oh, you know, jobs and stuff.' They'd usually moved when she'd made a mistake, got someone too interested in how she saw the world. She must remember not to go that route with Kel. It would be so lovely, though, to find a person who could see as she could, much less lonely.

'Will you stay with him, now you're eighteen?'

She hadn't thought of that. Theo's guardian duties were officially at an end as of today. 'We've not talked about it. He's like family to me. My only family.' Did Theo feel that way about her, she wondered? He always joked about stuff like that so it was hard to know. It would no longer be cute living with a young adult rather than a foster daughter. Maybe she should start thinking about what moving on would look like, how she would finance it, but that was hard when she was terrified of the world and her own future in it with faceless enemies wanting to end her life.

Kel took a gulping breath as if he was swallowing down nausea. 'What...what about eco-service? Will you stay at home for that?'

'Isn't it a lottery? They can send you anywhere.'

'Ah, no. Ade found out that you can apply early and put in a bid for a local position. We're applying for the Embankment project.'

'Can't really see myself working a digger or a dredger.'

'But...but there are jobs for support staff too.' He held the cool glass to his face.

She sipped her elderflower. 'You're feeling really grim, aren't you?'

'I've had better days.'

'Do you want me to leave you here for half an hour or so? You don't really have to talk when you're feeling like that. I'll go to the Egyptian gallery and come back and see how you're getting on. If you are still unwell, I'm taking you home in a taxi.'

His relief was visible in his eyes. 'Thanks, Meri. Yeah, I'd like just to sit for a bit. The fever roars in like a hurricane but it spins off as quickly. Sorry to rain on your birthday parade.'

'Catch your breath, big guy. I'll be back in thirty minutes.'

She left him slumped on the table. This was acutely embarrassing. Walking away might seem cruel, but she didn't know him well enough to be certain what was best to do. Giving him some space seemed the kindest option. Having to play at being her interested date had been torture for him so at least she had let him off that hook.

Looking to distract herself, she wandered among the granite slabs and fragments of hieroglyphs admiring the remnants of lost civilizations. Not so much lost as superseded. Thinking of her parents' letter, she decided to do some research of her own. Did the museum have anything on Atlantis? Going to an computer screen index to the collection, she typed in some key terms. References in the Flood Tablet came up first, the fragment of cuneiform from Nineveh telling the story of Gilgamesh and the Noah-like character, Utnapishtim, who survived a six-day flood that killed the rest of humanity. Scholars had taken it as evidence that there had been some world flooding event, at least in the Mediterranean if not wider than that, which had left its mark in the stories of the region. That was linked to the development of stories about the doomed world of Atlantis. She followed the onscreen directions and went to visit the tablet. Standing in front of the intricately carved stone she found it impossible to imagine that she could be linked to some civilization so old that its origins were lost and the only way of describing it had been left to the dubious area of myths.

Then a sudden revelation came—obvious to others, maybe, but new to her. Everyone alive on Earth was related to all these old objects; today's humans weren't a recent planting but a continuation of the old branches around her, the ones that had left behind these dusty fragments. That man over there could be related to pharaohs, the woman carrying a baby in a blue sling to ancient druids. The people who made these things weren't 'them'; they were 'us'. Meri had genuinely never considered that before; her imagination had been able to cope with a few generations on the family tree, but now she had to consider how it went back way beyond recorded history. What would survive if not genetic traces and distorted stories? Her biology teacher had told them you could pick up Neanderthal origins in many people's DNA so why not hints of other genetic inheritances if you knew what to look for?

'Maybe I really am from Atlantis,' she murmured to her reflection in the display case glass. 'Survivor of the flood: me, Noah and Utnapishtim.' She smiled at the thought of her in company with these hairy guys and their homemade boats.

Time was up. She returned to the cafe and found Kel had perked up enough to buy them both a round of sandwiches. That was a relief: she'd been worried how she could afford to pay the taxi fare home for him. If he had still been feeling unwell, she'd been planning to insist he bailed and went to bed.

'Feeling better now?'

'Yes. It's passed, thank God. Ham and cheese or roasted vegetables?' He did look much improved, light blue eyes bright but not glittering feverishly as they had been.

'How about half each?'

'Good thinking.' He divided the sandwiches between two plates. 'See anything interesting?'

She didn't want to confess her thoughts about Atlantis

and myths but she could mention a few of her musings. 'There's so much, isn't there? I was just thinking about how we're all related to the people who made this stuff, not just the things from the last few centuries but the really ancient artefacts.'

'I suppose we are.' He scratched at his sleeve.

'Are you really OK?'

'Bit of a heat rash. I suppose I should confess. Sorry I'm a mess today. I knew it before I left home but I was so wanting to impress you and not let you down, I came anyway.'

She smiled. 'I can truthfully say you've made an impression.'

'Ha-ha.'

'I mean, it makes a memorable first date, me going off on my own while you wilted in the cafe.'

'Cruel girl. No sympathy for the sick. First date, hey? I'm sorry.'

She smoothed her fingers over the back of his hand. 'Are you really feeling better? I wouldn't blame you if you wanted to cry off tonight.'

He raised his hand to cup her cheek. 'It's your birthday, Meri. I'm going to celebrate it with you if it kills me.'

'That's what worries me.' With a wry smile she tucked into her lunch.

THE WEAKNESS KEL had shown at the museum had passed by the time they arrived home to meet up with Theo and his friends. Meri was relieved that Kel was back to his charming normal behaviour which was just as well as he was about to face baptism by fire into her life. Theo had invited Saddiq and Valerie, two very alternative people in the arts world.

Valerie, a theatre designer, equalled two of sticklike Saddiq, an accountant in Theo's office. She had a great booming laugh that went well with her mop of frizzy dark hair and big brown eyes. She had dressed for the gig in an orange and yellow swirling print with a twist of material in her hair, part ornament, part turban. Meri settled her glasses on her nose to cut down the glare. Sensitive eyesight was not an asset around Valerie. Saddiq by contrast was dressed in a three-piece-suit, including waistcoat with watch chain, outfit accessorized with blue ankle-boots, his shit kickers as he called them. He had a neat beard and moustache, as well as a diamanté encrusted eyepatch which sent out mixed signals, hovering between pirate and Steampunk gentleman. He'd lost an eye in a terrorist attack as a child and made no bones about drawing attention to it.

As soon as Theo and friends heard her key in the lock, they broke into a squawking rendition of Happy Birthday. For people supposed to be promoting music, they were hopelessly tone deaf.

'Here she is: the newest adult in the British population!' Theo popped a champagne cork and poured them all a drink.

'Thanks, guys. This is Kel Douglas, a friend from school.' Meri pulled Kel into the kitchen with her.

'Into the lion's den,' he murmured.

'Kel, lovely to meet you! Make yourself at home,' Theo thrust a champagne flute into Meri's hand.

Valerie stood up and grabbed Kel to her generous bosom, kissing him on the cheeks. 'Aren't you just the most gorgeous thing ever!' She hugged Meri next, jolting champagne onto the floor. 'Well done catching this one, girl.'

Saddiq was not to be outdone in the 'how to make Meri squirm' competition. He also hugged Kel. 'A friend of Meri's is a friend of mine. But if you make her cry, I'm gonna kick your fine ass.'

'Geez, guys, what happened to tact?' moaned Meri.

'What's that?' asked Saddiq innocently.

'Makes me look good by contrast, doesn't it?' Theo shook Kel's hand and then passed him a flute of champagne. 'Theo Woolf.'

'Nice to meet you, Mr Woolf,' said Kel.

Valerie went off into a peal of laughter.

Theo mock-shivered. 'Mr Woolf sounds just wrong, like you expect me to eat you. Call me Theo.'

Kel smiled. 'OK, Theo.'

'Let's get the food on the table before we have to go out. Valerie's baked your favourite, Meri,' said Theo, bending over to check the oven.

'Cherry pie,' said Valerie happily. 'Made from the ones I froze from my allotment.'

'Oh wow: thanks!'

'And Saddiq brought in some fillet steaks so we're ready to have dinner now if you are?'

'Steaks? Amazing! I haven't had real meat since—'

'Lunchtime,' finished Kel.

'Pressed bits of what might once have been pig mixed with soya protein does not count, Kel. I'm talking proper red meat from a cow that mooed. How did you get hold of it, Saddiq?'

Saddiq smiled mysteriously. 'I have my sources.'

'Maybe I don't want to know, but thank you: this is epic. I'll just show Kel where he can put his jacket.' Escaping from the kitchen, Meri led him to her bedroom. 'Sorry about the hugging thing.'

'No worries. They're...colourful.'

'Yes, you can say that again. They mean well. I have a colourful adopted family.'

'And they love you.'

Meri wrapped her arms around her waist. 'I guess they do.'

'They absolutely do. And speaking of hugging.... I think we missed out that part at the museum. May I? A friendly one?' Hesitating a second, Kel closed the distance between them, dropping his leather jacket on the bed. He put his arms around her and drew her to his chest. 'There: that's better.'

With a sigh, she let her arms fall to her sides and leaned against him. Friendly had never felt so good. He rubbed his palm up and down the middle of her back, allowing her time to relax. It really was the best birthday present she had received.

'I didn't peg you as an enthusiastic meat-eater,' said Kel.

'Oh yes, when I get the chance. It blows the carbon budget to eat too much of the stuff doesn't it? Theo says it's the American in me—steers and cowboys and "How the West was won".'

'Yee-ha. You're American?' She felt the slight tension run through him before he returned to rubbing her back.

'Once, long ago. Been with Theo too long to remember much about my roots.' She didn't want to break the moment but they had an audience just beyond the door counting the seconds she spent in here with him. 'Saddiq's probably spent his entire carbon ration for the week on those steaks; I better get out there to check Theo doesn't burn them.'

Supper was as good as she anticipated, conversation raucous which was the only kind when Valerie and Saddiq were in the room. Theo was quieter than usual, words more guarded. As Meri feared, he was giving Kel a not very subtle interrogation, but then again, Kel seemed happy to answer and asked as many questions in return. Listening in, she learned a little more about him. Ade ruled the roost in their shared house because it belonged to his family. He got to choose his room mates.

'So your friend is from money?' Theo asked.

'Yes, once upon a time it was oil but that's all gone now obviously. I think they must've invested it wisely. Gone into solar and other renewables.'

'And you? Your parents come from wealth?'

Meri blushed. Next Theo would be asking if Kel could keep her in the style to which she had become accustomed. 'Ease up a bit. It's just a first date,' she whispered to Theo.

'It's OK, Meri, Kel knows I'm just getting to know him. I'm interested in people.'

'You're nosy.'

'That too.' Theo grinned at his friends.

Kel did seem to be taking it all in his stride. 'No, my family's not got anything like that behind them. We all have to work for a living—that's why we're spread out around the world, going where employment takes us.'

'But not you surely? You're at school still,' Valerie pointed out.

'Yeah, sure. But I'll soon be looking for a job too.' He mopped up the last of the meat juices with a fragment of French bread.

Valerie patted Meri's wrist. 'You can't have everything, dear.'

Her words confused Meri. 'What?'

'He's got looks, intelligence, an artistic soul, but no money. He was almost the perfect man.'

'Could you be anymore embarrassing if you tried?'

muttered Meri, feeling as if she was the one coming down with the fever now.

Valerie paused in thought. 'I probably could, sugar, but it's your birthday so I'll hold off.' She elbowed Kel who was sitting beside her. 'Anyway, this one doesn't mind me. He knows it's all teasing in good fun.'

'He does?' Meri met his eyes.

Kel smiled easily. 'I do. Just give me a few free passes, OK, when you meet the guys I live with? They'll probably give you a hard time too.'

AFTER A ROCKY START at the museum, Meri had to admit that she was having possibly her best birthday ever. They had prime seats at the concert, front row of the circle—not that they stayed sitting long because Tee Park was in good form, belting out his songs with the backing of a full band, singers and dancers. He looked great: an explosion of dreadlocks, warpaint and a graffiti patterned suit. The music went right through her, making her bones vibrate with the bass and drums. Despite knowing they'd all be deaf for a few days, her party were all on their feet dancing and clapping along with the crowd.

Meri thought she caught a glimpse of someone familiar down in the scrum in front of the stage. She tugged on Kel's sleeve then pulled him so her mouth was at the level of his ear.

'Is that Ade I can see down there?'

Kel turned his head to steal a quick kiss. 'Yeah—and you saved me from that. Lee had to go with him. For Ade being in the middle of that pack equals a good night out.'

Meri spotted Lee next, looking far from happy as he repelled the most enthusiastic bundlers from his friend with some neat moves that looked like they were taken from a martial art. 'Lee looks miserable. You both should leave Ade to it. He's a big guy; I'd put money on the fact that he'll emerge alive.'

Kel shook his head. 'Oh, we wouldn't do that to him.'

'Sweet of you.'

Kel just smiled. 'Enjoying yourself?'

Feeling bold, she went up on tiptoes and brushed her lips over his. 'Best night ever.'

He put his arms around her so they could dance together even though the number playing was as far from a slow romantic dance as you could get. He didn't mind being out of step with the rest of the world, Meri realized, which counted as an attractive side to his character in her books. This close though, she could feel he was a little too hot.

'Why don't you take off your shirt?' she suggested. 'Dance in your T-Shirt?' He'd kept his checked shirt buttoned all night.

'I'm OK.' He brushed off her fingers that had gone to the fastenings.

She let the issue drop as something down in the mosh pit caught her eye. 'Uh-oh: looks like things are getting nasty.' The dancing had turned into something more closely resembling a riot as Tee Park sang a song about this generation getting shafted by the old, thanks to their fossil fuel greed. Anger at this was never far from the surface and right now had boiled over into a fist fight between the guys in the mosh pit and the bouncers trying to keep them in their pen. As she watched, Ade took a punch to the face and went down.

'Gotta go—sorry!' Leaving her abruptly, Kel vaulted over the rows of seats between them and circle balcony. Leaping onto it, he ran along the narrow ledge, grabbed a lighting tower and shinned down to the lower level. Meri kept her hands pressed to her mouth to stop her yelp of alarm. She would never have anticipated him doing something so action hero.

Theo came to her side. 'What's James Bond up to now?'

'His friend's in trouble down there.' Meri pointed to the swirling mass of bodies. Bouncers were hauling people up and shoving them out of the exit while Tee Park carried on singing. From the glances the star was sending to the commotion at the front, he was close to abandoning his set. The rest of the audience started booing the scufflers.

'Take it outside, you fecking idiots!' yelled Valerie. 'Some of us just want to dance!'

Meri followed Kel's bright mop of hair to the edge of the pit. He leapt this too, despite the attempts of an usher to stop him. Diving in, he hauled Ade up by the back of his shirt. It came off in his hands as his friend staggered to his feet.

Oh God, Ade was blazing! Blazing with an almost neon light. His upper body was a mesh of irregular hexagons. Was she really seeing this? Heart racing, she glanced at Theo.

'Can you see Kel's friend, Ade?'

'The guy who's lost his shirt? Yeah, he looks OK.'

Was she the only one who could see the markings?

Flight and fight instincts kicking in, Meri wanted to scream at Kel to get away from Ade. Those markings meant danger, she knew that in her gut even if she hadn't seen them, or something like them, before when she was four. She ran to the balcony rail to signal to Kel, to beg him to come back to her where it was safe. The fight in the pit was subsiding as the bouncers removed the lead troublemakers. They tried to pull Kel out but he just shrugged them off, pointing to his mate, obviously explaining why he had dropped out of nowhere to help. They let him be. Kel slipped off his shirt and put it around Ade's shoulders. He then looked up and saw her standing above him. He waved and gestured to Ade with a rueful smile. Lee appeared beside him, nose running with blood.

He's bailing on me, realized Meri. He's staying with his friend.

Kel got out his phone and sent her a text. *Sorry. Got to take these two fools to first aid. See you Monday?*

Looking at the message, Meri wanted to demand he return to her side but that would be weird in the circumstances. If he couldn't see the markings then he was probably safe tonight. With his shirt off, she could see that Kel didn't have any of his own, so he wasn't one of them. She had to pretend she couldn't see his friend's patterns either but still think of a way of warning him away from Ade. She wasn't sure exactly what Ade was, but it spelt nothing good for either of them.

OK. I hope they're fine. Her hands were shaking as she typed. From this distance it wasn't clear but she thought she could also glimpse the edge of a similar kind of pattern peeking out the neck of Lee's ripped shirt.

Kel read the text and tapped his forehead in acknowledgement.

The noise and the shapes of people dancing blurred in front of her eyes. She had to get out of here. Had to go somewhere to think. There was too much noise, too many people. She stumbled up the steps to her seat. Kel had left his jacket lying on the floor under his. That gave her an idea.

'Theo, I'm leaving. I'm taking Kel his jacket. See you at home, OK?'

Theo put his arm around her shoulders. 'You OK?'

Her smile was a little shaky but passable. 'Yeah, this has

been great. I'm just going to check my friends are OK. I'm sure Kel will walk me home.'

At that hint of seeking some alone time with the new boyfriend, Theo grinned. 'Fine. I won't wait up.'

Ducking out of more goodbyes with Saddiq and Valerie, Meri grabbed her handbag and Kel's jacket and headed for the exit.

5

M eri kept her eyes down as she got off the Tube at Wimbledon station, ignoring the people heading out for the clubs and bars. Halfway back she had realized she didn't know exactly where Kel lived but, fortunately, she'd found a letter in Kel's jacket addressed to him in a curling female hand. She hadn't peeked inside even though she'd been tempted, but at least it gave her his location. She was undecided as to whether she should go there at all. He seemed fine with his friends and wasn't expecting to see her until Monday. Maybe the danger was all in her mind?

The flash of glowing skin in summer sunshine. Hot hay prickling her skin. Hours and hours hiding, not knowing if anyone would come for her.

Meri shuddered. Her instincts were telling her it wasn't imagination; she had lived through these things.

She really needed that second letter from her parents, the one that promised to tell her about her enemies. Only then would she know for sure.

'OK, Meri,' she whispered as she stood outside the little

row of closed shops, 'are you going to be that mouse you've been for the last few years, or Kel's friend? You can at least check that he's OK. He spent most of the day running a fever, remember?'

A cowardly part of her wanted to claim she was happy remaining a mouse but she chased that thought away and followed the directions on her phone towards Kel's address near Wimbledon Common. Kel didn't live that far from her, which she supposed she should have guessed from the fact the three boys got on at the next bus stop after hers. His house, however, was worlds apart from the little maisonette in which she lived. It was a big, double-fronted mansion set in its own gardens. You couldn't just walk up to the front door but had to buzz on the black double gates. Standing at the end of the drive looking in, she could see people moving in front of the lit windows and hear the thud of a music centre pumping out Tee Park's latest tracks.

She patted down the jacket again, tempted to hold on to it until Monday. It smelt so nice and had a soft buttery feel to the material. If it was fake leather, it was a really good simulation, but she suspected it might be real. Fingers meeting the bulge of a wallet in the righthand pocket, she reminded herself she had the perfect excuse for her impromptu house call. She pressed the buzzer. No response. She pressed again.

'Yo, can't hear you,' bellowed the guy on the other end. 'If it's the neighbours, sorry, we'll turn it down. If you're the police, then same goes I suppose.' The light flicked off and the music dropped so she could no longer hear it from the street.

She pressed the buzzer, holding on this time.

'What?' snapped the voice. The camera over the gate swivelled to take a look at her.

'I'm not the police or the neighbours. I've got Kel's jacket —he left it at the concert.'

'Oh right. OK.' There was a pause and the gate buzzed. Meri pushed it open, walked in and let it slam shut. Security was pretty tight; she could see more cameras on the outside of the house monitoring the path and the grounds.

As she approached the steps, the front door opened and a man stepped out, brown hair cut short like an army recruit. Dressed in white shirt and black trousers, he blocked her entry. Meri couldn't help but notice that the surround around the door was made from exquisite stained glass, light spilling on the marble steps in ripples. Disconcertingly, peril featured heavily in the colour-scheme, swimming before her eyes.

'Hey, thanks for bringing it back.' The man held out his hand to take the jacket.

She hugged it to her chest, fighting back her fear. He had a wrist band of leaf patterned markings showing, not bright like Ade's but definitely visible to her eyes. Her gut was screaming at her to run but she held her ground with difficulty. 'Is...Is Kel here?'

The man dropped his arm. 'Are you Meredith?'

'Yes.'

'I'm Swanny, short for Avon Swanson. Did Kel mention me?'

'No.'

He folded his arms, no give in his stance. 'I work for Ade and keep the show on the road in this house. So you can give me the jacket. I'll look after it for Kel.'

Meri bit the inside of her cheek. *You must not panic.* Was this guy like a butler or something? 'I'd really prefer to give it to Kel directly—check he's OK. He wasn't well earlier.'

Reflexively, Swanny looked back over his shoulder. 'I

can't let you in without Ade's permission, but I'll see if he's free, OK?'

'Um, OK.'

Meri waited miserably on the step while Swanny dipped back into the house. This didn't make sense: going to see a friend shouldn't require clearance from the householder—that was way too controlling. Maybe Kel really was in danger; maybe he was being held against his will? A ridiculous image of him being chained up in a dungeon popped into her mind.

Swanny came back a minute later and opened the door wide. 'You can come in. Ade would come down and say hello but he's lying down with an icepack on his head. Idiot.'

Her eyes swept over the spacious foyer. It was like something from an old movie: polished marble tiles, a curling abstract sculpture on a side table, a chandelier dangling like an ice-dagger aimed at the floor. She guessed the house dated from the 1930s, the lines clean and making full use of curves and swirls like an ocean liner saloon of that era. Not a smelly sock slum after all. 'Um, nice place.'

'Yeah, Ade's got good taste.'

Meri cleared her throat. *Act normal, act normal.* 'Is he OK? I saw him get hurt at the concert.'

'Oh yeah, he's fine. He's just keeping the bruising down, you know?'

She didn't know as she wasn't the type to dive into a mosh pit but she nodded anyway. It was a major relief not to have to face Ade.

Swanny gestured to a door on the far side of the hallway. 'Kel's down in the dojo.'

'What's that?' She gulped. Had he just said "dungeon"?

'A dojo? It's a martial arts training room—a gym I guess you might call it.'

She hugged his jacket a little closer. 'Thanks. I'll...um... just go and say hello then.'

Swanny's eyes sparkled with amusement. 'Yeah, you do that. Tell Kel I won't wait up but to lock the door behind you when you leave.'

Embarrassed now, Meri hurried down the stairs. It was clear why Kel's housemates were keeping out of her way. They all thought she'd come for a make-out session to compensate for the one she'd missed when Kel left early. Still, if it meant they weren't suspicious of her, that might be for the best.

The basement was brightly lit and full of identical doors. From behind one came the hum of a laundry and washing tumbling so she passed that by. She tried the next from which emerged the rhythmic sound of thumping. Peeking in, she saw Kel in the middle of a well-equipped martial arts studio, walls painted a dark red, black wood shelving, wooden rods and protective gear displayed on specially built racks. He was beating, what she could only call 'the crap', out of a humanoid sparring robot, the kind she'd seen advertised in high-end magazines but never encountered in the synthetic flesh before.

'I think he surrenders,' she said as Kel delivered a very fast kick to the groin area of the robot.

'Meri! What are you doing here?' Kel grabbed a black towel and swiped the sweat from the back of his neck, eyes shining with delight.

She held the jacket up by the collar balanced on her index finger.

'Oh yeah, I hoped you would pick that up for me. But I could've waited till Monday. Still, thanks.' He took the jacket and threw it onto a weights bench and registered the thump of the wallet hitting the top. 'My wallet too? I'd totally forgotten, so big thanks are required.' He glanced over her shoulder. 'How did you find me?'

'Letter in the pocket.'

'The one from Jenny? That's my sister by the way. In case you were worried.'

She smiled. 'I wasn't worried.'

'Theo waiting for you outside?'

'No. I came by myself.'

His expression clouded. 'You walked up here from the station on your own?'

Meri dug her hands in her pockets. 'That's what I just said.'

'But it's not safe. You never know who's out there so near the common—a girl on her own this late? Not safe.'

That was undoubtedly true but she hadn't been thinking about her danger but his. 'I'll be careful.'

'That's right, you will be because I'm walking you home.'

Her heart gave a little flip of pleasure—and she'd get a chance to talk to him away from this intimidating house. She had a feeling that it would be foolish to raise here the issue of the danger he might be in. 'Are you sure it isn't too much trouble? Are you OK now? You were so hot earlier.'

'Meaning I'm not now?' He arched a brow at her as he stripped off his black T-shirt to pull on a fresh one.

She laughed, feeling some of her nerves ease. Kel was acting normally; she was the one who had brought her fears into this situation. 'Well, I guess it was quite hot, seeing you take down roboman here.'

Kel patted the machine on the shoulder. 'Meet U-Can-Fight-2.'

'An overly cute name for a robot.'

'Droid, please. That sounds way cooler and more Star-warsy. It's one of Ade's favourite toys.'

'And one of yours?'

'I prefer the human touch but he'll do when there's no one to take his place.'

Intrigued, Meri circled the mechanism. It looked a little like one of the dummies car firms used to test crashes but some joker had painted a face on the head—a snarling bad guy. Little light sensors lay just below the surface of the smooth skin. 'How does he work?'

'I'll show you.' Kel tapped a remote. 'Easy pattern. You hit where the light flashes and he'll record how fast you react.'

'What, me?'

'Why not? Take off your jacket and I guess you'd best lose the shoes too.'

Intrigued, Meri did as ordered and stood barefoot on the mat. 'He won't hit back or anything?'

Kel chuckled. 'No. Robotics haven't got that far. That's the stuff of Sci-Fi films to think we'd get anywhere close to a really human-looking machine. It takes a lot of processing power for him to stay on his feet. He'll brace against you.'

'I doubt there'll be much to brace against.'

'Wear these.' He passed her some light leather gloves. 'Can't have you going home to Theo with grazed knuckles, can we? Fists for upper body targets, feet for lower.'

'You mean I have to kick him?'

'Absolutely, darling. This is primarily a kick-boxing training rig.'

She relished the endearment but didn't say anything in case it discouraged him from using it again. 'OK.' Meri bounced on her toes. 'Come on, big guy: ready to rumble? Be afraid, be very afraid.'

Kᴇʟ sᴀᴠᴏᴜʀᴇᴅ his amusement as he watched Meri take on the house mascot. She started slow but caught on fast, punching and kicking in a nice fluid rhythm. With a bit of training she'd be a half decent fighter; the chief lack was the absence of weight behind the punches.

The light went on in the groin area and Meri grimaced.

'Go on, champ: take him down,' cheered Kel.

With a distinct look of distaste, she kneed the droid in his theoretical manhood.

'A kick would be better,' Kel counselled. 'You come in too close if you use the knee.'

'I'll remember that...next time,' panted Meri, 'I take on a robo-mugger.'

'They'll be on the streets in a decade or two, I'm sure. Probably some socially maladjusted programmer in his bedroom devising that very thing right now, control alt delete to do a fast snatch.' He ended the programme and put her stats up on the screen. 'Not bad. Seventy-five percent accuracy. Force is measured at twenty per cent but for a fly-weight beginner, that's decent.'

Meri grinned and flicked U-Can on the nose. 'Not such a big guy now, are you, buster? Who painted this charmer?'

Kel held up a hand. 'I did.'

'And why does it look like Mr Beamish, the sports teacher?'

'Do you need me to join the dots on that one?'

'I guess not. Go on: you show me how good you are.' Slipping back into her heels, she got out of his way.

Vanity had Kel programming a really tough routine. The droid couldn't hit back like a human but it could change stance, throwing off the rhythm of an inexperienced fighter. Having been in training since childhood, Kel was far from that.

'Press that red button whenever you like,' he said, passing her the control.

'Ooo, a red button. I love a big red button to unleash mayhem.' Hoping no doubt to catch him out, she pressed it before she'd even finished her sentence. U-Can dropped to a crouch. Meri squeaked in surprise, but Kel's foot made contact with the throat, throwing the droid backwards. It balled into a very un-human shape to roll and then spring up, limbs shooting out again.

'That's so cool!' said Meri. 'Go, U-Can!'

The kicks and punches came quicker and quicker. Kel moved from the analytic phase of fighting to the instinctive where he anticipated without even being sure how he was doing it. He recognized it as the kind of headspace he got into when playing cricket, the ball flying from his hand, following a prompt from his subconscious awareness of his opponent's weaknesses. He worked up a sweat again, losing himself in the physical joy of hand and foot meeting the target almost at the same instant it illuminated. The bout ended with a crescendo of rapid strikes to the face and a foot planted in U-Can's stomach. This time the bracing mechanism couldn't counter his power and the droid flew onto its back and sprawled in a satisfying starfish display of articulated limbs.

'Game over!' crowed Meri, clapping his performance. 'How do I put up your stats?'

He took the control from her and pointed the remote at the screen. 'How did I do?'

'Wow: ninety-eight percent accuracy and eighty-five percent force!'

'I was holding back,' he said modestly.

'The last kick registered as a hundred percent.'

'Except for that one.'

Meri plucked at his damp T-shirt. 'Looks like you need another of these.'

This close, blood still pumping from the exercise, Kel was sorely tempted to haul her into his arms, even if he was a mess. *Just friends, remember.* 'I think I really need a shower.' A cold one. 'Can you hold on here for a moment while I run upstairs? No one will disturb you, I promise.'

'That's fine. Me and Buster here will have a chat.' Meri started pulling the sprawled limbs back to the droid's side.

'He's fine. You can just hit the reset button.'

'The red one?'

'Yep, the red one.'

Leaving her playing with the control pad, Kel raced up the stairs two at a time.

'Dibs on the shower,' he said, beating Tiber, another of his room mates, to the bathroom just as he came out of his bedroom with a towel around his neck.

'What's the hurry?' grumbled Tiber.

'I'm walking Meri home.'

Tiber made way, not without some cracks at Kel's expense. After the swiftest shower on record, Kel dressed in a fresh set of clothes. He put his head around Ade's door. His boss was looking very much like U-Can sprawled on his four poster bed. He'd dimmed the lights, leaving only a string of icicle shaped bulbs lit as they looped around the bedstead.

'How are you feeling, tough nut?'

Ade groaned. 'Not so tough.' He rubbed the egg-sized bump on his head. 'Did I hear right: you're walking Mouse home?'

Nothing stayed private for long in this house. Swanny was probably watching her on the CCTV even now to check they hadn't let a mad assassin onto the premises. 'Meri? Yes. She came to return my jacket.'

'Sweet. So you'll ask her about what she can see, right? Lee and I were both blazing tonight. If she has our vision then she'll have seen something.'

Kel wondered just how he could slip that casually into the conversation. 'She hasn't mentioned anything yet and you would think she might mention how bizarre you looked?' He'd worried about that in the back of his mind ever since she'd come in and not said a word about it. 'Maybe she'd been too far away to see anything, or put it down to the weird lighting at the venue?'

'Or she might believe she was imagining it.' Ade reapplied the ice. 'I mean, if the situation was reversed, would you raise it with a girl you were only just getting to know if you thought it was possible that you were going a little mental?'

'No, definitely not.'

'So ask her. You wouldn't want her to think she was hallucinating, would you?'

Ade had a point. 'I shouldn't be long but you get some sleep. I'll see you tomorrow.'

'If it turns out she did see the markings, then come and tell me immediately you get back in. Even if I am asleep.'

'Will do.' Kel turned to go.

Ade propped himself up on an elbow, dropping the ice on the floor. 'And, Kel, say just enough OK? Not too much so we have to do something about what she knows.'

A shiver ran down Kel's spine. 'What do you mean?'

'You know that we can't have people knowing about us. It's like the Star Trek prime directive—no first contact with those who aren't as advanced as us, as far as the UV sight goes. We have to keep apart from the rest to preserve our culture.'

Kel's frustration swelled. 'So you want me to talk to her but not? How does that work exactly?'

Ade shrugged. 'I dunno, but I trust you to find a way. Test her out. Innocent leading questions.'

'I already know she's got great colour definition—there's the painting and she did well on U-Can, spotting even the dimmest target lights.'

'Yeah, that's the way.' Ade flopped back. 'Baby steps. Piece together the evidence before you commit us by full disclosure.'

Outside the open door to the dojo, Kel paused as he could hear Meri talking. He was fairly certain no one would've come down to disturb her, not when they knew she was his guest, so wasn't that surprised when he found she was chatting to U-Can.

'So what do you think this thing does, Buster?' There was the sound of a thin bamboo sword swishing in the air. 'Take that, you jerk.' She was beating the weight's bench, not even able to bring herself to hit the droid now she'd made friends with it. 'I bet Kel can do real damage with this, huh? He's pretty awesome, isn't he? Looks so mild and then goes all Karate Kid when he gets in the zone.'

Kel chose that moment to enter. 'That's for kendo not karate.'

Meri grinned self-consciously, twirling the cane in her hand. 'Oops, busted.'

'You and your new friend getting on OK?' Kel picked up his jacket. The droid was upright again and Meri had parked him in his corner, ready for shutdown.

'Yep, me and the big guy are besties now. I found the manual.'

'That thing? None of us have read it.'

'You don't know all the things he can do then. We're talking about going on a date, exchanging corny messages, and he's buying a little robo-dog to take on romantic walks.' She slipped into her coat.

'He might make a better date than me: no high fevers, no rushing off to save his moron of a friend from a pounding.'

'Ah, yes, but his conversation is so, you know, limited?'

'There is that.'

'And he's totally lacking in any sense of humour.'

Kel squinted at the droid. 'I dunno. I think he has this ironic expression most of the time, like when I act as if I'm doing something worthwhile beating my own best score against someone who's not programmed to hit back.'

'Still, I can report that he can't hug for toffee.'

Taking the hint, Kel put his arms around her. 'Like this?'

'Yes. Just like that.' She rested her head on his chest for a second, ear pressed to his collarbone as if listening for his heartbeat. He could have told her it had picked up its pace as soon as she moved in close.

'You know something: you're no longer eighteen.'

'What?'

'You're eighteen and one day. It's gone midnight, Cinderella. I need to get you home.'

'OK.' She didn't move.

'Now would be good.' He made a half-hearted attempt to move her.

'Hmm.' She didn't sound convinced, and neither, come to think of it, was he. It was incredibly peaceful just standing here with her. He usually liked Ade's house but it had no quiet places, no soft touches, no long brown hair for him to sift his fingers through. His attraction to her had started as an instinct, an ember that was fast igniting other feelings.

This wasn't something, though, that he wanted recorded on the house security circuits. They really did have to go.

'Come on, darling. It's very late and Theo will worry.'

She stood up straight with a sigh. 'Yes, he will. You're right. I might be an adult but I think it'll take more than twenty-four hours for him to adjust.'

'With a dad, there are not enough hours for that. You'll always be his little girl.'

She took his hand as they climbed the stairs to the ground floor. 'So what's yours like?'

'My dad?' Kel was proud of Rill Douglas but their relationship had inevitably loosened with the distance between them. 'He's kind, loving, dutiful.'

'Dutiful?'

'Yes, he's in a kind of military service—as are all my family. We take our responsibilities seriously.'

'What rank is he?'

'Oh, it's not your regular military. He's head of a security detachment. A commander.' Kel felt himself skimming very close to the edge of what was permissible to say here. 'A bit like Swanny.'

'Swanny? I thought he was a butler.'

Kel roared with laughter. When he recovered his breath, he said: 'I'll tell him you said that.'

'Don't you dare. I didn't mean to offend him.'

'He won't be offended. He'll be delighted.' Kel locked the front door behind him. 'I'll tell him you thought he was Alfred to Ade's Batman.'

'This isn't how I imagined you living.' Meri gestured to the house. 'It's so much grander.'

'Ade's the one with the money. We get the benefit.' He made sure the gates were fastened as they stepped out onto the pavement.

'And...and you can come and go as you like?' She took a sideways look at him. Even if she was attempting to be subtle, her expressions were easy to read. She was fishing for something.

'Of course I can.' They walked along the quiet street with the Common on one side and a row of large detached houses on the other. A neighbour's cat streaked across the road and disappeared into the bushes.

'But you're tied to Ade somehow, aren't you?'

Where was she going with this? 'You could say that, if friendship is a tie.'

'But if that friendship turned sour, you could get out? I mean you can't know what might happen.'

'I could walk away today if I wanted.'

The tension left her face and she smiled. 'Great. Good. So you know you could come to Theo and me if there was a problem, right?'

'I suppose I do now.' He stopped walking and pulled her into the light of a streetlamp. He rubbed her cheek with his thumb, catching the corner of her mouth, willing her to speak. 'Meri, what's this about? Did you see something that upset you?'

Her eyes shifted away from him. 'No, no, it's nothing.'

'It doesn't sound like nothing. Tell me what you suspect.' *Please say you saw the markings. I want you to be one of us.*

'I don't suspect anything. I just want to know that you're safe—that you've got alternatives to living there.' She jerked her head towards Ade's house. There was a thread of bitterness in her tone that seemed unwarranted.

'So you really didn't see anything to upset you tonight?' He held her firmly by the arms, waiting till she met his gaze.

'I didn't like seeing the punch-up in the mosh pit.' Her

green eyes glanced across his and slid away again, taking their secrets with them.

'If you're worried about anything you saw, even if it sounds crazy, you can tell me.' He nudged her chin with his index finger, lightly pressing a little dent in the stubborn end of it. 'I promise I'll not judge you, or tell anyone else if you don't want me to.' That last promise was a bit shaky but he thought he could persuade her to let him tell the others if she did see the markings.

'I don't know what you mean.'

She was lying to him. He knew that because he was already coming to know her expressions. She was useless at hiding her reactions. But how to get her to tell him the truth?

A car drove by at speed and hooted, making them both jump.

'Could we go back to my house now?' she asked.

He slackened his grip, knowing he'd lost the moment and that nothing was settled between them. Something had spooked her but he couldn't be sure what it was. 'Of course. Stupid of me to keep you talking out here. It's ridiculously late.'

Having seen her to her door and exchanged a goodnight kiss that he hoped settled some things for them both, Kel walked home through the deserted streets. He kept replaying Meri's questions, her evident fear, and the veiled threat Ade had given him about telling her too much. Should he continue along this path? The cost of failure to Meri might be far too high. If he were to be anymore direct with her then Ade could consider that she knew too much. Was the risk worth it? But if he didn't do it, then someone like Lee would get the job of questioning her. She might blaze out soon herself and that would scare the crap out of her if no one had told her what it meant.

'Damned if I do, damned if I don't,' murmured Kel. Meri Marlowe was proving to be one very frustrating bundle of trouble.

6

Meri didn't see Kel at school for the next few days as the reports were that he had had a relapse and was still running his fever.

'Has a doctor taken a look at him? Malaria can be really nasty.' She was feeling boxed in on the front row of the bus because Ade had chosen to break habit and sit next to her. Giving herself a mental shake, she reminded herself that Ade wouldn't threaten her on a vehicle full of their school-mates for heaven's sake! She needed to get a grip. Glancing across the aisle she saw that her bad luck was someone else's good fortune. And at least it meant Sadie got to chat with Lee, data-stick earrings swirling in some enthusiastic conversation about a game they both rated. Vampire boy and comp-punk? Oddly enough, the pairing appeared to work for the two of them.

Ade turned from the view outside and gave her a strange look. 'Malaria? Oh yeah, malaria. Yeah, Kel's been seen by an expert.'

A siren wailed, phones chirped with automatic warnings

and the bus slowed to a stop on the High Street, taking advantage of a railway bridge.

'Looks like another storm.' Ade checked his phone. 'Hope it's not a long one.'

Sirens continued to sound from the weather towers. Pedestrians hurried off the streets, shopkeepers brought in their pavement displays. A homeless man, a climate refugee probably, moved from an exposed corner to the shelter of the bridge. He grinned gap-toothed at the passengers staring down at him and shook his ice-cream tub begging bowl. Ade leaned over Meri, cracked open the window, and threw out some coins. A couple bounced and ran down the gutter so the beggar shuffled off in pursuit before the rain swept them away.

'Does Kel want me to visit?' asked Meri. 'I can mop a fevered brow as well as anyone.'

'It's best if you keep clear for now. But he did ask if you'd like to go out on Thursday.' Ade nudged her playfully. 'I'm playing go-between.'

Meri didn't answer immediately, having caught a glimpse of his markings where his sleeve was pushed up. They didn't blaze this morning, just glowed softly. If they didn't scare her so much, she probably could have found them beautiful, like the subtlest of tattoos.

'No answer? Don't say it's bad news, Meredith? He thinks you like him.'

'I *do* like him. Yes, of course, I'd like to go out on Thursday. Sorry, I was just distracted by the storm warning.' *Meri, change the subject.* 'Have you ever got caught out in one of these?' The clouds had rolled in and the barrage of hail rattling the streets.

'Yeah, twice. Autumn and Spring ones seem the worst, don't they? Came home with bruises both times.'

'Me too. I got caught in the middle of the Common in April. Managed to run to a shelter but not without taking a couple of them on my shoulders.'

They watched the water churn down the gutters, carrying leaves and rubbish with it. The drain by the bus appeared to be blocked and soon the wheels were half submerged.

'I know the hail hurts, but I think the rain's worse.' Ade leaned back, legs crossed at the ankles, settling in for a long wait. 'So many areas keep flooding. I've got a cousin who lives in Amsterdam. They've lost several more districts last winter. Half the city is now on floating pontoons and engineers are thinking seriously about making the whole of it that way.'

'Oh wow. I meant that's terrible of course, but it sounds really clever.'

'Kel and I visited last Easter. They've got this cool floating railway track connecting the city centre to the mainlines—trust the Dutch to come up with something so brilliant.'

'You travel a lot?' Few people did these days, not abroad at least, now that the cost of exceeding your personal carbon ration was so high.

Ade shrugged. 'You know you can buy the miles from others who surrender theirs on the secondary carbon market?'

'I'd heard but I've never known anyone who could afford that.'

'It can be worth it. I have a big, scattered family. We like to get together once a year at least. How about you?'

'No, I've no one—apart from Theo—so nowhere to go.' She closed the subject by getting out her phone. 'I'd better just text him to let him know I'm OK. I hope he got to work before this hit. Except: no signal.'

'I guess that means the storm's taken out the local mast again.' Ade pulled out his phone. 'Look, I can get wi-fi here. Do you want to use mine?'

'Thanks.' Meri took the top-of-the-range handset and sent a quick message to Theo.

'You want to send a "get well soon" to Kel?'

'Um, sure.' It felt really wrong somehow, using a guy she thought might be an enemy as her messenger pigeon.

Ade found Kel's number in his favourites and she typed a brief acceptance of the Thursday plan and her hopes he kicked the malaria bout by then. Unashamedly reading over her shoulder, Ade looked very pleased by her message. By the time she had finished and pressed send, the bus had started moving again and normal life emerged back on to the streets. Ambulances already surrounded one victim who had taken a hailstone to the head. Blood seeped out onto the pavement as he lay face down.

'That looks bad,' murmured Meri.

'Don't watch, Mouse.' Ade turned her away.

Too late. She had already caught a glimpse as the paramedics rolled the victim over. The hail had hit the old man right in the face, leaving his features a bloody mess. He hadn't been able to move quick enough to reach safety. The other students on the bus fell silent, everyone chilled by the sight. Someone two rows back made a retching sound.

'God, I hate this. I hate what we've done to make what was a friendly planet into one that can kill us on an ordinary Tuesday morning,' said Meri. 'We should've done more much sooner.'

'Amen to that, sister.' Ade put an arm round her. At first she tensed but then forced herself to relax. He was just offering comfort. 'It might look worse than it is. Head wounds bleed like crazy. The doctors can do wonders with facial reconstruction.'

'Not like they don't get a lot of practice at it now.'

'That's true. Mouse, you can lean on me, you know?'

She was letting the guy who scared the heebie jeebies out of her put his arm around her shoulders. How mixed up was that? 'You can call me Meri.' She made herself rest against his side.

'I wondered how long it would take you before you said that. Thanks, Meri. On the subject of names, have you ever wondered what yours means?'

'No, not really.'

'You should look it up. You might find the result interesting.'

'And you're not going to tell me?'

'No, I think not. While you're there you could look up some other names too. It's worth thinking about.'

The bus pulled into the school lay-by.

'You're being very enigmatic, Ade.'

'Yeah, that's me. An enigma.' He removed his arm and politely passed her schoolbag that had been resting at their feet. 'See you around, Meri.'

IN DEFERENCE to the fact that Kel had been ill, Meri selected for their date an outing to the new holographic cinema in Leicester Square, deciding it would be most appropriate for a recovering invalid as it was both warm and inside.

While getting ready for what was their second date, she texted him explaining that the choice of films wasn't great: disaster movies or alien invasion.

Lady's choice, he replied.

Alien invasion. Watching yet another world city be destroyed by fictional fire/flood/hurricane held little attraction for her when you could see so much of the same on the news. The recently developed hologram technology made you feel you were sitting in the middle of the action and why sit thinking you were being fried to a crisp? She missed the old days where films stayed on the wall and played out for you to watch rather than be immersed in them.

'Suck it up, Meri,' she told herself as she plied the mascara wand. 'It's just your weirdo eyesight makes the impact all the more powerful. No one else complains.'

Bracing herself for a disturbing couple of hours where she might have to sit with her eyes shut, Meri insisted on buying the popcorn as a thank you to Kel for purchasing the tickets. Telling him not to wait, she joined the queue for refreshments, only then realizing she'd not asked him what flavour he preferred. When she carried the popcorn into the darkened auditorium she found Kel had selected seats in the middle of the back row. He looked so gorgeous, arm stretched out across the seats, sprawled like a well-fed lion, content but not safe. Never that. He had something of the same pent up energy as a big cat that indicated he might pounce at any moment and she was all too happy at the prospect.

'Back row? Really? I thought we were, you know, just friends?' she asked as she took her place next to him. The nearest patrons were several seats away as the film wasn't as big an attraction as the firefighting feature playing next door.

'It's still a date. Clichéd, isn't it?' Kel seemed perfectly happy with the admission.

'Just a bit.' She handed him the container so she could

take off her jacket. The seat was huge, more like an armchair.

'At least you know my intentions are entirely dishonourable.' He seemed a little feverish again, a glitter in his eyes that wasn't normally there.

She decided to ignore it and take it as his usual flirting. 'How do you know I don't want to pay complete attention to...' she couldn't for a second remember the title of the film, 'to...'

'Star-strike?'

'Yeah, that.'

'I made a very good guess.'

'Shut up and eat the popcorn.' She snagged a sample. 'Yum.' She had come out deciding not to be a mouse Meri but the person she wanted to become, bolder, funnier—and she was enjoying herself thoroughly.

'I hope you got salty.' He took a handful. 'Ugh. Butter.'

'Butter is the best. If you don't like it I'm sure I could manage it on my own.' She started to take the box onto her own lap.

'No way. I can force it down.'

A government advertisement for the fun to be had while on eco-service burbled unconvincingly on the screen, happy teens in waders repairing river banks giving cheesy thumbs up to the cameras.

'I'll remember next time—get you your own supply as I'm not polluting myself with all that salt.'

He brushed her earlobe, making the dangling pearl dance. 'I like the sound of there being a next time.'

She shivered. He was definitely more touchy-feely than normal. What was going on? 'Maybe. Subject to the usual terms and conditions.'

'Naturally. And they are?'

'That you don't hog my popcorn now.'

'*Your* popcorn?' He took a fistful.

She grabbed his wrist and stole a piece with her teeth from where it poked out of his fingers. 'Absolutely.' The main feature started, hologram technology clicking on and a planet appearing overhead as the screen became three-sixty degrees. Music soared, full orchestral score.

Kel opened his fist as stardust fell around them. 'Carry on. I think I like feeding you this way. Eating from my hand already.'

Keeping her eyes on his, she filled her palm with popcorn and held it up to him. 'Only if it goes both ways.'

'I can so get with that programme.' He took her wrist gently in his fingers and grazed off her hand.

'I...I think you've eaten it all.' Maybe she wasn't so bold after all?

His lips were playing over the skin, taking little nibbles. 'Just getting off the last of the butter.'

He dumped the popcorn he was holding back into the container to pull her closer.

'Kel!' Meri was annoyed her protest came out as a not very convincing squeak.

'You know the best thing about this cinema?' He murmured as aliens started their descent into the Earth's atmosphere.

'No.'

'The chair arm lifts so we can snuggle up.' He swung up the barrier between them creating something closer to a sofa. 'Very enlightened of the designers. We can take cover together from the little green guys.'

'Big grey guys with fangs actually.' Something was really odd about him tonight. Meri turned into his hug, free hand rising to test his cheek. The skin felt a little too hot under her fingers. 'Kel, are you feeling all right?'

'Honey, I haven't ever felt better. Now, sssh, and kiss me.'

Try it, Meri. You'll regret it if you don't. She closed her eyes and let herself sink into the sensation of his mouth on hers, the buttery sweetness of his lips, the tickling play of his tongue. He kissed as if there was no one else in the world and nothing else to do. It wasn't perfunctory: no first stop to go through before he got to other bases; it took his whole attention, and boy, was he good at the details. She'd never experienced anything close to this. She forgot she was supposed to be calming him down. Something new ran through her veins, something unstoppable—instinctive. She was about to go up in flames along with the Earth's space defences.

Light flashed behind closed lids, distracting her. She guessed the aliens had really got going now. It was so bright that Kel and she must be visible to other cinema goers. Self-conscious, she tried to pull away.

'Kel—'

'Sssh, don't stop.'

But the light grew brighter and brighter. Her rucked up skirt and half-reclining stance would be on display.

'Kel.' She pushed at his chest, making a space between them. Opening her eyes she found her nose pressed up against the open neck of his shirt. It was pouring out bright peril-coloured light. 'Oh my God!' She leapt to her feet, causing a fountain of popcorn to rain over the seats in front, passing right through a holographic alien like buckshot. Kel was covered in swirls—glowing skin markings just like Ade and Lee. She couldn't—didn't want to believe it. 'No. God. No!'

'Shit!' Kel was looking down at himself with horrified amusement.

Grabbing her jacket and shoulder bag, Meri bolted for the exit.

'Meri! It's nothing.'

She ignored his shout behind her. Nothing? She had to get away—had to run. Bursting out onto the street, she looked in vain for a taxi but the rank was empty. He mustn't catch her. Making a dash across the square, she sprinted to the station. If she could get on a train before him, she'd be home and packed before he could get to her. Swiping her travel card over the sensor she barrelled through the ticket barrier and half ran half stumbled down the station escalator.

'Careful, lady!' called one of the station staff.

'Come on, come on!' Frantically praying that there'd be a train along imminently, she scanned the board. Due in one minute. She ran down the platform, hoping to get out of sight before Kel had a chance to overtake.

Hiding behind the protection of a vending machine, she watched the friendly profile of the front of the Tube train emerge from the tunnel. The driver even smiled at her as their eyes met, helping Meri settle her shredded nerves. Normal people still existed. This was just a brief nightmare from which she was going to escape. The doors opened and she got in, taking a seat beside the largest passenger she could find, a well-padded woman in a fake fur coat. The doors hissed closed and the train set off. First stage of her escape completed.

Peeking around the woman, Meri looked along the entire length of the Tube train. She could see the front winding first into the tunnel, the passengers swaying in their seats or hanging from the bars overhead, guarding bags or fold-up bikes. She thought maybe she caught a glimpse of a blond head moving through the crowds, coming towards her down the carriages.

Oh God.

Meri got up and began working her way through the people as fast as she could. One party of tourists blocked the gangway with a mini-Manhattan of various sized rolling cases.

'Can I get past please?'

The women gazed at her without comprehension.

'Meri, wait!' Kel was gaining on her.

Meri climbed over the suitcases, ignoring the protests from the owners. She began to run even though she could see that she was out of carriages to escape through. She had to hope they reached the next station before he caught up with her. If she timed it right, she could be out and into the crowds before he knew what she was doing.

The train began to slow for Piccadilly Circus. Almost there.

'Meri, just wait a damn moment. I can explain.' Kel seized hold of her arm just as the doors opened. Rather than have it out in front of a carriage full of spectators, he hustled her onto the platform and pulled her down to take a seat on an empty bench.

'Let go—let go!' She slapped at his hand like she would a hornet.

'I'll let go if you promise to listen.'

Chest heaving, heart thumping, Meri nodded. She just had to get out from under his touch.

The doors closed and the train pulled out. Kel lifted his hand now she had no easy escape. The glow at his neck was fading, becoming the subtle lines she'd seen on Ade and Lee. She sank her teeth into her bottom lip to hold in a sob.

She should never have lost it like that. He knew what she'd seen—she couldn't plausibly deny it now. But why did he look so pleased by that?

He raised his hand to cup her cheek but dropped it when she jerked away. 'OK, OK. Look, I know what you saw in the cinema, besides scary aliens of course. You probably think I'm a scary alien, now I come to think of it. It was unexpected for me too.' He gave an embarrassed laugh. 'Just...just trust me when I tell you it's completely normal and completely human. I'm going through a special kind of puberty thing; that's why I've had a fever these last fews days. We—you—develop these markings when we reach full maturity.' He pushed up his sleeve. 'See: gone now. They only flare out at times of...' he searched for the right words, 'stress or exertion. That kiss, it kinda lit the touch paper.'

The markings hadn't gone to her eyes. They were still right there, spirals of intricate lines like patterns on a seashell. She didn't want to hear about this, but knew she had to listen. *Know your enemy, Meri.*

'We suspected you might be one of us when you did that painting. Ade asked me to get to know you a little, see if I could establish what you were either way.'

'What!' She shot to her feet. 'You've...you've been dating me as a favour to Ade? Well stuff you!' Bleeding bloody hell: didn't that make her feel stupid?

'No. No! Feck, that didn't come out right. I asked you out because I wanted to but I also wanted to find out if you are one of us.' He grinned hopefully at her. 'And you are.'

'I am not one of you, OK? No markings—nothing.' She shoved up her sleeve to show him. 'I'm going home.'

'You don't have the markings yet but you will do. Eyesight like yours, the ability to see colours into the UV spectrum—that's what people like us do.'

Meri decided flat out denial was her best of bad options even if he knew she was lying. 'I can't see anything. I've got a headache. I need to lie down.'

The next train rattled into the station. Kel took her hand. 'I know it's a shock. Don't bolt. Please, just trust me. I can make it all right for you.'

Trust the people who took her parents from her? Never. Retreating into silence, regrouping, she followed him onto the train and didn't speak a word as he chattered beside her about how great it was to find another one, how he'd been hoping she'd turn out this way even if he regretted the circumstances in which it had been revealed.

'The guys are going to tease me about that for years,' he admitted, rubbing the back of his neck. 'Most of us flare out first time when we're exercising; only a few have the dubious honour of going that way when...well, anyway, Ade's going to be so pumped that we've found another one of us. We don't have enough girls in our population.'

She was sick of hearing about Ade. Everything revolved around him like he was a dictator and they his faithful troops.

They got out at Wimbledon and exited the station. Lights were on in the windows of the nearby restaurants and bars, showing ordinary people going about ordinary dates where they ate and chatted and no one turned into a glowing nightmare. Meri wriggled her hand from his. 'Right, we're back. Sorry you didn't get to see the film. I'll see you around.'

Her attempt to flee was thwarted when he took her elbow and pulled her towards a taxi. 'I'll take you home.'

'I haven't got carbon credit to spend on that.'

'Humour me. We'll put it on my account.' Kel handed

the driver his ration card and gave the address of Ade's mansion.

'Yeah, I know it. My best customers, you guys,' said the driver out of the side of his mouth as he chewed on a nicotine stick. The electric vehicle zipped up the hill with the softest of whines.

'That's not my address.' Resentment was mounting in Meri's chest. She had every right to go home if she wanted. Kel might have to report in to Ade but she certainly did not. The whole set up in the mansion was wacky, like some cult nestled among the normal citizens of Wimbledon.

'Let's go there first. We can walk the rest of the way to your home like the other night.'

'You can let me out at the next corner,' she told the driver.

'It's OK, mate, keep going,' countered Kel. 'Meri, just give me five minutes. It's the last thing I'll ever ask you to do for me.'

As if. Meri did not want to walk into the fortress even for five minutes. 'Why do I have to go to your place?'

'Because there are things you need to know and it's best if you hear them there. It's not a conversation to be had in the back of a taxi.'

'So after five minutes I can walk straight out again?'

Kel put his hand on his chest, pale blue eyes sincere. 'I promise. You did before, remember?'

'Fine. Whatever. Let's get this over with.'

The taxi dropped them at the gate and Kel entered the code on the touch pad, keeping a wary eye on her.

'We need this security because Ade's in danger from our enemies,' he explained. 'It's not a trap or rigged to keep you inside.'

'Please, I don't want to know.' Meri bunched her hands in fists in her jacket pockets.

'You have to understand. We're not the bad guys here.'

Tell that to her parents. 'Five minutes. I'm starting the count right now.'

Kel smiled. 'That's all it'll take, darling.'

'Don't call me that.' Entering the house, Meri wanted to scream, to shove the sculpture on the hall table right through the peril-coloured stained glass windows.

'OK, I'll park that for now, until you've calmed down.'

'I am calm!'

'Yeah, right,' Kel muttered and led her into what looked like a recreation room: sofas, big screen, bar area, table tennis table at the far end. Most of the inhabitants of the house were gathered in there, some reading or doing school assignments while plugged into their own music, a couple playing on handheld screens, others watching football on the massive curved wall television. Kel smiled his reassurance but to Meri it felt like she was in the scene in the classic Indiana Jones film when the heroine is dropped into a pit of snakes wearing a flimsy white dress.

'Four minutes,' she whispered.

'I'd better make this fast then.' He whistled to gain everyone's attention. 'Hey, guys!'

The screen muted, ear buds were removed, as Kel's friends took in the fact that he'd brought a guest home. Lee moved between Meri and the rest of the people in the room.

'What's she doing here?' he asked Kel.

Ade got up from the sofa where he'd been sitting in front of the football game. 'Meri, didn't expect to see you tonight. Thought you two were at the cinema?'

'It didn't work out. Instead of aliens causing all the trouble, I kinda had a flare out,' admitted Kel, flushing a little as his friends whooped and applauded.

'Man, that must have been awkward!' laughed one guy, shaking his head apologetically at Meri.

'Scared the crap out of her. But there's no doubt she saw.'

Ade slapped Kel on the back. 'Pretty hard to miss the first flare. So, you're a spiral like your dad?'

'Yeah, running true to the Douglas DNA.' Kel rubbed his forearm.

Meri folded her arms, hands kneading her elbows, wishing she could disappear. If they could see UV, why couldn't they perceive that the markings were still there? She could see each of their different patterns. Ade had an interlocked design like a tortoise shell; Lee the rosette spots of a leopard; Swanny a leaf pattern.

'Congratulations.' Ade put his hand out to Swanny. 'You owe me fifty.'

'What? Swanny, you didn't think I'd be a leaf like my mother, did you?' asked Kel.

Swanny sighed but his act was undercut by his wide smile. 'I lived in hope, bro, now I'm out of hope and out of pocket.'

'We'll break out the champagne later but I guess we've some explaining to do to Meri.' Ade turned to her.

Meri felt like her mind was undergoing an emergency evacuation, all thoughts streaming to the nearest exit. 'Actually, I really just want to go home. I don't want to hear any more about this. I'm not one of you, as I told Kel. I won't say anything to anyone though, so you don't have to worry about that.'

'Sweetheart, I'm afraid it's not that simple.' Ade pointed to the picture which had been hung on the wall behind the table tennis table. 'You did that—you can see that?'

'I can't see anything right now but a loads of badly placed blobs. You should chuck it. Look, I've got to go. Kel, you promised.'

'What did you promise her?' asked Ade.

Kel reached to stroke the back of her head but she ducked out the way. 'I promised her she only had to come in for five minutes. She's pretty spooked.'

Lee came to Ade's side. 'She knows too much already, sir. We can't let her go until this is settled and she understands what's expected of her.'

Panic levels soared again. She should never have trusted Kel even this far. 'You can't make me stay!'

'We can. Ade's your prince now. You're under his authority.'

'Like hell I am! This is so bogus!'

Ade clicked his tongue in anger. 'You're going way too fast for her, Lee. This has all been dumped on her with no preparation whatever. Shut the hell up. In fact, you're dismissed for the night, OK?'

Lee left the room with a poisonous look at Meri.

'Sweetheart, what you saw at the cinema on Kel's skin— that's all completely natural. We're a small group of humans who have developed some specialized characteristics way back, an evolutionary distinction like red hair being found among the Celts or almond shaped eyes among some Asian peoples. What's different for us is that only a few can see it so we can live pretty much under the radar—a society within a society. It does give us great definition in eyesight and a few other advantages which I won't go into right now. It's nothing to be scared of.'

'Then why do you lock yourself away in this fortress?'

she asked, not really wanting an answer. 'Five minutes is up, Kel.'

Ade held up a hand to stop her marching out. 'Good question. Because, while very few know of our existence, we do have one very powerful enemy—a kind of natural predator I'd guess you'd say, if we're using Darwinian language—and we have to protect ourselves against them.'

'I've already said I won't tell anyone but I insist on going home right now. You can't keep me here. Even if that pissy-cat Lee thinks he can.'

Ade tapped his lips thoughtfully. 'Ah, so you did see Lee's markings at the Tee Park gig. I wondered. I thought you might be too far away.'

She had been too far to get a clear view then but not now, not with everyone's markings right there before her eyes in their T-shirts and rolled up shirt sleeves. She had to be more careful. 'I thought it a special effect of the lights or something.'

Ade rocked on his heels a second, hands dug down in his jeans' pockets. 'Look, OK, I get that you're freaked out. You're right: we can't keep you here, not without your guardian calling the police and getting us into deep shit. Go home tonight and think about it. Let it settle. But remember: it's natural and one day soon you'll get your own markings. I don't suppose you remember what your parents were?'

'My parents were good people.'

'I meant what markings they had?'

Meri pressed her lips together and shook her head.

'No matter. It'll become clear all too soon. Kel, see she gets home safely.'

Kel slipped his arm around her, moving quickly so she couldn't duck again. 'Come on, darling, you're free to go as I promised.'

'Party when you get back, Kel, OK? And just one more thing, Meri?' Ade's tone demanded that she listen.

She paused in the doorway, looking back at her schoolfellow in what she understood now was his court. 'What's that?'

'I'm holding you to that promise not to tell anyone, OK?'

Lee was waiting in the hallway to see them out. 'He's letting her go?' he asked Kel.

'Yes, of course.' Kel smiled reassuringly down at her.

'That's not procedure.'

'It's what needs to happen now to make this right for her.'

'And when was it our job to make this about her rather than Ade?'

'Lee, please.'

'All right. I'll back down for now as it's Ade's direct order but I'll be watching her. See you around, Meredith Marlowe.' Lee released the locks on the front door.

Not if she had anything to do with it, thought Meri, pushing past him.

KEL WAS in two minds whether it was a good idea to leave Meri while she was so distressed, but his presence was obviously making it worse. On the doorstep, she ducked out of the good night kiss he wanted to give her, body language screaming that she'd prefer him at a distance—at least a million miles. All he could do was give her what she wanted.

'Take it easy, OK? It's really nothing to worry about, Meri,' he promised as she closed the door. He could hear the drum of her footsteps climbing the stairs as fast as she could go. He dug his hands in his pockets, a little depressed by this, anticipating how much repair work lay ahead if he wanted the relationship back on track. 'Good night to you too.'

Keep watch or go? Knowing Swanny, he'd send a team to keep an eye on her as a freaked out newcomer was a clear security risk. Besides, Kel was expected back and Ade had promised a party. Kel had been to Flare-out parties before when a housemate had gone through his change but never had a chance to take part. There was no point waiting here on the step like a stray cat she wouldn't allow in.

With a last glance up at the lit windows of Meri's flat, Kel jogged home. He was passed by Tiber and Jiang in one of the cars, heading out on the watch detail he had anticipated. They tooted the horn and he waved. As the only two late developers in Ade's house who had not yet got their markings, they'd drawn the short straw and would miss the party.

'I'm back!' he called, chucking his jacket on to the newel post in the foyer, too rushed to take it upstairs as per regulations.

'In here, Kel!' called Ade. The guys had been getting things ready. The furniture in the club room had been pushed back, the music turned up, and food and drink laid out. They gave him a wild round of applause as he entered.

'Yo, let's hear it for the spiral-back!' hooted Swanny, who usually acted as Master of Ceremonies on these occasions.

Ade jumped on a sofa, taking his favourite role of baiter. 'But do we believe him?'

'No!' yelled the others. 'Flare out! Flare out! Flare out!' Each stripped off their tops and began taking mock punches and slaps at each other.

'We need proof!' bellowed Ade, beating his chest where the turtle back marks were just beginning to glow.

'Oh God, I think I'm gonna need another drink if we're doing it this way,' said Kel.

'And it's gotta be champagne!' Lee popped the cork on the waiting bottle and let it spray over Kel. Swanny and a couple of the others grabbed Kel's shirt and pulled it over his head.

Kel downed a swig of champagne direct from the bottle and passed it on. The music went up a notch, trash rock with a driving beat. Turning off the main lights, Lee hit the switch for the UV lamps hidden in the ceiling. Immediately, they picked up the beginnings of the flare out from some of the guys who like Ade were already pumped up by the dancing and scuffling. As Kel bundled into the middle of the crowd, one tiny part of him looked at this chaotic scene with an ironic detachment. They were like a bunch of primitives not far off hitting each other over the head with a club as part of some male bonding ritual; mostly, though, he was seduced by the atavistic pleasure of thrashing about with his best mates. This time he would be with them when they all went glow-bal.

Pushing through the bodies, Ade grabbed him round the neck. 'Where are these markings then? Or do you need a big sloppy kiss to get revved?'

'Not from you, mate.' Laughing, Kel threw Ade off in a neat pitch and tumble move.

'With no green-eyed girl to get you flaming, it'll have to be the old stand-by of FIGHT!' With that yell, the others took Ade's word as a signal to come at Kel. Well aware of his skills, they didn't hold back. He sent a few flying over the sofas until Lee and Swanny got him pinned.

'Dig deep, Kel. Find those battle flares!' yelled Ade. 'Or was it all a one night wonder?'

Suddenly afraid that he was going to disgrace himself and not blaze, that it had been just kissing Meri that had triggered the reaction, Kel began fighting for real. He couldn't stand being mocked, humiliated in front of his friends, and the attacks were suffocating. 'Get off me!' With a kick, he pushed Lee away, shook off Swanny and sprang up.

'Uh-oh, lads, there he goes!' shouted Ade.

With a great rising roar, the boys all yelled as Kel's skin marking erupted into a massive flare out, blaze emphasized by the UV light bathing the room.

'Whoa, dig out the sunglasses! That's one hell of a skin pattern you've got there!' Ade slapped him on the shoulder. 'Welcome to the world of the big boys, Kel.'

As his panic ebbed, so did the intensity of the skin-glow. Kel looked down at his arms and torso, intrigued by his first clear sight of what had been hidden so long. The pattern curled and looped its way up his arms and down his chest, coming to a halt at his hips. Tendrils and curves like the patterns on a fossil ammonite. So cool.

He grinned at his friends. 'Pleased to be here.'

7

M eri waited until she was absolutely sure that Kel had turned for home before she burst into Theo's bedroom. Her guardian was still awake, sitting up in bed with his usual nightcap of a camomile tea and a good book. The picture of contentment bought a lump to her throat. She was about to put an end to all that.

'We've got to go—I've got to go,' she began, wringing her hands. 'Right now. Tonight.'

Theo put aside the novel he was reading and threw back the duvet. 'Whoa: slow down, Meri.'

Spinning on her heel, she rushed out and into her room. She started pulling clothes at random from her chest of drawers, dumping them on the bed. 'I can't slow down. I've only got a few hours to escape.'

'What are you talking about?' Following her and standing in the doorway, Theo ran his hands through his hair, making it stick up in wild tufts.

'Kel—his friends—everyone in that house is one of them.'

'One of who?'

'My enemies. Theo, I haven't got time for you to be dense. They're the same kind of people as took my parents from me.' A suitcase wouldn't do—too cumbersome. She'd have to take a backpack.

'I don't like the way you are talking to me right now, Meri.' Theo dragged the backpack out of her hands and threw it into the hallway out of reach. 'Now, just stop. Sit down. Despite what you say, you do have time to tell me what's going on.'

Meri almost chucked in his face that she was an adult, that she didn't need to explain, but her more rational half recognized that he deserved the courtesy of an explanation. Like the droid hit by a kick in the midriff, she slumped on the bed. 'OK, OK. At the cinema I found out that Kel is part of it.'

'Part of what? Meri, could you be any more mysterious if you tried?'

Her promise to Ade to keep the secret and her resolution at the lawyer's office came back to her. Theo would be put in danger if she told all. She had to measure out the truth in tiny doses. 'It's something to do with the UV vision I have.'

'They can see like you do? That's good news, isn't it?'

'No, because I'm not exactly like them. Mine is different —more powerful somehow. I see far more than they do.'

Theo was still on completely the wrong track. 'But they'll understand you. You won't be so alone with it.'

'No, Theo, they'll hunt me. They are exactly like the people who took out my parents with no mercy. I can't explain how I know. Just believe me that I'm not making this up.'

'We're not talking organized crime, are we, and mafia vendettas?'

She shook her head.

'So what are we talking about?'

She scrunched up a T-shirt, twisting it in her hands to form a rope. 'This thing, it's much older—much deeper. I'm on one side, they're on the other, and they don't wish me well.'

'They threatened you? I find that hard to believe. I'd've said that Kel was really fond of you.'

'He might be at the moment as they don't know yet but they'll work it out. I'll slip up or they'll have some test I don't know about.' Realizing she was ruining the top, she dropped the shirt back on the bed.

'This is a lot to absorb.' Theo's expression was an appeal for her to take it all back, to unsay what she had claimed. Their neat little life was about to be blown out of the water. 'How can you be so sure?'

'I saw them chase my parents and me that day. Theo, I saw them.'

Theo held his hands spread, helpless. 'You were four.'

'Old enough. It's not something I'll ever forget.'

'So if you're right, what do you want us to do?' Theo paced the short distance between the door and her bed. 'I'm not sure how easy it will be to disappear. The other times I had a chance to prepare, line up the next job.'

Meri swallowed. 'I guess I'll have to start out immediately. You can follow when you're able.'

'You're not doing this on your own.'

She thought that would be a problem for him. 'Just temporarily. We'll make mistakes if we try to run too quickly. I'll need a new ID and so on. Can you get me that?'

Theo rubbed his forehead. 'I don't know, Meri. I'll ask around. Saddiq has some relatives that might have connections but I'm not exactly up to speed with the criminal underground. I hoped I'd never have to use it again. Where are you going to go?'

'Not sure but I'd welcome some ideas.'

'What about staying with Saddiq—or Valerie?'

'Kel's met them. Your friends are the first places they'll look. I can't drag them into this.'

He nodded, coming to the same conclusion. 'Then stay for a couple of nights in a hostel, pay cash, while we think of something better. There are lots of them in the city for eco-volunteers. You'll blend in with people your own age.' He paused. 'Are you absolutely sure you are not over-reacting?'

'Theo, I'm sure.'

'God, Meri, what is this madness? From the way you're talking, I'm afraid for you.'

'So am I. And for you. Don't let them put pressure on you, OK? Snow them. You know nothing.'

'How will you get in touch? If this crew are as dangerous as you claim, we can't trust usual methods of communications and you can't come here or to my work.'

'What about the lawyer's office? No one else but you and me knows about that.'

'That's a good idea.' Theo started picking up her clothes and helping her pack. 'Meet you there tomorrow afternoon around three, OK?'

'Make sure you don't have anyone following you.'

'Meri, I'm not newly hatched from the egg.'

'Sorry. Just...just....'

'You're just scared, and stressed, and feeling as if life is spinning out of control.' He pulled her head to his chest. 'I get it.'

She let out a sob, finally safe to let it go. 'I really liked him.'

'I know, sweetness.'

'And then…and then he turned out to be just the same as them.'

'Not knowing exactly what that means, I'll have to take your word on it. But, Meri, we've been running for fourteen years. When are we going to turn and make a stand? Involve the police or seek some kind of official protection?'

'I don't think that would work. They're too wealthy, too well connected, with too much at stake.'

'Think about it, huh? You can't keep running for the rest of your life.'

'Maybe not, but if I stop running then I'm dead, Theo. I mean it.'

MERI DECIDED to leave at five in the morning, planning on catching the first train into the centre of London and lose herself in the commuting crowds. Putting the final things in her bag—a photo of her with her parents, her copy of *Jane Eyre* and the little sketchbook Theo had given her—she settled the backpack on her shoulders. Theo handed her a print-off of the address of a hostel in Wapping not too far from the lawyer's office if she decided to walk.

'Reviews online make it sound OK but don't leave your bag lying about,' he said as he zipped up her jacket for her and settled a beanie over her hair, a last paternal gesture before he let her go.

'What was your phrase about not having just hatched?'

'But you are sheltered, Meri, whatever you might think. I wanted it that way. This time I can't be there to stand between you and the crap that's out there. What do you want me to tell the school?'

'My exams—all that work and I'm throwing it away?' She'd only just thought of that. And what would Sadie think when she just didn't show up? She'd have to get some word to her friend so she didn't believe Meri had dumped her without a thought.

Theo looked as unhappy at the prospect as Meri. 'I guess that's the price you're going to have to pay. But, love, your life is worth far more than a few exams.'

She squeezed those regrets into a corner of her heart and slammed a door on them. 'Tell school I've moved to be with other relatives.'

'OK, that'll fly. Makes it sound like once past eighteen you couldn't wait to get shot of me.'

'You know that's not true.' She went up on tiptoe to kiss his cheek. 'Will you check there's no one watching?'

He rolled his eyes but did as she asked, peeking through the living room curtains. His stance stiffened. 'Actually, Meri, I think there might be. I was hoping it was going to be mainly in your imagination.'

She joined him. A car was parked just down the street, windows slightly fogged indicating there were people inside. She didn't think it was a couple making out: it was too public. There were many better side roads on the edge of the Common. 'Neither of us are imagining that. I'll go the back way, climb over the wall onto Parkside Avenue.'

'Do you want me to report them to the police? I could claim I suspect they're burglars waiting to break in. That should keep them busy. I'll do it anonymously.'

'I like the way you think.'

Meri waited for the patrol car to pull up alongside the surveillance team before she headed out through the garden they shared with Mr Kingsley downstairs. Using an old stone birdbath to give herself a boost, she threw the bag over the wall, then followed, taking care not to cut herself on the broken bottles cemented along the top under the covering of ivy. She felt better now she had taken the necessary evasive action, her churning emotions smoothing out to a determination to get out from under this snarl of troubles. If only Kel hadn't turned out to be one of the enemy; if only she hadn't ever tried to venture out from her self-imposed island of no-friends....

Suck it up, Meri. There was no point in regrets. He wasn't who she thought so the quicker she put that relationship behind her the better. She had to let go of the silly dream that she could be the special one for him. Lesson learned.

KEL LOOKED for Meri on the bus the next day and was disappointed when she was a no show. At first he didn't think anything of it—she'd need time to get over the shock so a day off school wasn't unreasonable—but then the art teacher didn't call her name when she took the afternoon register.

'What about Meri?' he asked Mrs Hardcastle as she sent the data off to the office.

'Who, Kel?'

'Meredith Marlowe?'

'Oh, yes, the pointillist. There was a note in the register. Apparently she's switched schools suddenly—family crisis.'

'To where?'

'It didn't say. If you're a friend, I'm sure she'll get in touch.'

Kel went back to his potter's wheel, using the circling motion and hands pressed lightly on cool clay to calm his thoughts. Swanny had reported at breakfast that Tiber and Jiang had got moved along so they had had to stop their surveillance of her flat. Had Meri taken the opportunity to bolt? That seemed an extreme reaction and far too quick.

She'd not even given what Ade had told her a chance to sink in.

He'd have to report her.

He muttered a curse.

Seeing the comp-punk friend of Meri's frowning at a wire sculpture over on the far side of the room, Kel turned off the wheel and wiped his hands. Sauntering over, he came to perch on the bench beside her.

'Hey, Sadie.'

'Hey, yourself, Kel.'

'Looks good. Abstract?'

'Ah no: that's where you're wrong—and exactly what I want you to think.' She tied her hair back with an off-cut of flexible wire, bundling the long black mop up in a messy bun. The action revealed a row of little jewellery guys climbing along the outer rim of her right ear. 'It's a scaled-up model of the inside of the quantum chip.'

'Very scaled up then. Clever. So, er, did you hear what Miss Hardcastle said about Meri?'

'Yeah, I got a text from her. Seems she and Theo had a serious bust up and she's moved to other relatives. They've been wanting her to come for ages so it just brought that forward. It's a bummer changing schools in her last year but she'd made up her mind.'

And that was a total lie. Meri hadn't argued with Theo and had no relatives. 'Where's she gone?'

'She said she'd let me know the address as soon as the dust settled. For the moment she said to text.'

'I'll do that then.'

Twisting a piece of wire around her index finger, Sadie looked away, a little awkward. 'I don't mean to be rude, Kel, but she might want to cut you loose, you know? She told me on Saturday that the first date was a data-dump.'

Humiliation crawled hot under his collar. What if Sadie was right? 'We went out again last night so it can't've been that bad.'

'But she didn't say she was moving? That doesn't sound to me like a girl wanting to keep seeing you. Maybe she is just too nice to tell you?'

He couldn't get into that now, not with someone who had no idea of what really was at play here. 'Just say I'm worried about her if you talk. Say I want her to get in touch urgently.'

'Sure—as long as you understand I'm her friend first.'

'I've no problem with that—she needs her friends.'

Leaving Art to join the crowds mingling in the hallways on lesson change, Kel decided to put off mentioning anything to Ade until he got home, hoping that the delay would give Meri time to calm down, come back and reply to his messages. He kept circling what he had said the night before, what he could've done differently to give her a softer landing.

Doubts edged in like rain-bearing clouds at a cricket match. Granted that the markings were unusual, it didn't add up that she had gone off like a rocket into panicked outer space. He would have imagined most people would be intrigued, even want a closer look, once the initial shock had passed. The markings were beautiful, something to be proud of and displayed when visible. That had been their original function: a mating and battle signal like a peacock's tail, a little bit embarrassing to admit now but surely no different in essence from cultivating sexy long hair or designer stubble?

But had she stopped to think about any of that. No. Meri had totally freaked, lashing out at all of them. It hadn't been helped that Lee had been hostile. *Mr Pissy Cat*, as Meri had aptly named him.

Kel's steps slowed, thought of making it to his next lesson fading. But when had she been close enough to see Lee's jaguar markings? Not at the gig despite what Ade assumed. In that bundle in the mosh pit all she could've seen up in the balcony was the glow, not the definition. He was sure he hadn't mentioned any specifics either. And if she didn't see it clearly then, when else would she have had the chance? Lee had been running cold rather than hot last night, not blazing out, or they all would've seen.

Oh hell, no.

That was impossible.

Kel stopped in his tracks in the middle of the chemistry corridor, not caring when a younger student bumped into him. The girl muttered an apology even though it had been his fault. Ignoring her, Kel turned on his heels and headed out of the school building. The chances must be so slight as to be microscopic. He had to check but could only do that at home in the library.

Swanny met Kel at the door, surprised to see him back before end of school and without Ade. 'Everything OK, Kel? Not ill again?'

'No.' Kel bowled straight past and into the library that opened off the foyer.

'Who's looking after Ade?'

'Lee I expect. If not, Ade'll have to cope. He's a big boy. I've got something more important to check first.'

'That's not the deal, and you know it.'

'Get out of my face, Swanny.' Kel slammed the door, knowing he was probably in for a reprimand for insubordination but right now he could only think of one thing. He grabbed the first volume of the archive history of his people off the shelf and turned to the index. *Atlanteans: distin-guishing marks, p. 82.*

Flipping to the entry he had read so often but never thought he would have to take seriously, he checked his facts.

At the lawyers' office in the city, Meri sat in the same room to read her message, exactly as she had as on her first visit. The same noises played outside: the murmur of voices and tapping of keys. The only thing that was different was her. She was the one who had gone through a life-changing experience, ousting her from her safe nest to have to fly free well before she was ready.

Shaking off her paralysis, she put the little key into the lock. According to Mr Rivers, she had timed her visit perfectly, the box having arrived from New York that morning with a special courier. Theo had arranged for her to read its contents with her own cup of coffee while he tried his Cockney chappie act again with Sultry Sophia. Sniffing the drink, Meri hoped the real caffeine would punch through her sleepiness. When she'd booked her bed at the hostel in Wapping, she'd been tempted to fall facedown on the mattress but knew Theo would go out of his mind with worry if she didn't make her afternoon appointment. She took a sip. Ugh: was that what real coffee tasted like? Heavily diluting it with milk, she tried again. Better, but to be honest it wasn't her drink, not like it was for Theo. Another gulp and she could feel her heart beginning to react. Should this stuff be legal?

OK, quit stalling, Meri.

Turning the key in the lock, she lifted the lid. As well as the expected letter there were some old photographs, Victorian by the looks of their age and styling. Shuffling through them, she didn't like them one bit. Always a back view, the subjects, male and female, were stripped to the waist. Someone had traced their skin markings with black ink to make visible to the camera what her kind could see with the naked eye. She looked at the little notations on the reverse of the ones she recognized: turtle shell, warrior; leaf, cultivator; snowflake, domestic servant; panther, fighter; spiral, poet. But there was something very wrong with them. The people did not seem willing participants in this categorisation. She could see the muscles straining in the arms as they fought their restraints but they had been tied so tightly to a frame there was little or no give.

Putting them aside, she turned to the letter, hoping that would provide the answers. Once again, she came face to face with the curling script that belonged to one of her parents. She ran her finger over the paper, feeling the connection where they had once touched it. Her father, she guessed, as the writing seemed masculine somehow. As she remembered it, he had been the one to take the lead at home when it came to matters affecting their safety.

Darling daughter,

As we said in our first letter, we are sorry beyond words that we are not there to stand by your side as you face your enemies. I'm writing this in our house in California and trouble seems very distant. Seeing you today playing outside in the yard with your mother, hearing your laughter, it is hard to imagine such a future, that anyone could want to harm a child so bright and beautiful. Yet I write this knowing from bitter experience that such people exist. You would not be the first innocent they try to cut down, but the last in a very long line of Atlanteans who have lost their life to the Perilous.

Meri took a moment to study the first paragraph, noting how careful her father was not to mention her by name or give any details that would tip off someone who came across the letter. Looking quickly ahead, she could see no mention of Theo this time. If an enemy had broken in and stolen one of the boxes, they would only get half the information and not enough to locate her—a wise precaution considering what she now knew.

I don't write this to frighten you needlessly but to instil a proportionate sense of danger in you. The fact that you are reading this tells me that they have indeed lived up to their reputation and removed us from your life. I imagine your mother and I went kicking and screaming—but undeniably we went.

So let us tell you about the Perilous. We have fought many battles with them over the centuries but we have to admit to having lost that long war. They live on gaining power and influence in the shadows and our people have dwindled to a handful, maybe to just a single person: you.

Originally the Perilous were our neighbours and shared the island with us. Our stories say we called them that because even then, long before we started writing such things down, our superior perception of the UV spectrum meant we saw how their skin would blush in the colour we had called 'peril'. Our vision developed through generations of choosing mates with these skills, a physical trait the Perilous shared to a lesser extent. This is how we noticed that with those we called 'the Perilous' the source wasn't a rush of blood to the skin, but unusual natural skin markings that absorbed UV from daylight and released it back in fighting or mating situations—what the Perilous called the blaze or flare up. These markings appealed to both peoples on an aesthetic level and over many centuries, partners were chosen for the Perilous to define and refine these characteristics.

The island society was highly stratified. Our kind, the Atlanteans, were the ruling class. Unfortunately, it amused some less enlightened of our leaders to use the markings to decide which professions the Perilous should go into, even if temperamentally they were not suited to that role. Eventually what started as a muddle-headed piece of social engineering became tradition and our two nations, Atlanteans and Perilous, settled to many centuries of coexistence, one ruling, one serving.

As you might imagine in an unfair society such as that of old Atlantis, there were attempts at rebellion from the Perilous but in those days we were much stronger than them. Our more developed sight meant we always knew in advance if it was a Perilous or an Atlantean who was confronting us. And we had one weapon they could not defend against, not while there were enough of us to protect ourselves. Like the Perilous we absorb ultraviolet light but at a much greater intensity. When deliberately turned on a Perilous it causes their markings to flare out. The result will be burns that can reach the worst, third degree of seriousness, resulting in death. One or two executions by this method in each rebellious generation was enough to keep the Perilous quiet. These are shameful episodes in our history but they demonstrate that you aren't as powerless as you might think. A skill that was used to oppress a people might also be used as a last resort in self-defence.

Meri stared at her hands. No, that wouldn't be something she would be trying even to save herself. It sounded beyond cruel.

Then the inevitable happened: in the aftermath of a natural disaster that destroyed our homeland and resulted in exile for the survivors, a rebellion took place. Rather than sue for peace, the two sides chose war and have been fighting ever since. From being oppressed, the Perilous have become our oppressors, killing on sight as they fear our powers to what is now an irrational degree. They never give us a chance to speak, never choose mercy when we are vulnerable. They believe that for them to live happily ever after we must be eradicated. There is no shifting them from that view despite the brave attempts of our diplomats of recent times to reach out to them. My parents were two of these peacemakers and lost their lives when they went to broker a treaty.

Our advice to you, therefore, is to avoid contact with the Perilous at all costs. Run if you must. Choose to live quietly. The full strength of Atlantean culture only lingers in your existence. Blend with the ordinary population and snatch a final victory by passing on some of your traits to a new generation.

Be happy. Prosper away from the cruel disputes of the past. Know that you are loved always.

Dad and Mom

P.S. I found these photographs in my father's archive. I would prefer to destroy them but you might find them helpful in identifying your enemies.

MERI TURNED BACK to the pictures. Sickened, she saw now that it hadn't been ink but burns that marked the skin of the subjects. Someone had released their power into the captives to a very deliberate degree to bring to the surface that which only Atlanteans normally could see. God, she could've done that by mistake to Kel when she had panicked yesterday. He'd had a narrow escape. She didn't want to look but made herself go through the rest. So many kinds. It was like some perverted human butterfly collection: the photographer hadn't stopped until he'd got a specimen of each. Meri didn't want a copy of them, or even of this letter. She locked it all back in the box, like caging a savage beast back in a cage.

Her dad hadn't spelt it out but she had understood his message. The Perilous had been the Atlanteans' serfs, kept under because the masters had a deadly force at their fingertips. From having been intrigued and even a little proud of her Atlantean heritage, Meri now just felt disgusted. Just as well a disaster had wiped out the whole pack of them. They'd deserved it.

Pushing away from the table, Meri stood, head hung, at the window. A mother was pushing a child on one of the swings of the garden in the play area built in the centre of the square. The child was laughing, looking rosy-faced buttoned up in his Paddington duffle coat.

Something inside her softened. Thoughts of Atlanteans deserving their fate were unfair. Not everyone had been guilty. There were always innocents hurt in any war, any disaster: children, non-combatants, refugees. And did a blood tie mean Meri deserved to be hunted now? Of course not. But what responsibility did she bear for things that had been done long before her birth, in a world so ancient it was no more than an archaeological trace? When did you stop having to say sorry for crimes others who might be distantly related to you had committed? Tired out by that conundrum, Meri rested her head against the windowpane and wished the swing of this mad world would stop and let her get off.

8

A clock ticked in the silence of the library while Kel wrestled with his conscience as to what to do about Meri. She had run, most likely because she had known exactly what she could expect from a household of Perilous once they unmasked her. It might well be best to let her go. The problem was that, now Ade thought she was one of them, he'd not leave it there. As a Tean—if she really was a Tean—she was dangerous and if Ade or anyone went after her unprepared they could get seriously hurt or killed. Kel had lost his mother to Teans so he knew it was no idle threat they posed. His friends had to know the truth.

But what then? Though the historic policy was to kill on sight, the Tean threat had dwindled to almost nothing over the last few years. As far as Kel could see, there was no need to make Meri into a big deal. Test his theory and then come to a special arrangement for her: that was the best way to handle it. The others would see sense surely? Make an exception for her? Even imagining killing someone outside self-defence just seemed so unreal; he couldn't believe anyone he knew would take that step.

Burying his face in his hands, Kel ran through what he would say, the tone he would employ. This was an eighteen-year-old girl, not a Tean hit squad like those who killed his mother. No need to go off on a witch hunt. They should be gentle, make sure she posed no threat but basically leave her be.

Right. OK. Best get this done.

Kel found Ade in the kitchen chatting to Swanny over the toaster, his first port of call when he returned from school.

'Uh-oh, someone's in trouble,' said Ade. 'Swanny here was just telling me that you should be sent to bed with no supper for dissing him.' The toast popped up and he moved quickly to spread the margarine while it was hot. 'I told him it was just the hormone rush of flare out still working its way through your system. Am I right?' He leant back against the counter and took a bite out of his toast.

'Look, Ade, can I have a word?' Kel gestured to the garden terrace that lay beyond the double doors. It had assumed an unattractive autumnal messiness, net on the tennis court sagging. The leaves on the vine were dipping and dripping to the flagstones. Unpicked grapes rotted on the stalk, dusted with mildew.

'You're joking? It's raining. Besides, there's nothing you can say to me that Swanny can't hear. That's how we work, remember? So not hormones. What's up?'

Kel supposed Ade would have to tell Swanny anyway so maybe it was better to get it over with in one briefing. 'It's about Meri.'

Ade winked at Swanny. 'Thought it might be.'

'She's gone.'

'Gone where?' He tore the crust off his slice.

'I mean she's run away.'

'Did we scare her that much? I thought she'd, you know, come round with a little time?'

'She can't come round. She's not one of us.'

'Not yet, but the sight—'

There was no way of sugaring this pill. 'Ade, I think there's a chance that she's Tean. In fact, I'm pretty sure.'

The toast dropped back on the counter as Ade swore fluently. 'How do you know?'

'She could see our markings even when we weren't flaring.'

Swanny grabbed his mobile from the charging point by the radio. 'Where do you think she is? I'll send a team to pick her up.'

'I don't know where she is—and I don't think sending a squad after her is appropriate. She must be frightened enough as it is.'

'*She's* frightened? Wake up, Kel: we have a Tean on the loose in London. She could kill anyone of us!' Ade began pacing.

'Really? Did she show any signs of that yesterday when she had all of us at her mercy? As I read it, she just wanted to get away.'

Ade waved off that argument. 'She was outnumbered then. Swanny, get on it. The Tean must be captured at all costs. Shit. Shit.'

'Her name is Meri,' Kel said. 'Meri that you nicknamed Mouse. Someone you were friendly with just last night.'

Ade poked a finger at Kel. 'Put aside your personal feelings on this. Meredith Marlowe is a clear and present danger to our existence, Kel. You should know this better than any of us.'

'How? She's just one girl.'

'She's an Atlantean, one of the race that bred us for their

amusement, the reason we have these.' Ade shoved his forearm under Kel's nose, markings starting to flare as his fight instinct surged. 'Captive breeding programmes, artificial selection to raise a slave population that pleased them.'

'Millennia ago.'

'But never forgotten, never forgiven. And it's not such ancient history. Your own mother, only a few years ago, burned with four others by the last Tean squad in America.'

'I know that.' Kel felt like Ade was driving a spike through his head.

'Then you know your dad had to dump her body along with the other victims in a river to hide the evidence, not even give his wife and our brothers and sisters a decent burial. But the threat never ends, does it? Meri can do the same to you right now, or sterilize you, bleaching your organs from the inside with lower doses of her power. Have you ever seen one of us after a Tean has finished?'

Kel shook his head.

'I've been shown the pictures—and they're not pretty. You wouldn't think I was overreacting if you had.'

'Just because she can, doesn't mean she will.'

'She's been exposed, now she'll be hunted so of course she will. She'll have no choice.' Ade turned to Swanny. 'Bring in the guardian, Theo Woolf. Take Lee with you. Let's find out what he knows.'

This was horrible, like watching a multi-vehicle accident with no way of stopping it. 'You can't just snatch a civilian off the streets,' protested Kel.

'Why? Woolf won't involve the police if that means more people looking for the Tean. He'll answer our questions, I promise you.'

'Ade, don't do this.'

'It's what we've all been trained to do. Are you letting your feelings for the girl overrule a lifetime of training?'

'Then let me be the one to bring Meri in.'

'Can you do that? No one will blame you for stepping back from this. The only way we'll be safe is if we put her out of action. Permanently.'

What had he started? wondered Kel with growing horror. 'Not acceptable. This is the twenty-first century. You can't go around executing our enemies without due process, certainly not when they've done nothing but be born.'

'Fine, as a concession to you and to check our facts, she gets a trial. With any luck she really is the last of her kind and we can put this to bed now once and for all.'

'A death sentence is not an option here, Ade.'

'Death comes to us all as you well know. I'm trying to stop us finding ours too soon.'

'And she's the sacrifice?'

'Damn right she is. Rather a Tean than you or me.'

Anger blazed, Kel's skin markings flaring. 'And you can live with yourself when you say that, you murdering bastard?'

'I'm one of the ruling house, you disrespectful prick! It is our responsibility to protect our people, take the hard decisions.'

'So you've already tried and condemned her in your own mind. Bringing her in is just the first step to the gallows? God, Ade, did I ever even know you?'

'Don't start bleating now about human rights, Kel.'

'Why? Because you know you are acting like...like some kind of fascist? Kill the undesirable. Send her to the gas chambers for being who she is, not what she's done? Christ, you make me sick.'

Ade turned his back in an effort to calm down before

either of them was tempted to throw a punch. 'Swanny, see that Kel is secured in his quarters while he has a chance to cool off. We'll review his conduct tomorrow.'

'Sod that. I resign.'

'Resignation not accepted. Swanny.'

'Come on, Kel. Don't make this more difficult than it need be.' Judging Kel's mood, Swanny took out a taser from the holster at his belt. They knew not to take Kel on in hand to hand.

Kel backed towards the patio doors. 'If you think I'm sitting quietly confined to quarters, Swanny, while you back this homicidal maniac then you know nothing about me.'

Swanny cooly checked the setting and took aim. 'I'm sorry, but Ade's right. Teans are too dangerous.'

'Then sod you too.' Though the chance was slight, Kel made a break for the doors. The dart hit his back, delivering its payload of electricity. He crumpled to the floor, body shrieking with a pain to match his mental anguish.

Lights out.

WHEN KEL CAME TO, he was in his own room, lying on the bed, storm blinds lowered on the window to keep him in, door shut and probably locked. His whole body ached and twitched, little cramps running up his calf muscles like someone was sticking in needles. He could hear a commotion outside, voices raised, the sound of things being moved as if they were preparing for a siege.

One little Tean and they lost their heads. Flight or fight instincts kicking in and the Perilous assumed battle readiness.

And it was his fault. He should not have said anything. Instead, he should have gone after Meri, told her to hide and never make contact with the Perilous again. He should've helped her disappear. He had to hope she'd done a good enough job of that herself as he had so monumentally cocked up. How had he not understood? He'd gone and pushed the big red button without realizing the consequences, thinking everyone would see it like he did.

From being proud of his heritage as part of an oppressed race who had turned their fortunes around and beaten their masters, he felt utterly disgusted with Ade, and with all his so-called friends. Could no one else see what they were becoming by hounding a girl like this? They were becoming as bad, if not worse, than the people who had originally persecuted them.

No wonder she had run in terror. She was right to do so.

Kel heard a scuffling at the door, a scrape of a key in the lock. Lee came in wearing his black combat gear, expression all business.

'Ade wants you downstairs. Will you behave?'

Anything to get out of this room. 'Yes.'

'He wants your word of honour.'

'Honour? Do we have any of that left?'

Stance softening a little, Lee held out a hand to help him up. 'We all get it, Kel. You like her. Ade liked her. It's tough when personal matters conflict with our people's policies.'

Fine for Lee to speak. He hadn't spent the last week with Meri. He didn't know her like Kel did. 'Our policies are wrong.'

'Then give your word and come and argue that downstairs.'

'All right. I'll behave.'

'No escape attempts?'

'So I'm a prisoner now?'

'You're being held for your own safety. We all know that

you want to go and find her. Ade is just trying to protect you.'

'I resigned.'

'Doesn't matter. He's still your prince and he's trying to be your friend.'

Kel's heart sank yet further. 'I'll appeal to his uncle. He's our king and can overrule him.'

'And you think he'll be more merciful than Ade who actually knows the girl?'

Another door slammed shut in Kel's mind, limiting his already narrow options. 'Then maybe he and his family have been ruling us for too long.'

Lee shot a glance over his shoulder. 'Shut the hell up, Kel,' he hissed. 'You're in enough trouble without spouting treason.'

'Me? In trouble? I'm not the one advocating murder.'

'You brought a Tean right into the court of the crown prince.'

'On his fecking orders.'

'We know, but it doesn't change what you did.'

Kel felt a drag on his anger, a heavy weight of despair. 'Lee, when will we change? When after all these centuries will enough blood have been spilt?'

'It's not personal to Meredith.'

'I bet it feels pretty personal to her right now. I could be killed by a tiger tomorrow if I had the misfortune to meet one of the few survivors in the wild but I don't say we should go round shooting all the ones in zoos. How is this different?'

Lee dug his hands in his pocket, rocking on his heels. 'Look, maybe caging her will be enough. If you calm down, then you can make that argument.'

'I shouldn't have to.'

'I'm not arguing with you. I know we won't agree.' Striding across the room, Lee picked up a flannel from the sink and tossed it to Kel. 'You'll want to wash your face. You're messed up. Hit your nose when you did a face plant.'

Kel scrubbed off the dried blood. That explained the crashing headache. 'What's happening downstairs?'

'Swanny and I scooped up the guardian on his way back from work. He seemed to be expecting us and came along willingly. He's downstairs now, hurling abuse at Ade, but it's you he really wants to see.'

So that's why they wanted him. 'Fine. I want to see Theo too.'

'Your promise?'

'I promise not to try and escape tonight.'

Lee nodded, accepting that was as much as he would get. 'Don't try and go out into the garden. We've orders to stop you if you do.'

'And you're OK with that?'

'I'm just following orders, Kel.'

'The cry of storm troopers throughout history. You'd better do some reading. Start with the Third Reich.'

'And you'd better decide where your loyalties lie.'

In razor-edged silence they walked down the broad flight of stairs, through the elegant foyer and into the reception rooms.

Theo Woolf had been shown into the library. He was currently standing over Ade, voice raised in fury, while Swanny looked on with amusement, something that stuck in Kel's craw. This was far from funny even though Theo was a bit of a lightweight to take on Ade and Swanny at the same time.

'This has gone way too far. You will tell my daughter there's nothing to be scared of. You will let my girl come home and finish school without fear or I'm reporting you to the police!'

Ade steepled his fingers, every inch the prince. 'I'd be delighted if Meredith came home.'

Theo tossed his head, his fair hair rippling like a mane. 'Don't say that in those tones, you little shite. I'm not stupid. I know that means you aren't calling off the hit on her. What did she ever do to deserve this persecution? Sod all, that's what. Well, she'd not a four-year-old anymore, not alone, and I'm not scared of you. I've got friends—contacts in the government.'

'Mr Woolf, no matter how many friends you have, I'll always have more,' said Ade calmly. And that was true: the Perilous made sure they had people planted throughout government and law enforcement in each country where they had a community. 'Just tell us where she is.'

Theo was saved from answering by spotting Kel's entrance. 'You!' Then to everyone's shock, maybe even his own, Theo launched himself across the room and threw a punch that connected with Kel's jaw. Kel ricocheted into Lee, both of them only prevented from hitting the floor by collision with a bookshelf. Theo stood over Kel, panting. 'You lying bastard! I hope you're ashamed of what you've done. She's running—she's terrified—she's got nothing now thanks to you. Not even a home!'

Kel wiped his wrist across his mouth and nose. Bleeding again. Not a bad hit for a scrawny fella with more ear jewellery than sense. Theo should never have come here.

'What? You've got nothing to say for yourself?' Theo looked ready to take another punch but, as Kel hadn't struck back, had no excuse.

'Mr Woolf, we understand that you're angry but I really

can't have you beating up one of my men like this,' said Ade. 'Kel, are you OK?'

'Sod off,' said Kel, accepting a bundle of tissues from Lee.

'He's OK. Mr Woolf, as you may have worked out, Kel isn't that pleased with us either. It's not his fault. He didn't want Meri to make a run for it. Why don't you tell him where he can find her so he can persuade her to come back?'

'Don't tell me anything, Theo,' Kel said quickly.

'What? Why?' Theo's eyes went from Ade to Kel. 'What's going on here?'

'What has Meri told you?' asked Ade.

'Don't say,' hissed Kel.

'She's told me nothing, apart from the fact that she knows you are her enemies.' From the alarm that now travelled across his face, Theo had only just now worked out that he might also be in danger here.

'And why did she say that?'

'She wouldn't tell me.' Theo got out his mobile. 'I'm calling the police. This has gone far enough.'

'Please do,' said Ade graciously. 'But what will you say? We have CCTV in the house. All that you can report is yourself for taking an unprovoked swing at Kel here.'

'I'll report that you are terrorising my girl.'

'How? What exactly have we done?'

Theo struggled with his temper, then pocketed his phone.

Kel knew that Ade was at his most dangerous when he used that cool I'm-in-charge tone. 'Ade, let Mr Woolf go. This doesn't involve him.'

'Of course it does. He knows where she is.'

Theo bristled with outrage. 'I'll never tell you. There is

no threat you can think up that would make me do that, I promise you.'

'I'm not going to threaten you. I'll just point out that it will be kinder to Meri if we could pick her up without a fuss. She won't like being tracked down and I can't be sure how my men will react if they feel personally in danger when hunting her.'

'He means you to lead her to the slaughter,' said Kel. 'Don't do it.'

'Keep quiet, Kel.'

'Not in this lifetime. And never again on your orders. You and I, we are way past finished.'

Disquiet flickered across Ade's face before being ruthlessly suppressed. 'Mr Woolf, you really should tell us. It is the kindest way of handling this for all concerned.'

'Tell him to piss off.'

Theo's eyes glittered. 'Yeah, I think I will.'

Ade shrugged. 'I didn't really expect you to give us the information but I do know you're in contact with Meredith. Tell her that if she wants everyone she cares for to remain safe and well,' his gaze went to Kel then back to Theo, 'then she'd better turn herself in. We'll track her anyway but if she does this she makes a good case for no one else to get mixed up in this mess.'

Theo lifted his chin. 'I'm not telling her that.'

Ade leaned forward, hands dangling between his spread knees. 'I know it sounds harsh but I guess you don't know what's really at stake here. She doesn't mean to be, but she's dangerous, like the carrier of a deadly virus. I feel sorry for her. I'm just trying to stop something worse happening.'

Theo studied Ade's earnest expression for a moment. 'That's what you think you're doing but you're so wrong. Sitting there like the bloody junior Godfather! You've lost sight of the fact that this is a real person's life you are playing with for some stupid reason of your own—an innocent. I wasn't sure at first if she was right to run, but she was, wasn't she? You're all fanatics—terrorists—and I'll tell you something: I'm bringing you down.'

Ade shook his head. 'Take Mr Woolf home, will you, Swanny?'

'This way, sir.'

'I'll find my own damn way home.' Theo stomped to the door.

'Then just make sure he leaves,' amended Ade.

Theo paused by Kel on his way out. 'Sorry about the, you know?' He mimed a fist connecting with his face.

'I'm not. I deserved it.'

Theo gave him a nod. 'You OK? Do you want to come home with me?'

More than anything. 'I don't think they'll let me leave tonight.'

'Well, when you do, come find me. I seem to have a spare bedroom all of a sudden.' And then he left, slamming the front door behind him. One of the stained glass panes cracked.

Kel made no effort to break the silence that followed Theo's departure. He'd been tasered by his best friends and now imprisoned—his disappointment with them was so huge, life altering, shaking him on a fundamental level. He knew he wasn't going to be able to get past it.

'Kel, I need you on my side on this,' Ade said at last.

'Back at you, mate. I'm on the humane, let's give the innocent a chance side. Which one are you on?'

'The protect my people one.'

'At all costs?'

'I'll do what's necessary.'

'Then we really have nothing more to say to each other.'

Ade ran his fingers down the spines of the books on the shelf by his chair. 'My uncle's coming to deal with this personally. Your father will be with him.'

'No surprises there.'

'They both want to talk to you.'

'I bet they do.' Kel folded his arms. 'Did you tell them I resigned?'

Ade gestured to Lee and Swanny to leave them alone. 'Kel, sit down.'

'I'd prefer to stand.'

'Fine. I told them we argued. I wanted to give you a chance to rethink.'

'Just stop and consider what you're asking me. How can you yesterday be a reasonable human being and today turn into a tyrant?'

'You think I don't care about her?' Ade got up and went to the window. 'You think I don't know what I'm saying when I give the order for her to be brought in? Sod you if you think I want to do this.'

'Then don't.'

'I swore a vow—to protect us.'

'I get that. But I don't get how murdering a friend achieves that. You'll destroy us.'

Ade turned to look at him. 'No, you'll destroy us if you choose her over your people.'

'I don't see that you're giving me a choice here.'

'To use your own words, back at you, mate. What options are you handing me by your behaviour?'

'So what are you going to do with me?'

'I don't know. Let your father talk to you tomorrow, I suppose.'

'We shouldn't have to hurt her.'

'I agree, but biology has made it a necessity. She's our last natural predator; we're her prey.'

'Then why is she the one being hunted?'

MERI STUDIED the other young people in the hostel kitchen while trying not to make it too obvious that was what she was doing. Meals were cooked on an 'everyone muck in' basis and she had been given the carrots to peel. A huge mound. Not that she minded. Anything to take her mind off what was really bothering her.

A girl sat down opposite her with a basket of onions. She had a a snub nose and a strong no nonsense build to match her expression. Meri felt an instant liking for her. She looked like she didn't put up with any crap. 'Hi. I'm Anna.'

'Hi Anna. I'm...Em.'

'Short for?'

'Emma.'

'Cool. So are you an Idippy like me?'

'What's that?' Meri watched a perfect curl of carrot skin slip to the board, pleased with the peeler she'd been given. She was making herself take pleasure in small things as the big picture was so grim.

'You are green, aren't you? An I.D.P. or internally displaced person. I'm from Lincolnshire originally. We had to move out when the sea moved in. There're special grants for us to relocate.'

'Oh yes, I did know that. No, I'm not an I.D.P. Just here to...you know...?'

Anna nodded, supplying her own answer. 'See a bit of London before eco-service.'

'Yes, exactly.'

'Where are they sending you?'

'I'm not sure. Didn't get the paperwork in time.' She started chopping her first batch of carrots for the casserole.

'Bad luck. That probably means they'll put you on sewer duty or something gross.' Anna leaned forward, pointing at Meri with the vegetable knife. 'Between you and me, the eco-service admin is all over the place. My sister works in the Climate Change ministry and is always moaning about it.'

'Any chance they'll just plain forget me?'

'You wish, but they might lose you once they've got you.' Anna grinned. 'In a bog probably.'

'That doesn't sound too bad. I wouldn't mind getting lost.'

Anna diced an onion with impressive speed. 'Depends on who you take along for company in my view. My eco-team sucks out loud. The leader is a total arse. If he comes up with another, "we're all in this together" slogan, I'm going to deck him.'

'Where are you working?'

'Essex marshes—or what's left of them. Trying to save Canvey Island. We won't win. As I keep telling Dexter: hasn't he heard of King Canute?'

They chatted some more while finishing their task, Meri learning the names of the other girls in the hostel kitchen and the boy carting out the recycling. All were proud Idippies.

'So it's like a club?' asked Meri, handing round some peeled carrots that had escaped the pot.

'Yeah, a totally exclusive one,' agreed a girl called Zara. She had long black hair and an ink tattoo of a Celtic symbol on her bicep. Her taste ran to layers of lacy clothes accesorized with navy blue lace-up boots. 'Hippies? So last century. Idippies is where it is at. Now everyone wants to be part of our subculture. All you have to do is have your home wiped out by nature. They're simply clamouring to get in.'

'Where are your family, Em?' asked Anna.

'I'm an orphan.' It was the first time Meri had ever admitted this. It rather killed the conversation.

'I'm sorry.' Anna looked rather desperately at the others to say something to help.

'No, it's fine. Well, not fine, obviously, but it happened a long time ago. Anna, can I borrow your phone a moment? Mine's dead.' Theo and she had agreed not to call each other on their usual numbers in case they were being monitored. He had asked Valerie to swap his for hers for a day or two.

'Sure. Dinner will be in about an hour so you've plenty of time.'

'I won't take that long.' Meri took the phone into the cold porch where the eco-service volunteers left their boots and overalls and dialled Theo. 'Hey, it's me.'

'You OK?' Theo sounded odd, not his usual self at all.

'You alone?'

'Yeah, thank God. I've just got back from seeing those madmen you went to school with.'

'You didn't! Theo, I told you not to!'

'Well I did. Didn't have much choice as they met me at the station.'

'So they know.' Meri had hoped she had a little more time to make her escape.

'They certainly suspect something, though what the hell that is I don't know as none of you will give me a straight answer. Meri, I don't think Kel's part of it. In fact he looked as though they've roughed him up a bit before I came. I didn't help things by throwing a punch at him.'

Meri squashed a surge of concern for Kel. Theo was the

one she should worry about. 'Are you completely mental? He's an expert in martial arts!'

'He didn't fight back. I feel really bad about that. He let me get in a free shot.'

Meri pinched the bridge of her nose. 'He may not be part of it but he is one of them.'

'And that makes absolutely no sense.'

'I can't explain.'

'I'm sick and tired of you saying that. Why can't you explain? Why can't I go to the police? Why are we living in some Alice-In-Wonderland world where we're running scared of a bunch of boys living in a posh house?'

'Theo, please.'

She could hear he was breathing heavily, trying to regain control of his temper. 'OK, OK. Let's deal with what you can tell me. I presume you rang for a purpose?'

'I've had an idea. How about I slide into an eco-service programme. A girl here says the administration is hopeless. I can probably pretend they just lost my papers. They issue you with a new ration card, don't they, when you join up?'

'That's right. You get extra travel credits as a perk, so you can go home to visit without spending your annual allowance. That's not a bad idea.'

'I've got to do it sometime, so I could just do it now. Pick up school in the new year, do online courses or something so I can still take some of my exams in the summer.'

'And you'll be more protected as part of a team, rather than just you and me. They'll be looking for me too and I'm much harder to hide. Yes, yes, I like it.'

'I'm going to ask one of the girls here if I can go with her. I think she'll welcome the company.'

'Just make sure you get registered so the time is racked up. You don't want to have to do it all over again.'

'I will.'

'What name do you want to use? Saddiq came through with a shady connection. They can make you an ID card.'

'Emma,' she looked around for inspiration. 'Boot. Emma Boot. Only child. Orphan. Make me an IDP from the Fens. You took me there once, remember, that concert on Ely Island? Most of the guys here are idippies so I'll blend.'

'OK. They'll get that to you tomorrow night. I've told Saddiq your address.'

'What else did you tell him?'

'The truth as I know it: that enemies of your parents are after you. He already knew there was something weird in our past so he took it in his stride. Valerie knows as well. They're rooting for you.' Theo cleared his throat. 'And look, if anything happens to me, go to them, OK?'

'Nothing's going to happen to you, Theo. I won't allow it.'

'Love, you might not be able to stop it.'

9

A sleepless night did not improve Kel's mood. His sheets looked like a war zone, twisted in the knots, pillows punched into submission. He finally ended up face down in exhaustion on top of the mess. He wasn't surprised when the next person he saw early on Saturday morning was his father bearing a breakfast tray.

'Hello, Kel.' Rill put the tray down on the desk. 'Got a hug for your old dad?'

Kel got off bed and walked into the embrace, struck that he was now an inch taller than his father. So much was changing. 'Good to see you, Dad. You're here with Osun?'

'Yes, the king's here. He's meeting with Ade to discuss the crisis.'

'And you've been asked to come deal with the prisoner?' Moving to the sink, Kel splashed water on his face. He could see in the reflection that his room was a mess, guitar half buried under sports gear, new marks on the wall where he had thrown a cricket ball at it last night, his Japanese art prints hanging at a precarious angle.

'Something like that. Let's eat first, OK? Tell me how you've been, aside from the obvious.'

Kel cleared yesterday's clothes off a chair for his father to sit down. 'Not much to say.'

'Ade said you flared out?'

'Oh yeah. I'm a spiral.' He rubbed at his arm. Most Perilous remembered their flare out as a great moment; he'd always associate his with Meri's terror.

'I'm proud of you. Your mother would've been so thrilled too. Come, eat something. They said you missed supper.'

'You mean between tasering me and locking me in here? Funny that.'

'Kel, please.'

He picked up his guitar and tucked it back in its usual corner, then sat on the edge of the bed. 'OK, let's eat. Tell me the news from you and Jenny.'

Grateful for the distraction, Kel listened with half an ear as his father gave the run down of the family news. The other half of his attention was on what exactly they could say to each other. Would his father back Kel through family loyalty, or go with his training and tradition?

Finally, Rill kicked back his chair, cradling a mug of tea. He leafed through the history of art book Kel had left out on the desk. 'So, Kel, do you want to tell me why you're locked up here—why Ade doesn't feel that he can trust you any more?'

'We don't agree about Meri: it's as simple and as complicated as that.' Kel reached for his cricket ball and began tossing it hand to hand.

'The Tean girl. I must admit I never thought I'd see the day when my son would break ranks over one of them.'

I mustn't lose my temper, Kel reminded himself, rubbing the ball on his thigh. 'Have you ever met a Tean, Dad?'

'Only when we fought them. I don't have to remind you what happened then.'

'Then you don't understand.' Kel tossed and caught the ball.

Rill dropped down so all four legs of the chair were firmly planted on the carpet. 'Put that damn ball down. It's you who doesn't understand, Kel. What you're not getting is the bigger picture. This poor girl—and yes, I feel sorry for her: she can't help being what she is—but she can't be ignored or swept under the carpet. Left at large, she could potentially pass on her traits to her children. There's something you have to get about Teans: they know who we are and we never suspect them, not unless something extraordinary happens like it did the day before yesterday, something which makes them drop their cover. Otherwise they can slide right in among us like sharks. None of us can live freely knowing there are people out there who can burn us from the inside out. I watched your mother die at the hands of a Tean. I don't want my son to go the same way.'

Kel gripped the ball tightly, not putting it down but no longer playing with it. 'I get that, but I don't get why we talk as if there's only one solution. I can probably kill with my bare hands—I was trained to do so—but no one is talking about culling me because I'm dangerous.'

'That's different.'

'Is it?'

'How old are you now, Kel? Eighteen-years-young. Can't you trust that those of us who have gone round this course a few more times might have a better grasp of this situation? We might have weighed how you feel, balanced that against the very real risks, and decided that we can't let her run?'

Kel dragged the fingers of his free hand through his hair. 'I can't believe that you're defending the idea of killing someone who's never harmed a fly. I thought you were better than that.'

Rill sat back. 'Actually, I'm not in favour of killing her.'

Finally someone talking some sense. 'Well, good.'

'I'm for neutralising. We catch her, contain her and make sure she lives happily somewhere, but so she can't hurt us or pass on her abilities to another.'

'That's not a life. At least Ade is honest. You're talking about condemning her to a kind of life sentence where we control her completely. She wouldn't even be a slave like the Teans did to us, but a zoo animal.'

'It might be the best offer on the table, Kel.'

'Then we need another table.' Kel threw the ball so it fell with a satisfying thud into the sports bag at the foot of the bed.

Rill closed his eyes a moment and sighed. 'This is a problem, isn't it? I can tell you're going to throw everything away on her. We Douglases do loyalty well, but this time you're being loyal to the wrong person.'

'You know nothing about her. You don't know that she's sweet and kind, talented, bitingly sarcastic at times, but under it all, quite shy. These facts don't add up to a stone-cold killer.'

'But any child she has in the future might turn out to be —or any other relative that she is hiding from us. It wouldn't take more than one or two Teans to overthrow the peace we've forged for our people, start the whole cycle again.'

'It's a peace that I now see has been built on the smoking corpses of a whole civilization.'

'There was nothing civilized about the Teans.'

'I'm not playing word games with you. You know what I mean.'

'Yeah, I do.' Rill scratched his chin. 'Put it another way, if you thought she had an infectious killer disease, Ebola or Bird Flu, wouldn't you quarantine her?'

'Yes, but she doesn't.'

'That's how we see her.'

'You see her wrong.'

'What if the person she touched, the person she tortured was me or your sister?'

'But she wouldn't.'

'People do all sort of terrible things when pushed.'

'Then don't push her.' Kel's headache was back, pulsing like a great red light in the middle of his forehead.

'You're looking at this from the perspective of one person; we have to look at it on behalf of all our people.'

'Maybe it's time we stopped thinking of ourselves as separate then and started thinking of us as sharing one race —the human race? What you're advocating is nothing but genocide, a war crime that the Reformed United Nations would prosecute you for if they knew what you planned.'

Rill placed his mug on the tray, signalling the end of the debate. 'I can see that we're not going to agree. Get dressed, Kel. Osun wants to see you at the briefing.'

'Yes, sir.' Kel gave him an ironic salute. 'I've resigned, did Ade tell you that?'

'He said you wanted to.'

'I'm out even if he doesn't accept it.'

'That means out of this house, out of our community.'

'Out of my family too?'

Rill put his hand on Kel's shoulder and squeezed. 'Kel, never that. But it'll make things very difficult.'

'And they're not already?'

THE CLUB ROOM as the largest space in the house had been

turned into a briefing room. When Kel entered, a couple of his friends said a guarded hello, but most pretended he wasn't there. Feelings were running high on both sides so it was just as well. No one had thought to take down Meri's picture. It remained on the wall—a threat curling over their heads or an image of what they were to the artist?

'Kelvin, good to see you,' said Osun in his deep tones. With skin like polished teak and dressed in a maroon suit, he made an impact on the room by his very presence. Add to that his air of command, and no one had any doubt who was in charge. Ade had by some family instinct dressed in a shirt of the same colour tucked into black jeans. King and Crown Prince. The future of their people right there.

'Sir.' Kel forced himself to give the king a respectful nod. Though his hopes were low, he might still find more mercy in Osun than anticipated. He didn't want to start by pissing him off.

'Sit by me. You know the Tean best. You might be able to predict what she'll do next.' Osun gestured to the chair beside his at the conference table.

'Sir, did no one explain that I'm not happy about this process—that I've resigned as Ade's bodyguard?'

'They did. But you haven't resigned as a Perilous, have you? Sit down and listen to the briefing. You might find things are a little less muddled when you are in possession of all the facts. You can start.' Osun nodded to Rill.

Kel's father clicked a remote at the wall screen. Old images started to flicker across the surface and Kel felt a rising tide of horror in his chest.

'These are the CCTV pictures of the last Tean attack,' said Rill. 'You can see that two adult members infiltrated our Washington base in the guise of tourists. We never identified them for reasons that will be made clear shortly. They brought with them a minor, age three or four.' He froze the picture on the mother leaning down to wipe ice cream off the face of the child, highlighting a pony tail poking out through the back of the cap. 'Odds are this is a female. Since Kel identified her yesterday, we think it might well be the young woman now known as Meredith Marlowe. The dates agree.'

He pressed resume. 'They made straight for the exhibit hall where Rayne Mortimer was employed as a talking guide. My wife and I happened to be visiting her that summer as part of our training. Rayne, as many of you know, was the investment manager for the North American branch and a lovely person. The Tean intelligence must have been good as they went right to the heart of our opera-tion. Unfortunately there was no video inside the room and we don't know exactly what transpired but their plan hit a snag and they tried to flee. All Perilous were called in to take up the pursuit. We tracked them across the site.' He flicked through a series of grainy images, skipping quickly the parts that showed Kel's mother die but even this brief glance of the material was enough to haunt Kel for the rest of his life.

Kel's knuckles were white where he gripped the arms of his chair. 'Dad, do you have to?'

'Sorry, Kel, but you have to see this. You won't get it unless you see what these people can do.'

Kel couldn't understand how his father could sound so cool showing snatches of what had to be the worst day of his life. 'It proves nothing about Meri.'

'I beg to differ. Looking more closely at these last ones, it is now apparent that the Teans made a switch, dumping the girl and picking up a decoy. I don't know how we missed that. They were cornered at the river and threw what we now know was not Meredith in the water before engaging with our defenders. Five Perilous were killed, including my wife, Kel's mother, Marina, just before I got there with the other guard. The two Tean adults were shot four times, probably fatally. We don't know for sure because they chose to jump into the water with their injuries rather than be captured. We thought they were going after the kid. With so many casualties the place was in chaos. A search was, of course, launched but none of the three were found. Until now.'

A sunny day turned to bloody violence for Meri and Kel's own father and mother had been part of it. Wasn't that a kick in the head? Kel couldn't bear to watch, to see his mother's death played out before his eyes, then that of Meri's parents. It was pure torture. He'd loved his mother with all his young heart. But he didn't buy his father's voice-over explanation. 'How do you know the Marlowes were there to hit Rayne Mortimer, Dad? Would you take your child along with you if that was your plan?'

Rill scrolled back to the initial shots. 'How do you explain that they went right for Mrs Mortimer?'

'Because they were visiting one of the premier historic attractions on the East Coast? Look at them in that queue: eating ice cream, chatting to the other visitors—do they look like they've got assassination on their minds?'

'They're Tean. That's what they do,' muttered Ade on Osun's other side.

'They're people taking their kid to visit George Washington's home like thousands of other parents. If the community over there wanted to hide why did they pick such an obvious place?'

Osun held up a finger. 'I'll answer that. The first president was a good friend to the Perilous and sheltered us during a resurgence of the Tean threat at the end of the eighteenth century. We preserve his house as part of the valuing of our culture and in thanks to him.'

'Good for George, but can't you see that you are jumping to a conclusion that the Marlowes had hostile intentions when all the violence seems to start with us?'

'Five people died, Kelvin. Your own mother.'

He swallowed past the lump in his throat. 'And Meri's parents. Looks like self-defence to me and leaving a little girl orphaned.'

Osun tapped his fingers together, evaluating Kel. 'You know, you may be right. You're looking at this from a fresh point of view when I've studied it so many times I see it with my eyes shut.' He held up a hand to stop Ade interrupting. 'Maybe Meredith Marlowe is the victim here today. She certainly was at four—none of us would argue she had any hostile intent at that age. So where does that leave us? One lone Tean, afraid, desperate. Can't you agree she needs to be pulled back in, persuaded that there is no need to harm anyone?'

'She has the right to live without having to fear for her life.'

'And so do we.'

'So does that mean that you're not going to put a kill order out on her?'

'No, I'm not. I'm suggesting we retrieve her. Your father was quite persuasive when we debated this. He said you were a good judge of character and if you said she was basically a nonviolent girl, then we should not assume she was out for vengeance.'

'Retrieve? What does that mean? The prison sentence Dad talked about?'

'We would have to talk to her—see how her needs and ours can mesh.'

'Uncle, when have Tean and Perilous requirements ever meshed?' asked Ade.

'There's always a first time. So what do you say, Kel?'

Kel studied his king's face. He was used to trusting Osun, believing in Ade, but he was still too deeply shaken to drop his wariness. It could be a ruse to get him to cooperate. They'd see it as justified. 'I'd say that was a good idea. You do that. You mesh.'

'And you?'

'Are you asking if my resignation stands?' His eyes slid to Ade. 'Yeah, it does. I don't like how this community handles someone who disagrees so I'm out. I won't betray you but I won't stay with you.'

'Kel—' Ade raised a hand as if to grab him back.

'No, sir, I can't be your guard or your friend any longer so don't ask me. I'll pack and go this morning.'

'That wasn't an ironic "sir" was it?'

'No, sir. I'll see you around at school I suppose.'

'Wait.' Osun interrupted Kel's attempt to exit. 'I'm not stopping you leaving but I do want your best guess what Meredith will do now. You owe your fellow Perilous that much.'

Kel shrugged. 'I've only known her a couple of weeks really.' It felt like a lifetime. 'My guess is she will get as far away from me as she can, so look for her where I'm not. That's the only tip I can give you.'

'I don't want our years of friendship to end like this. My door's always open, Kel,' said Ade quietly.

'I'll shut it carefully on my way out then.'

'YOU WANT to join the Canvey Island crew?' Anna couldn't believe her ears. Meri and her two friends were sitting on the top deck of a bus on their way to the Saturday craft market at St Katharine's Wharf, wheels splashing through the run-off from the high tide.

'That's right,' said Meri. She'd left her sketchbook behind but her eye was caught by the cables of Tower Bridge on the lefthand side of the bus. Now the Victorian edifice spanned the river south to a pontoon extension built by the army in the early days of the flooding. Only pedestrians and emergency vehicles were allowed to use it.

'Are you absolutely sure? Canvey Island, famous for its caravan parks for idippies and deserted fun fairs?'

'Sounds a blast.'

'You have to be crazy.'

'No, I just want a better gig than sewer duty and I heard there's a girl on the team who needs some company. Do you think your sister can slip my record into the ministry files?'

Anna chewed a fingernail, already nibbled to the quick. A glance checked Zara, sitting in the seat in front, couldn't overhear. All was clear as Zara was plugged into her playlist, humming along to some dirge of a folk lament. 'I guess she could. Can't see that it matters. My boss won't care. Just tell him you're in it together with him and he'll love you. This is our stop.' She tapped Zara's shoulder.

'I'll get my application together then tonight.' Meri followed Anna and Zara down the stairs.

'Fine. Better than fine,' said Anna. 'You might've saved me from committing justifiable homicide on Dexter.' She offered Meri her fist to bump.

'Glad to be of service.'

The craft market was on a network of barges lashed together in what had been the old dock just east of the Tower of London. As the Thames rose and flooded the riverside buildings, rendering them unfit for habitation, squatters had moved in—or squirters as they called themselves in honour of their water-based existence. They had brought with them a craft-based alternative culture, famous for quilting, knitting, furniture making and other handicrafts using recycled or salvaged goods. Zara was a frequent visitor to the market and it was the main source for her clothes so when Meri had mentioned she could do with some more off ration card, Zara had suggested they all come for a little shopping.

'So, Meri, what are you looking for?' Zara asked, fingering the fluttering silk fringe of a stall selling scarves. 'You don't have to spend your ration here as it's all recycled.'

'I'm not sure.' Some of the colours popped too intensely to her eyes. There seemed to be an awful lot of peril in the mix for a small place. She'd noticed that at Chelsea too. River squatters went in for the colour without being able to see it. How did that happen? It seemed beyond coincidence.

'Then you should browse. What's your budget?'

'Maximum twenty pounds.'

'You need the second hand rather than handicraft stalls —better deals. If you're good with needle and thread, you can do your own customisation. Wow, that's a nice piece of lace. Spanish?'

As Zara got chatting to the stall holder and Anna started picking through some old magazines, Meri wandered on down the pontoon aisle. What would Theo be up to now? Normally on a Saturday they would be doing the housework together, perhaps getting in some groceries for the week, popping into the high street chapel he liked for tea and a cheese scone baked by a local lady. If she hadn't been over eighty, Theo swore he would've married her. Smiling at the memory, Meri revolved in her mind the issue of how to contact without endangering him. Stopping at an intersection, she saw one bargeman advertised an internet cafe on board what was called Big Ben's Boat. Meri climbed up the ladder and ordered a tea from the huge, grizzly bear of an owner who sat at the hatch leading to the kitchen. He looked like either an extra from a pirate movie or a retired biker—maybe he'd been both in his time. She would bet the house on his music taste running to heavy metal. That wasn't her stereotyping him but what the tattoos on his biceps advertised.

'How much for screen time?' she asked, checking her change.

'You get fifteen with the tea.' His voice didn't match his demeanour, coming out as a light tenor. 'After that, you pay a pound every fifteen.' He passed over a surprisingly delicate shortbread biscuit on a plate. 'The cookie's free to first timers.' He grinned, showing a shiny gold tooth. 'Signal can be a bit hinky as the wireless is come-and-go but if you hit a poor patch, you deal. Not my problem.'

'Thanks, um, Ben.'

'Big Ben, lil'chick.'

'Thanks, Big Ben.' Taking her tea and biscuit to a free seat in the narrow lounge, she opened up her mail account. Sadie was online.

Hey, comp-punk, how's things?

Like an inbox of spam without you in Art. No one to bitch about Miss Hardcastle. Kel was asking after you.

What did you say?

That you'd migrated your site to a new server. You did move, right?

Yes. The situation is a little more complicated than I said and I think I need to be careful about what I say online.

Sounds icy.

More like out in the cold, thought Meri. *Do you know any*

way of adding more secure layers to my email so I don't have to worry about it being hacked?

Do digi-bears do their data dumps in the woods?

Is that some weird comp-punk way of saying yes?

Affirmative.

Can you do that so I can talk to Theo without being traced?

Ditto the bear thing.

Can you set it up now?

Growl yes. I'll send you a new message when I've got the programme running. Shouldn't take more than a few hours and we can go into stealth mode. Bye-bye creepy eavesdroppers.

The green light by Sade's name went out, telling Meri she'd gone offline. With still a few minutes left out of her fifteen, Meri started running names. She'd forgotten to do this when Ade had mentioned it on the bus during the storm and now she wanted to know what hint he had been dropping. That was before he found out that she was the enemy.

Adetokunbo, the crown that came from over the sea. *Lee*, a water meadow. *Kelvin*, narrow water.

The Perilous gave themselves names that referred to water, like a kind of secret marker. Intrigued she ran her own name. *Meredith*, protector of the sea. Surname meant 'ghost lake'. *Naia*, her mother's name, meant 'wave' in Basque. Her father, *Blake*, had a body of water locked in right there.

So the Atlanteans did the same. Maybe they were all commemorating the earthquake and the ensuing tidal wave that took out their homeland?

Whatever the reason, it was useful. Something she could employ as an early warning signal before anyone got close to her. She would have to remember to check the names of those on the Canvey Island crew in advance and take a long look at the ones who rang that particular bell.

Talking of bells, Big Ben was back. 'Want another fifteen, lil'chick?'

Meri cleared her search history. 'Not today, thanks. Do you know any good second hand clothes stalls in this part of the market?'

Ben picked up her cup and plate and wiped the table. 'Try the Frobishers, two boats down. They're decent people. Don't be a stranger, lil'chick.'

Taking the genial Ben's advice, Meri wandered down the pontoon to the barge he indicated. It was piled high with castoffs arranged in types rather than sizes: a pile of paired shoes, a mountain of trousers, a drift of skirts. Bargain hunters pawed through the goods like sniffer dogs hunting drugs, an obsessed glint to their eyes. Meri joined them, noticing the defensive looks she got if she had the temerity to go too close to someone's rooting zone. She moved off, spotting a pile which no one else had bagged as yet. Hand-made bunting fluttered overhead, seeming to lead her to it. Blinking, she realized that everything in the mound was sparkling with peril. To normal sight the clothes would look unremarkable; to her, she could see they were patterned in intricate interlocking designs not unlike the Perilous body markings.

That gave her a moment's pause. Did this mean she had stumbled upon another Perilous community? The back of her neck itched: nerves or was she being watched? Checking, she couldn't see anyone paying particular attention to her. The flags rippled, luring her on. Kel and his friends couldn't see peril unless it was flaming out at full intensity, she reminded herself. They could see into the UV but not as far as she could. These designs were too subtle for them. Who had made them then?

Intrigued now, Meri drew closer and knelt down among the clothes. She couldn't stop herself reaching for a blouse with a spiral print, so like Kel's skin. She ran her finger over the fabric, wishing...she wasn't sure what she wished.

'Are you buying that old thing?' A woman appeared from the cabin, mug of tea in one hand, e-cigarette in the other. The end glowed violet.

'Thinking of it.'

The woman, a buxom redhead in a multilayered skirt and sturdy black boots, took a puff, releasing a cloud of vapour. 'If thinking turns to spending, then I could let you have it for a song.'

'Which one do you want me to sing?' Meri pressed the blouse to her chest. It was already hers.

The woman smirked and replied with matching sarcasm. '"Oh, I do like to be beside the seaside"—or fifty pence.'

Meri dug into her pocket. 'As I sing like a frog, I'll do you a favour and give you the money.'

'See anything else you like? What about that nice leopard print under your knee?'

Meri looked down and saw that she was indeed squashing a skirt in that design. But it was in peril again. Was this a trap? 'What leopard print? I don't see anything.'

The woman hooked a stool from behind her counter with her boot and dragged it beside Meri. 'Of course you don't. Just like you can't see that cloud pattern on that table-cloth and the waves on that jacket.' She pushed up the sleeves of her sweater, rotating them so Meri could see that she had no Perilous marks on her.

Puzzlement tangled with excitement. Could the barge-woman possibly be another Tean? Meri noticed she was selecting all the pieces with the boldest designs in peril, the most obvious in the heap. 'I was looking for a floral pattern myself. Shame you haven't got one.' Meri was actually holding a scarf with the palest design of tiny interlinked flowers.

'No, I haven't got anything like that on show.'

'Are you Mrs Frobisher?'

'That's me. Who's asking?'

'Emma Boot.'

'Nice steady name, but not your own, I'm thinking. Show me your arms.'

Meri slipped off her jacket.

'Interesting.' She stuffed the e-cigarette in a pocket. 'And interesting that you didn't question the need for me to see. I wonder. Emma, I think you and I should talk.' She glanced over to where a customer was arguing with another over who had spotted a pair of suede boots first. 'But not right now. I've got to stop World War Four.' She pressed a card into Meri's hands. On the front it appeared to be a standard business card but on the back there was a name—Tea and Sympathy—and a further set of numbers printed in peril coloured text.

'Thanks.'

'You see that, don't you? Without any help?'

'See what?'

Mrs Frobisher just smiled. 'Nice to meet you, Emma.'

10

O n the top floor of the science block, Kel gazed out at the snow falling on the playing fields. Last day before the Christmas holidays and the mud between the rugby goalposts was being erased, a little like his old life had been wiped out by this new existence. Two months had passed since he left Ade's house. That meant eight weeks in a lonely bedsit sharing a bathroom with two refugees and an IDP family from Dorset. Fifty-six days of avoiding Ade and Lee. One thousand three hundred and thirty four hours of worrying that they would catch Meri.

He hadn't taken up Theo's offer of a spare room, thinking that would only bring yet more attention to Meri's guardian. He had called round a couple of times for dinner but Theo and he had both studiously not mentioned the subject that was closest to their hearts. Both of them believed they were being watched. As for Meri, Kel was working on the no news was good news basis. That gave him a little hope in an otherwise bleak situation.

'Kel, your yeast isn't going to respire unless you add that

solution,' warned the teacher. 'You won't have time to record the results if you don't get a move on.'

'Sorry, yes.'

Dr Morrison, an owlish woman in round spectacles who only clocked in at just over five feet, came to stand at his shoulder so she could share the view from the second floor window. 'I can see why you're finding it hard to pay attention. Very pretty. Shame it means it's here until February.' She flashed him a conspiratorial smile. 'Reminds me of certain members of my family at Christmas who have the unfortunate habit of far outstaying their welcome.'

'You think it'll last that long?'

'We seem to get either unseasonably mild or super cold winters. This year, with the Gulf Stream weakened, no warm current keeping the cold at bay, I'd say it is time to dig out the woolies and wellies.'

Kel thought grimly of the inadequate heater in his bedroom and the howling gale through the ill-fitting window frame. Though by law landlords were supposed to have insulated their properties to the highest eco standards, there were many that had only done so on paper. It was times like this when he missed his old home with its comforts. He had taken much for granted.

'And I definitely don't want to stay after school waiting for you to finish this up,' continued Dr Morrison, 'if the snow's going to make the journey home a nightmare.'

'Right. Yes. I'll get on with the experiment.'

Going through the required steps, Kel scribbled his results into the table on the handout and quickly put away his apparatus. He could see Ade and Lee had already completed the assignment and were watching him from the other side of the lab. He really didn't want to talk to them right now, not when he'd hit a low point. He knew he was vulnerable: lonely, directionless, torn between his people and protecting someone who didn't want him anywhere near her. It was hard to keep on believing he was handling this the right way.

And, great, they were heading for him. That was the mouldy icing on his stale cake.

'How's it going, Kel?' asked Ade.

'Fine. You?'

'We're good. Look, we're having a party tonight. Tiber flared out this morning at training so we're having a gathering. You want to come?'

'Thanks for asking, but I've got plans.'

'Yeah, to sit in that flea pit you call a home these days,' muttered Lee.

Ade elbowed him. 'You wouldn't be committing anything, not coming back in as a guard or whatever. We want you there just as one of us.'

And Kel wanted to be there with the only family he'd really known, but he knew a slippery slope when he saw one. 'I really appreciate that you've reached out, Ade, but I just can't.'

'If you change your mind...'

'I won't.'

'There's no news of her—and I'm not snowing you on this.'

'Ha-ha.'

'Do you realize she may never surface again and you're holding out for no reason? We might never have to do anything about her?'

'But I'll still know what you were prepared to do, won't I?'

'Yeah, you do.' Ade shifted a step away. 'And it shouldn't have been such a surprise. You're the one who went off on a tangent. I think you've made the wrong choice. We're ready to forgive when you see sense.'

Kel couldn't thank Ade for that so just nodded. 'Understood. Tell Tiber congratulations.'

'Have a good holiday.'

'Yeah. You too.'

It was even harder to return to his bedsit after that conversation. The room smelt damp, the sheets never seemed quite dry, and his few books were beginning to swell with the background moisture. Even his guitar felt slimy when he picked it up. Rather than stay in this dump, he wrapped up in his warmest clothes and headed out to the station. His dad's allowance for living expenses only went so far. Money being more than tight now he no longer had a wage, he made rent by busking. A Friday evening before Christmas should be a good time to earn the rest of the next month's payment.

His usual spot at Kensington High Street was taken so Kel got back on the Tube and headed for Covent Garden, an open space in the heart of London right on the edge of the water that lapped at the Strand at high tide. Once a fruit and vegetable market, the white arcades had been turned into a dining and tourist shopping destination many decades ago. There was a risk in such a popular place that he wouldn't get to play. The police were notorious for moving people along there unless they forked out for the expensive street entertainer licence but the upside was that it was guaranteed to be busy. Even an hour busking there was well worth it. Wandering the cobbles of the yard inside the covered market, Kel scouted the possibilities, banking on some of the regulars having been kept inside by the snow and that he'd find a prime spot. He wasn't disappointed. A space was available under the arcade near the Royal Opera House and there were queues forming for the night's ballet, The Nutcracker Suite, according to the lit posters festooned with holly and tinsel. As if on cue, a droid street sweeper, size of an industrial vacuum cleaner, hummed passed, clearing a patch for him. Tucking his plectrum between his teeth, Kel got out his guitar to tune up, half an eye on roving police patrols.

When Kel finished tightening his strings he found a little girl in a blue winter coat watching him expectantly, tugging at her mother's hand as they waited for the doors to open. Smiling, Kel broke into a medley of Disney classics, not his usual repertoire but it went down well with the pre-theatre crowd. His guitar case began to fill up with coins. Once that early audience went inside, he switched to the songs he preferred by the Sharks and Renaissance Man, adding in a couple he'd composed himself, and a few Beatles, Ed Sheeran and Adele golden oldies. That drew him a new crowd, people on their way to Christmas parties or drinks after work. After a drag of a day, Kel was almost beginning to enjoy himself.

And then he looked up and found Meri standing in the snow right in front of him.

ECO SERVICE in winter was a bitch but Meri loved every awful day of it. Her team was working on a patch of river-bank that felt more like an alien planet than somewhere within half an hour's boat ride from Tower Bridge. A flat, wind-swept island, big grey East Anglian skies, this was the battlefield on which the ecological war was being waged. Fighting the rising tides on Canvey Island, heaping mud into embankments with mini-diggers, planting what Dexter called 'habitats for wildlife' and the rest of the team called grass: it all gave her a sense of purpose and the satisfaction of making a difference. Like every other sane teenager she hated the cheesy advertisements online and in the cinemas but she had a sneaking suspicion she agreed with the underlying message: the eco-service was doing a necessary job and people, at least on this vulnerable island in the Thames estuary, really were grateful. She was surprised she enjoyed it so much.

The locals in the caravan park near the eco-works threw a party for the young volunteers on the last lunchtime before their Christmas break. The Idippy primary school, a miserably inadequate structure made up of portakabins, had been decorated with cutout snowflakes and strings of stout paper reindeers. The parents stumped up for crisps, sandwiches and fizzy drinks. It was like being five again, but as Meri had missed out on most kiddie parties due to trauma and then shyness, she found the whole event hilarious. That also might have been something to do with preloading on a bottle of wine sneaked in by Anna who had vowed it was the only way to get through the torture. Whatever the cocktail for success, Meri found it easy to chat, laugh and play silly games with all ages standing in her boot socks, as she had left muddy protective gear at the door.

The late afternoon was spent back in overalls putting the equipment to bed for the two weeks leave. Dexter, team leader—and didn't everyone know it—masterminded operations. A good-looking guy with sandy hair and tanned complexion, camera friendly square jaw with a little cleft on the chin, he made a perfect advertisement for the eco service.

'Let's crack on, people,' he called cheerfully. 'Looks like that cloud is going to dump a load of snow on us and I'd prefer to be snuggled up warm before that happens.'

When he turned away to take a call, Anna rolled her eyes at Meri.

'Herr Commandant has spoken. Let's put this baby to bed.' Together they hurried to pull the tarpaulin over one of the machines that wouldn't fit in the shed. The wind picked up, carrying with it the first flakes of snow. Meri wrestled her end of the sheet down and tied it tight with a few heaves on the rope to the ring set in the ground.

'Impressive. You wouldn't've been able to do that a few weeks ago,' said Anna, tying off her side.

'Do what?'

'Miss Peanut-biceps has actually got some strength now.'

Meri flexed her arm, showing off her new muscles. 'Funny what two months of eco camp can do to you. We should make a book and video, sell them as the next big Get-In-Shape regime.'

'And they worried about childhood obesity twenty years ago. All they needed was to send us out for a couple of years, semi-starve us and treat us like slave labour and problem sorted.'

Meri snorted.

'So, you still on for the team Christmas night out, Em?'

'You bet.'

'Even though Dexter's coming?'

'I guess Christmas needs some irritating relatives to make it feel really authentic—he can be my stand-in.'

'I think he wants to be more than your stand-in irritation. He looked at you when he talked about snuggling up.'

'Get your mind out of the gutter, Anna Brackley.'

'Just saying how it is, sister.'

'Nope: don't even speak it out loud. Speaking it puts that into my head and I really have enough bad dreams without that.'

'Don't worry, Boot, I've got your back. I'll protect you from the handsome but yet disappointingly annoying pain in the arse.'

'That can be my Christmas present then.'

Back at the hostel showering off the estuary mud, Meri let her mind circle back to the conversation with Anna. Her friend was probably right about Dexter. He'd been making moves in her direction, sounding out if she had a boyfriend and what were her off-duty interests. She could hardly answer truthfully that, no, she was unattached as her last boyfriend turned out to be a mortal enemy and that her main interest was staying alive.

Tucking in her favourite shirt, the one with the peril-coloured pattern, into a pair of black jeans, Meri checked her appearance in the small mirror in her bedroom. She thought that maybe her face had also changed a little over the last two months. Some of the strain had gone as she felt safe with her team. No one could creep up on her stuck out in the middle of the estuary and, if anyone tried, she now had friends who would come to her aid, no questions asked. That was what the team did.

'Em, are you ready yet? We're going to be late!' called Zara.

'Coming!'

Her friends were waiting for her in the hostel sitting room. Anna was dressed down like Meri in jeans and a shirt, though Anna's had a sprinkle of sequins for that festive feeling. Zara had gone uptown, wearing a plum lace dress over a black corset and leggings. She looked like a funky Christmas fairy, particularly when you factored in the silver lace-up boots with killer heels.

'Did I miss the note about dress code? I didn't know we

were supposed to go as gothic Christmas tree decorations,' said Meri with a grin for Anna.

Zara slapped her arm. 'You know, Em, the day I see you wearing something other than black, navy and brown, I swear I'm going to have a heart attack. Live a little: put this on!' She pulled a red Santa hat from her coat pocket. 'I was going to wear it but I think I'll go with tinsel.'

'For you, dear, anything,' quipped Meri, pulling the hat over her ears.

The eco team met up in Leicester Square right in the heart of the flourishing theatre and cinema district. Coming out of the station, Meri had a poignant flashback to her disastrous date here with Kel two months ago. She wondered what he was doing now?

'Yo, team, bad news,' said Phil, the guy who had been responsible for the itinerary for the evening. 'I totally screwed up—forgot to make a reservation—and everywhere is booked up till January.'

There was a round of 'Oh Phil, you moron!' from everyone until Dexter took charge, as usual.

'Never mind, team, I know a place in Drury Lane that's usually quieter than this. I'll just ring ahead and get us a table. How many are we? Seven?'

'Yes, squadron leader,' muttered Anna.

'Follow me. I know the way.'

'I bet those are his absolute favourite words in the English language,' she muttered to Meri.

'But what I want to know is why the restaurant isn't booked up like other places? I mean how bad does it have to be?'

'Excellent deduction, Sherlock.'

Dexter slowed so Meri and Anna had to catch up with him or look churlish.

'Enjoying yourselves?' he asked brightly.

'Every minute. I just love wandering aimlessly looking for a place to eat with the snow falling,' said Anna, brushing flakes off her black winter coat.

'I know, it's just so atmospheric, isn't it? So Christmasy. How are you going to spend the big day, Em?'

Meri blew on her fingers, cursing her oversight of leaving gloves behind. 'No plans yet.'

'Ah. Is it against your religion to celebrate it?'

'No.'

'She's an orphan, Dexter.' Anna shifted to put herself between Meri and their team leader. 'Give it a rest, will you?'

'Sorry. Sorry. Difficult subject. I get it.'

Taking pity on Meri, Anna linked arms with Dexter and moved ahead. 'So tell me where we're going, Dex. Is it Mexican? I love Mexican, Dexican. And how many people exactly have died of food poisoning after eating there?'

Meri smiled as Dexter spluttered his defence of his restaurant recommendation. He was just so serious about having a good time. She couldn't work out why he was attracted to her as Meri spent most of the time out at the project making fun of having a bad time. In that she was his absolute opposite.

Maybe that was it: he had fallen for the cliché of opposites attract? The magnetic pull went one way in this case.

Her party straggled into single file as they hit the crowds in Covent Garden. The market looked really pretty with its Christmas lights in the shape of stars, fir trees dripping with glowing icicles, retaining a pre-flood glamour. Someone was busking on the corner—a talented someone from the audience he had gathered. Meri slowed, drawn in by hearing one of her favourite songs by Renaissance Man. Squeezing into a gap, she caught her first clear view of the singer.

Kel.

He looked amazing in the snow, guinea-gold hair shining in the Christmas lights.

She hadn't known he could sing, hadn't known he played the guitar.

You only knew him for a couple of weeks.

But so much had happened in those two weeks it felt much longer.

Rooted to the spot, she couldn't think what to do. Theo had sworn Kel had stood up for her, wasn't out for her blood like the others, had left Ade's house because of her; but he was also a link to her hunters and she had promised herself she wouldn't do anything that would give away her hiding place.

Besides, after giving her a couple of the best kisses of her life, he would probably be scared of her now. Did she want to witness him flinch away from her touch? Should she even trust herself around him now she knew what she could do?

Her moment's indecision took away the choice of disappearing. His wild blue eyes met hers and he stopped singing. An awkward pause followed.

'Forgot your words, mate?' jeered an onlooker.

Kel shoved the guitar back in the case, not bothering to collect up the coins people had thrown inside. 'Sorry, show's over. Don't move.' The last comment was to Meri.

The crowd melted away leaving them standing facing each other. Snow had settled on Kel's shoulders and hair.

'You need a hat,' said Meri. 'Have mine.' She took off the Santa one and held it out to him.

'And then what would I do when you get cold ears?' Taking it, he put it back on her head, letting his hands rest over her ears to warm them. 'It's good to see you. Merry

Christmas, Meri.' His lips quirked at the pun. 'I guess that's
not very original?'

'I'd be lying if I said you were the first person to say that
to me. But Merry Christmas to you too.'

'What are you doing here?' He shook his head. 'Actually,
no, I don't want to know. Don't tell me anything. Just tell me
how you are.'

'Fine.'

He raised a brow.

'Really,' she assured him.

'But you're...one of them?'

'Yes. So, it would seem.' Testing him and herself, she
held out her hand. 'Does it bother you?'

Hesitating only a fraction, he touched her fingers. 'You
should remember to wear gloves.' He lifted them to his
mouth and blew on them. She could have loved him for that
alone, overcoming his whole upbringing in a simple gesture.

'Remembering gloves is one of those life lessons yet to
sink in.'

'Hey, Em, are you OK?' Dexter strode up and threw his
arm around her shoulder. Kel immediately stepped back
and dropped her hand, expression blanking. 'We thought
we'd lost you.'

'I've just run into an old friend.' She didn't want to—and
couldn't—risk giving names.

Dexter had no such scruples as he sized up the competition. 'Hi, I'm Dexter, Em's team leader.'

'Hey, Dexter. Nice to meet you both. I'll see you around.'
Kel picked up his guitar case, grimacing as the loose money
rattled against the wood. 'I should probably find somewhere
quiet and sort that out.'

Dexter dismissed him with a nod. 'Come on, Em, the
others are waiting.'

Glancing over her shoulder, Meri allowed Dexter to steer her away and towards their party. She knew exactly what Kel was thinking: that she was out on a date, that she'd moved on. Would it be better to let him believe that? Kinder in the long run? But for some illogical and completely insane emotional reason, she just couldn't do it.

She slipped out from under Dexter's arm. 'Sorry, Dex, but I really need to catch up with my friend—the chance is too good to waste. Tell the others I'll text them when I know what I'm doing. Don't wait for me to order.'

Dexter put on his kicked puppy expression. 'But Em—!'

'See you later—or in two weeks after the holiday if we get caught up chatting. Have a good Christmas.'

When she got back to the corner, Kel had gone. Desperate not to lose her chance now, she took a gamble that he'd consider his day over and would head for the nearest station. Weaving through the crowds, she caught up with Kel just before he entered Covent Garden Tube. 'Kel! Please, wait!'

He turned, eyes scanning the street behind her. 'Where's the boyfriend?'

'He's not a boyfriend, not exactly a friend either. I was out with a big party of mates and he'd been sent back to round me up.'

Kel's stiff body language softened. 'OK then. That's good.'

'Can we go somewhere to talk?'

'I'd like that, but it's ridiculously busy and expensive round here.'

'Let's walk until we find a quieter spot then.'

'Which way: north, south, east or west?'

'South. Let's find a spot by the river.'

They walked side-by-side, the guitar between them.

Meri had so much to say but yet wasn't sure if she should say anything at all. Maybe she should just enjoy being with him this one last time? That didn't seem enough though. She hadn't had a chance to say goodbye because she had been in panic mode after his flare out. She didn't want to leave him with the impression that she hated him for being what he was. He couldn't help that any more than she could help her Tean inheritance. How could she tell him this when no words could capture what she felt?

In the end, they both spoke at once.

'Meri, I don't—'

'I'm sorry I—'

Kel smiled and gestured for her to go first.

'I just wanted to say that I was sorry I panicked on you. I didn't know what I was dealing with. I just knew that the people who attacked my parents were patterned like you. It was a flight instinct kicking in—survival. I think I know you well enough to realize you wouldn't hurt me but I wasn't being rational.'

He shifted the guitar to the other hand and took hers in his. She could feel his fingertips exploring the new calluses and rough skin on her palm. He wouldn't ask, she knew that already. He would protect her by keeping ignorant. 'You were right to run, Meri. My kind are trained to eliminate Teans. If I'd been taken by surprise, realized that night and not the next day, then maybe I would've reacted badly, more like the others did.'

She hoped not. She was trusting her life to the conviction that he was different. 'So there is a kill order out on me?' The words caught in her throat. 'It's really hard to believe that Ade and the others would go that far.'

'I can't tell you what was decided—that would be betraying trust the other way—but I can say you must keep away from them. My advice is that you stay hidden, well hidden. Move if you can. Theo's a weak point—they'll watch him.'

Meri knew what he was hinting. 'If I cut myself off from Theo then I have no one. He's my family. Can't we negotiate peace or something with the Perilous? I don't want to harm anyone.'

'I know that, but they're thinking about what happens if you pass on your powers to the next generation.'

At least he talked about the Perilous as 'they', which confirmed Theo's opinion that Kel had not aligned himself with them. Still, it didn't solve her main problem. It was like being caught in a tangle of barbed wire that cut each way she pulled to escape. 'Children? That's such a long way off. And why would my children want to kill anyone if we aren't under attack?'

'Call it a lesson learned after centuries of experience.'

Meri remembered the torture photographs in the box. 'But I think I'm the last. From here on any Tean DNA will get diluted, changed. I might not even be able to have children—might not want them. I'm eighteen: what do I know? Aren't your people worrying unnecessarily? It's all a bunch of "what ifs".'

'That's not how they see it, but if it helps, I totally agree with you. I think we should declare peace. We shouldn't push you into a corner where what we fear is made to happen by the fact that you have to defend yourself.' Kel stopped outside a little cafe with windows looking out on the Thames. It was low tide so the abandoned buildings of the area that had been lost stuck out of the mud like a ghost town, all lights off. 'How about here? That couple have just left so there's a table in the window.'

'Good choice.'

When they had placed their orders with the waiter, Meri took Kel's hand. She made herself trace the spiral on his wrist, telling herself it was beautiful rather than a threat. He got full marks for not shuddering and she hoped she got some points for overcoming her instinctive fear. She kept tight control inside, not daring to let any power leak out and put him at risk. It was hard though, like holding her breath underwater. She wasn't sure what she was doing or if she was doing it right.

She looked up into his blue eyes. 'I'd never use my powers to hurt you. I don't think I know how and I certainly wouldn't want to.'

'I get that. It's not in you.' He touched her finger with his, tracing the same pattern. 'You can see them, can't you?'

'Yes.' She pushed up his sleeve. 'I don't understand how a human can have developed anything so perfect.'

'Generations of forced breeding.'

'What?' She removed her fingers quickly. 'Forced?'

'Yeah. Systematic and deliberate. The Perilous that didn't fit pattern were culled or not allowed to breed.'

'My ancestors did that?'

'It's not on you, Meri. They existed so long ago that I'd no more blame you than I would present day Egyptians for using slave labour on the pyramids.'

'I want to say it's beautiful but how can I now that I know it's the result of such suffering?' She started to roll his sleeve back down but he stopped her.

'We've long since embraced the markings as a sign of pride in our families and culture. As I said, it's not on you. An apology from you doesn't mean anything as you're not to blame.'

'Can I feel sorry for your people then?'

'Absolutely. And a kiss better would be appreciated.'

She raised his palm to her cheek, then turned her head to lay one in the centre. 'There.'

'I hope that was just a first instalment.'

'You want me to touch you, even though you know what I can do? I'm not sure I can control it, not if we're...you know....' She'd never felt more embarrassed and was sure she had to be as red as a fire engine.

'It would be a magnificent way to go.'

'Don't make fun of this. I'm serious.'

'Meri, I'm not afraid of you. Please believe me.'

The waiter was back with their orders so they moved away from each other. Meri drank in the sight of Kel making easy conversation with their server, his eyes warm, smile genuine. She remembered how her first impression of him had been that he was filled with light; even on this dark December evening, he dispensed a glow to everyone that was nothing to do with his Perilous inheritance.

'You're just a good soul, aren't you?' she commented when the waiter moved on.

'What? What have you been drinking?' Laughing, Kel poured half his coke over the ice in his glass.

'You've just got this...' Meri twirled her hand, 'ease about you that other people catch. They become nicer in your presence.'

'That makes me sound like a cold.'

'Ah-choo.'

'What?'

'I'm seeing if I can catch it from you.'

He smiled. 'Let's see if I can raise your temperature.' He nibbled on the ends of her fingers sending lovely little shivers up her arm and down her spine. He was back to flirting again, which she took as a good sign. She'd missed him so much over the last months. It had been like a part of her was left behind. 'What have you been doing, Miss Marlowe? Digging ditches?'

He meant it as a joke but, as that wasn't far from the truth, she gave what she hoped was a mysterious smile. 'I thought you didn't want to know.'

'I want to know every single thing about you but I can't ask. This is taking risks as far as I dare, just sitting with you here. Now.'

'But no one followed you?'

'I wouldn't endanger you by sticking around if I thought there was the slightest chance of that. They're all at a party at the house tonight. I don't think Ade would waste the manpower on having me watched. I've been busking often enough. They'd've got bored freezing their butts off watching me work the crowd.'

'I didn't know you could play like that.'

'Did you like it?'

'Loved it. You didn't busk before?'

'No. I didn't have to. I do it now to make rent.'

'Theo said you moved out.'

'Yes, and lost my wage as Ade's guard.'

'I'm sorry.'

'Another thing that's not your fault.'

'I don't know. I think this might be.'

'It's a small sacrifice compared to what you've lost.'

With her drink finished, Meri feared that she was going to have to bring this to an end, that her stolen few minutes with Kel would be over and their goodbye would be final. That felt so wrong. Despite their differences, being with him was perfect; she felt like she had finally arrived home to a crackling fire after a long cold walk in the dark.

She then had an idea. Totally outrageous. Insane even.

'The holidays have started, yes? Is there anyone waiting for you at home?'

'Only the mould on the window ledge—my digs are a dump. I think the mould's not far off turning into a sentient being.'

'Then don't go back yet. Spend Christmas with me. I can't risk going to see Theo so I'll be alone. You'll be alone too by the sounds of it.'

'Meri, I—'

'Is the only reason you're about to say no that you think it'll put me in danger?'

'Yes, but—'

'I'm going to be in danger for the rest of my life. Don't you think I should grab my chance of a little happiness when it comes along?'

He rubbed his chin, considering. 'I just don't go home?'

'Exactly. You weren't followed so no one will be tracking you.' As she laid out the reasons, she found she was persuading herself how absolutely sensible the mad plan was. 'You've not made any preparations so there's no tip off as to what you're doing. There'll be plenty of space in my hostel as everyone else is going home to family tomorrow. They don't even have to know. I can smuggle you in. And you can keep your phone switched off.'

'Meri, I don't even have a change of clothes.' From his tone she could tell he was persuaded. His protest was token.

'That sounds just about perfect to me. Spend Christmas with me.'

11

L ying with her head on Kel's chest, Meri discovered a sense of contentment she'd never before experienced. He was so warm. A haven—yes, that was the right word. She let her fingers explore the spirals, getting to know his pattern. All her life, she'd associated Perilous markings with terror, but now she recognized them for what they were: beautiful, exquisite. The pattern was like a butterfly's wings, a mirror image on his rib cage, scrolling out from the breastbone.

While she did her investigation, his fingers were stroking her upper arm, the other hand resting behind his head. Beyond the door, the rest of the hostel was busy with people having a late breakfast, laughter, a few groans as people regretted the night before. The snow continued to fall, softening the light coming through the window, building up on the sill.

There came a brisk rap at the door. 'Em, I'm off. Just want to say goodbye.'

Meri had been expecting this. No way would Anna leave without getting the gossip. She leapt off the bed and threw the duvet over Kel, burying his mischievous eyes under the cover. 'Ssh, OK?' She opened the door. 'Anna, have a great time with your parents.'

Booted and hatted, Anna was all packed and ready to go. 'You can still come, you know?'

'I'll be fine here.'

Anna leant against the doorpost trying to see around her. 'What happened to you last night? Dexter said you'd run into a friend. He was very dischuffed.'

Meri couldn't help a betraying glance over her shoulder. 'Yes, I did. From my old school.'

'Oh, I see. A really good old friend? Or the deliciously bad sort?' Anna wiggled her eyebrows.

Meri could feel a blush rising. 'A mixture of both.'

'Oh, right then. I'll make myself scarce. Two's company, three's a crowd. I'll tell Zara you're *occupied*.'

'Thanks, Anna.'

She came closer for a hug, keeping her arms around Meri a moment longer. 'I expect details,' she whispered.

'You can wish.'

'I can hope, though you are always so annoyingly private. I'll just have to get you drunk one night. See you in the New Year.'

As the front door banged a final time after the last person, the hostel fell silent. Deciding it was safe to emerge, Meri went down to the kitchen and brought back a breakfast tray. It would be safer to keep Kel out of sight until she was sure no one was coming back for something. Entering her bedroom, she found Kel standing by the window, holding her shirt up to the light.

'Hey, can you see that?' she asked.

'Sorry.' He dropped it back on the chair where she'd

dumped her clothes. 'I wasn't pinching it. I was looking for something to wear.'

Meri thought it was a shame to cover up so much gorgeousness but she couldn't keep him locked up half naked in her room all holidays, more's the pity. 'I'll raid one of the boys' rooms in a moment. They're bound to have left some of their stuff behind. Have some cereal.' She set out the breakfast on the rickety desk. 'What I meant was: can you see the pattern on the shirt?'

'I think I can see something faintly. Swirls, right?'

To her they were as plain as checks on a chess board. 'Yes. I bought it because it reminded me of you.'

Kel grinned and held the shirt up again against his chest. It was an uncanny match.

'Snap,' she murmured.

'It's in peril, isn't it? How would anyone know to put that on a fabric?'

'I guess because they can see it too.' Meri explained where she had bought it. 'Do you know if the river people are Perilous? The woman who sold it to me could see some, but not all the patterns. She checked my arms for markings but there were none on hers.'

He frowned, thinking. 'That's weird. I've never heard that they were connected to us in any way.'

'It was really odd. She gave me this card.' Meri showed him. 'Can you read it?'

Holding it up to the light, Kel squinted. 'There's something there. Text and numbers but too faint for me to make it out. I think I'd need to put it under a UV light to read. What does it say?'

How far she could trust him? Maybe that was no longer the question, she acknowledged, as she'd really made the choice when she invited him to stay. He felt right to her—

safe. Added to that, Kel was her only source on Teans and the Perilous. There was nothing more coming from her parents. 'It says "Tea and Sympathy". It didn't take me long to run that together and you get—'

'Tean Sympathy.' His eyes widened. 'Wow.'

'I wondered if it was a trap? If I'm the only one who can see this, see what's on the clothes, she might have been laying it out like sticky fly paper, to see what she caught.'

'But there are hardly swarms of Teans walking around to be snapped up and she had no idea you were coming that day. Seems too elaborate, too unfocused.'

'That's what gets me wondering. She couldn't see all that I could see but she did recognize a few of the patterns. She saw the spirals, that's for sure.'

Kel rubbed his face with the heel of his hands, an adorable effort to wake up some more so he could puzzle this out with her. 'Where does that get us? Her ability sits between yours and mine?'

'Exactly.'

'Then what does that make her?' He sat down on the foot of the bed and pulled a blanket over his shoulders.

Meri delayed her answer by moving the bowls off the tray She was worried that her guess might make Kel freak out. There was a real risk this might be too much for a Perilous, even an enlightened one like Kel, to take in his stride. But she wouldn't know unless she tried him, would she? 'Our two peoples made a fuss about breeding for different traits, a dangerous kind of racial purity deal. But still, it seems hard to believe that my kind are down to just me, like I'm some sort of last white rhino. OK, maybe I'm the last full blood Tean, but humans being humans, I imagine Teans have, you know, diddled with others throughout the centuries.'

'Diddled?'

'OK, that was childish. I mean had sex and produced babies.'

'You're talking watered down gifts out there. You're probably right.' Kel frowned as the idea sank in.

Not freaking out but he wasn't happy either, Meri noted. 'That can't be something to get your knickers in a twist about. I doubt they'd be able to do the full attack-a-Perilous thing—might not even know about that aspect of a Tean's power.'

Kel got up and walked to the window, trailing the blanket like a prince's cloak. 'We've not talked much about that—among the Perilous I hang out with—but of course that would be the case after all these centuries. Life isn't tidy. And we've left our traces out there too—we call them the lost ones. That's what we thought you were. And I suppose if a Perilous can diddle, so can a Tean.' He smiled at her, teasing her with her own word.

'I bet they can.' Scooting up the bed to rest against the headboard, Meri hugged her knees to her chest. 'I'm not sure what I should do about it. The lady I met, she might be a good contact, help me maybe, but it's a risk exposing myself to her. If I'm wrong, and she's a Perilous despite not having the markings....'

Kel shook his head. 'She won't be. You said she was a mature woman. Her markings would've been through long ago. But I could come with you if you go back. Just in case.'

'Thanks. That makes me feel better about returning.'

He started pacing, picking up the few things she had scattered around the room, a postcard from Canvey Island, a piece of drift wood she'd picked up off the beach, a pebble with a hole in it. 'You know, a watered-down Tean community might be good news.' He held up the bleached twig to find the most pleasing curve.

'Really?'

'Yeah. It might persuade my friends that you can find a way of living that poses little or no threat.' He replaced the driftwood on the mantlepiece in its new position.

'I really hope so. And you know something else?'

He approached her on the other side of the bed and crawled across the duvet towards her, playful mood returning. 'That you are incredibly kissable at ten in the morning? And at eleven. And all other hours of the day come to think of it.'

She reached out to take the kiss he wanted to give her. They had stopped pretending they were just friends at midnight. The months apart had proved they wanted so much more from each other. They ended up flat on the bed again, but this time with his head on her chest. 'That wasn't what I was thinking.'

'Shame as I think about kissing you all the time.'

'Let me be serious a second.'

'OK.'

'So stop tickling my ribs.'

'Oh. OK. Spoilsport.'

'I was thinking that Tean and Perilous must've started as the same people once upon a time.'

His questing fingers stilled. 'How do you mean?'

'Well, obviously, in evolutionary terms all humans came from some ancient ancestor but I mean closer than that. Our abilities are similar, linked to our ability to process UV in a different way from other humans. It must be that something switched on in the DNA to allow us to do that.'

'Aren't you the clever clogs this morning?'

'I might be a high school dropout but I can still put a few biological facts together.'

'So somewhere back in the day some caveman on the island noticed a few of us were developing these skin markings and decided "hey, that guy's different from me: let's make him our slave"?'

'More or less. I think the changes must've been made more quickly than by natural selection. You told me about the captive breeding. That fits.'

'And the Teans, marrying among their own kind. Choosing partners with the strongest UV vision?'

'They artificially selected themselves too, but it was framed as a cultural thing, marriage practices.'

'And built a civilization on it. Teans to the top, Perilous to the bottom.'

'History is littered with cases where people persecuted others for the stupidest reasons. We don't ever seem to get beyond it.' She ran her fingers through his hair, feeling the silk tug and tickle. She treated him gently, afraid to let her attraction to him get out of hand in case she inadvertently hurt him. 'I wish we could.'

Going up on an elbow, he leaned forward and kissed her. 'Maybe *we* can. You and me. Maybe we can be the end of this vendetta?'

'I'm all for that, if only others would let us.'

MERI'S SUGGESTION that the barge people could be connected to Teans nagged at Kel. How had his own people not known? Could he square it with his conscience that he had no intention of telling his fellow Perilous if this river community was a way out for Meri? He spent some time over the next few days researching the possibility on the internet, wishing he had access to the library at Ade's where the resources were much better than anything that had gone online. By typing in a few key terms, he did come across message boards and websites that could have fitted the bill but they required passwords to get beyond the initial page and he didn't have the skills to hack beyond that.

'I'm getting possible hits worldwide,' he told Meri.

'Hmm-hmm.'

That wasn't an I'm-following-every-step-of-your-investigation sound. He looked up. She was drawing again, this time sketching him as he worked on the hostel computer. This was an ancient machine on a desk in the shared lounge, positioned strategically below a cork board of take-out menus—its main function in life being to order in—but it could still run a basic search. Slowly.

'Six in the US alone that have some mention of Tea and Sympathy.'

'Hmm.' She flicked her gaze up then corrected a line on the sketch, tip of tongue poking through her teeth. She said she loved sketching him almost as much as she loved tracing his markings. Personally he preferred it when she did the latter. Much preferred.

'It could be the tip of the iceberg, Meri.'

'Mmm.'

'And there is a party of Martians about to land on the doorstep. To have tea. With us.'

'Um, good.'

He cleared his search and swivelled round on the chair. 'And you hereby promise to do the washing up for all eternity. Say "hmm" if you agree.'

'Hmm. What?' She'd twigged from his grin that she'd just made an unwise bargain. 'What did you say?'

'Now she listens. Too late. I have your word.'

She closed the sketchbook. 'What word?'

He patted his lap. 'Come here and I'll tell you.'

She frowned. 'I wasn't really listening. It doesn't count.'

'Look on it as a penalty then for not paying attention. I might let you off if you come here.' He patted his lap again.

With a huff, she uncurled from the beaten up armchair and moved to sit on him in the swivel chair. 'Satisfied.'

Resting his forehead on her chest he breathed in. Over the last few days, he'd come to love every little thing about her but especially the scent that was pure Meri: a little flowery from her favourite soap and then her underneath it. 'Yes, I am.'

'And I'm let off whatever it is I promised?'

'Maybe.'

She kissed him. 'And now?'

'Yes, you're forgiven.' He spun the chair in a circle so they both took a ride. 'Do you want to hear what I found out?' He dipped her back and gave her a playful kiss on the lips.

'Sure.'

'There are groups coming up globally when I enter the key phrases. All are membership only. We'd require a hacker to get beyond the first level.'

Running her fingers through his hair, Meri frowned in thought. 'I could ask Sadie.'

'Sadie?'

'She set up a secure link to Theo for me in case one of your guys has computer skills and was listening in to his communications.'

Kel didn't say anything—couldn't—but it was just the kind of thing Ade would order. Lee and Tiber both had the training to do that. He hoped Sadie was as good as her reputation claimed.

'But if I ask her,' continued Meri, 'then I'll have to explain something about why I'm interested.'

'You could take the direct approach: ring the number on the card.'

'Or go back and see Mrs Frobisher. We already talked about that.'

'You think that's better?' Kel wished he could keep her safely behind closed doors for ever but that wasn't a workable life plan.

'It's hard to gauge what side these people are on unless I talk to them face to face. I might just be walking into that flypaper if I ring the number.'

'Going back might be another trap too.' He caressed her waist, wishing they could just be them in a simple world where they weren't supposed to be enemies. She felt so slight to him; having all this weighing on her was just wrong. 'OK, we'll pick our moment so they don't have time to prepare and we'll go together. When?'

'Let's go today. It's Christmas Eve and I haven't even bought you a present. You obviously rock Phil's old hoodie and Terry's jeans but I could get you some of your own clothes while we're there.'

'Sounds like a good plan.' He gave her a final squeeze then let her slip off his lap. She danced off across the room, energized by the idea of going out to find some answers. 'And don't worry: I've got your back.'

She left the room to get ready for going out in the snow. Kel remained at the computer, smile fading. He had her back. Simple, true words, but they set off an ugly echo. Backup was what he had spent his entire life training to be for Ade. Guarding the Perilous was his family's pride and profession throughout generations, the cause for which his mother gave her life. Meri was what he had been taught to fear and he'd sworn to defend the royal line from any threat she posed. To his kind, there was no bigger betrayal than what he was doing now. They'd say he was in bed with the enemy.

With a sigh, he shutdown the computer and switched off the screen.

If that was what they believed, then so be it. He could only do what he thought was right.

WHEN THEY ARRIVED at St Katharine's dock, Kel wondered why he'd never been to any of the riverside markets before. It was a fabulous sight, lit by solar-powered lanterns and candles, humming with live music and crowds of bargain hunters. Wooden walkways had been raised above the submerged pavements so that people could walk without getting their feet wet at high tide. The rhythmic thud of footsteps added a bass to the tenor and soprano of the voices. Behind the masts of the barges and, further off, beyond the turrets of the Tower of London, the city skyscrapers blazed bright white. No one in those buildings worried about carbon budgets or bills. They still partied there as if it were the Year Two Thousand. Kel preferred the wavy yellow light of the riverside lanterns, slowly dimming at the solar batteries faded, the flickering shadows cast by the candle-flames, the intrigue of the faces glimpsed in fragments among the shade. The snow highlights on roof and ledge made the market appear like a scene ready to be turned into an Advent calendar.

Just lift a hatch or open a window to find the hidden chocolate, mused Kel.

'Like it?' asked Meri.

'Love it. This market runs all day everyday?'

'I think so. They live here now. When the buildings got flooded and the firms moved to higher ground, they sailed in and used some of what could be rescued.' She stopped by a stall selling iced gingerbread biscuits. 'Aren't they pretty, Kel? Can I have two, please?'

The stall-holder swept his hand across the display. 'Which shapes, Miss?'

'Oh, a Father and a Mother Christmas.'

'I'll add a Rudolph with my compliments.'

'Thanks. That's really kind of you.' Meri took the paper bag he handed her and opened it up under a string of fairy lights a few paces away. 'You can choose.'

'Lucky dip then.' Kel plunged in his hand and came out with Rudolph. From the flicker of disappointment on Meri's face, he could tell that was the one she had really wanted with its dab of red icing. 'Here's what I picked for you.' He brushed it against her lips until she bit into it. He put his hand in the bag again. 'And it looks like I'm eating Santa. I'm sure that's probably a black mark against me and I'll get coal in my stocking.'

Going halves on Mother Christmas, they washed down the gingerbread with a mug of hot apple juice while sitting on a thick coil of rope which served as table and chairs at the bar. A violinist and a cello player busked nearby, playing a selection of seasonal songs.

'What do you normally do at Christmas?' Meri asked, watching the little band amuse the crowds by taking requests.

'I like to go to Midnight Mass—feel a bit of the awe and mystery, you know?'

She nodded. 'Hmm, me too. Theo has this thing for carols.'

'Then in the morning we unwrap presents—one big one

each, bought by everyone in the house—and then all chip in to cook a huge dinner. It's normally not ready until late afternoon. It's fun.' It had always been his favourite day, he realized with a pang of yearning. 'That's how we got U-Can. Last year's most popular present. I think we let the turkey burn playing with him.'

'You have turkey? Real turkey? No way!'

'Yeah.' He rolled his shoulders, uneasy at the reminder of the privileged life he had taken for granted.

'And let it burn? Geez, meat is wasted on you guys.'

He was relieved that she could still joke about a household of people who were her sworn enemies. 'So what do you and Theo have for dinner?'

'A little turkey once or twice—Saddiq has his ways—but usually chicken.'

'So Theo will be with his friends this year, like at your birthday?'

'Why do you want to know?'

'I just don't want to think of him being alone.'

'No, he won't be. They'll rally round.' She brushed off the crumbs from the biscuits. 'I wish I could see him though. I miss him so much.'

He knew she would prefer that above any other kind of present he could organize for her. 'Maybe we could arrange something. We seem to have got away with me being with you. We could set up a meeting somewhere Theo won't be watched.'

'Any ideas?'

'Somewhere that seems random, like a big crowd, that would be good. It's almost impossible to follow someone in a situation like that.'

'New Year's Eve then. For the fireworks at Trafalgar Square.'

'Perfect. I won't tell anyone that's what you're up to.'

'Wouldn't that, like, blur your loyalty lines rather too much?'

Kel trailed his fingers down her cheek. 'Meri, I think they got blurred a while back, don't you?'

'Right. OK. I'll message Theo tonight and start the ball rolling. Shall we go and see what's going on with Mrs Frobisher now?'

'Yes, sir.'

'Oh, and, keep your jacket zipped, OK?' She pushed the fastener all the way up so no betraying hint of skin showed. 'We don't know what we're dealing with.'

Mrs Frobisher was busy with customers when they climbed on board the secondhand clothing barge. Meri led Kel over to the pile she said blazed with peril, not that Kel could see it. At most he could see a faint bluish glow to some of the fabrics.

'If we look here, she'll come to us. At least, that's what happened last time. What about this?' She held up a hoodie. 'That'll fit you. And how about these jeans?'

'What's on them?'

'You really can't see?'

'Why would I be asking if I could?'

'Sorry, it's just odd to be reminded of that. OK, this hoodie has a nice graffiti-style zigzag and the jeans have a kind of fleck in peril mixed in the weave.'

Kel held them up against himself. 'But if I go round with these on, aren't I marking a target on myself to those who can see?'

'Oh, I guess so.' She dropped them back on the pile.

'But if I'm hanging with you, then it'll be more like a disguise. People will assume I'm the same as you.' He picked them up. 'And you like them.'

She grinned. 'I do. Finally some clothes that actually look right to me. Usually people look as if they've been dressed by someone with all the fashion sense of a circus clown.'

Kel glanced down at his current outfit. 'You should've said.'

'Not you—not normally. Mostly girls really as they wear the brightest colours. Valerie frequently gives me a headache. And Saddiq when he wears his orange waistcoat with the gold pinstripe trousers. Just something about those colours that sets my teeth on edge.'

'The downside of having a superpower, hey?' He tapped her nose.

'Back again?' Mrs Frobisher arrived at their side. She was bundled up against the cold in a padded coat, red hair tucked into a hat with earflaps.

'How much for these?' asked Meri.

Studying the two customers, Mrs Frobisher went through a pretence of checking the garments. 'These are good quality.'

'I hope so as they're a present for my friend here.'

'He likes the graffiti logo, does he?'

'Love it,' said Kel quickly.

Mrs Frobisher named a price and Meri accepted it without trying to bargain. She dug in her purse.

'I can do a special rate for friends,' Mrs Frobisher said carelessly, not taking the offered money.

'I see. Who qualifies as a friend?'

'Did you have a look at that card I gave you?'

'Yes.'

'Make anything of it?'

'You know that I did, Mrs Frobisher, I just don't know what it means. Care to explain?'

Mrs Frobisher got out her e-cigarette, a delaying tactic, Kel thought, to buy her thinking time. He glanced around. He wasn't sure what was making the back of his neck itch, but he didn't feel happy.

The barge woman blew out a puff of vapour. 'Well, it's tricky, isn't it? Cart before horse, chicken and egg.'

'You mean who goes first?' Kel admired Meri's level tone. She'd certainly gained in confidence over the last few months surviving on her own. 'I'd prefer it if you make the running here. I'll just say that I can see what you see.'

'OK, ducky, I'll give it a whirl. Pull up a stool.' Keeping an eye on her customers, Mrs Frobisher led them to the shelter of her cabin towards the stern. 'It's like this: your ability to see these patterns means you share something with me and those like me. Have you heard of Teans?'

Meri nodded.

'You, sunshine?' Mrs Frobisher pointed her cigarette at Kel.

'Yes.'

'Seeing colours like you do means you've got some of their blood in you. There used to be many more of them, pure bloods, strong, powerful, a civilization with a long history, but it's dwindled. We're left with a network of people who have one or two ancestors who were Teans. My grandfather was one, and a great-grandmother on my mother's side, so I've got pretty good sight. Do you know who your ancestor might be? We might be able to match you up with family.'

'Can we get to that in a minute?' said Meri. 'I'd like to know more about what the Tean Sympathizers do.'

'Suit yourself.' Mrs Frobisher crossed her booted ankles. 'Look, the Teans have become distant, almost mythical, like those ancients who built Stonehenge; but we live on, the people who come from them. The difference for us is that we can tell who we are by this physical distinction.

'Originally, we used to try and help the full blooded Teans, offer sanctuary when we found any, because they were hunted by a rival people called the Perilous. Heard of them?'

Meri squeezed Kel's hand, an unnecessary warning to keep quiet. 'We have.'

'As far as I'm aware, we've not been called on to do that for some years so now we protect ourselves. The Perilous are fanatics. They see anything Tean as bad news and will destroy what little is left of the culture so you'd better be careful about not flashing that power of yours in public.'

'I'm not one for flashing.'

'No, you don't look the sort. Him? Maybe.' She smiled at Kel. 'Our job as we see it is to keep the stories, the relics, the cultural practices alive.' Mrs Frobisher sucked on her cigarette, letting the violet light shine between them for a moment. 'What? Wait!' She grabbed Kel's wrist, holding the cigarette up to his skin. Too late, Kel realized it glowed with a UV bulb, picking out the pattern on his arm. 'What's your game, you two? Have you been sent to spy on us?'

Kel pulled his hand free. 'Come on, Meri: we'd better go.'

'You're not going anywhere.' Mrs Frobisher reached up and rang a bell hanging over the cabin door. 'You can't. I told you too much. Stupid! Stupid!'

'You don't understand,' protested Meri. 'He's with me.'

Alarmed by the bell, the ordinary shoppers looked up from browsing. Several of the other barge owners abandoned their businesses and swarmed up the ladder. Big Ben, the affable giant from the internet cafe, was the first to reach Mrs Frobisher.

'Got a problem, Mabel?'

'Big one of the wrong colour. Clear the decks, Ben. Ah, Francis, thank goodness you're here,' she said as a man emerged from the lower deck of the barge. With his white beard, peaked cap and thick knitted jumper, he looked the epitome of an old sea dog, the sort of man habitually seen fishing at the end of a pier.

'Mabel, are you all right?' asked Francis.

Kel wasn't too worried for himself. He was sure he could take down the big guy and evade the rest but he had no idea how Meri would react. 'We're going to have to run for it,' he muttered, pulling her close to him. If pushed they could jump to the next barge and make their escape that way.

'Move along, ladies. Little issue with some shoplifters to sort out so Mrs Frobisher is closing early tonight,' rumbled Ben, shepherding the stragglers off the deck.

'What's the story with the youngsters, dear?' asked Francis.

'He's Perilous. She's not, as far as I can tell, but she lured me into telling her about us.'

Meri was trembling. Kel rubbed her arm in reassurance. They were in a fix but he could probably still get them out.

'She lied to me—caught me off my guard,' continued Mrs Frobisher.

'I did not lie to you!' exploded Meri, pushing past Kel and coming to stand toe to toe with Mrs Frobisher. Kel realized what he had read as fear from Meri was actually fury. 'We answered every question truthfully.'

Mrs Frobisher waved that away. 'Hid the truth then. But the point is, he knows about our network: I'd got that far in the induction.'

'And you didn't check?' Francis frowned.

Mrs Frobisher looked flustered. 'I checked her last time

when she came on her own. Sorry—I made a mistake. I would never have imagined...'

'Who would?' He patted her on the shoulder. 'Don't worry: we'll fix it.'

'You don't need to fix anything!' snapped Meri. 'Kel is not a problem. He's my friend. And I will not have racist comments made about him in my presence.'

'I'm not a racist!' Mrs Frobisher seemed genuinely shocked at the accusation.

'You said he was a problem of the wrong colour: that's pretty straight forward to me.'

'I'm not against his skin markings but the fact that he's Perilous. He probably wants to kill all of us!' Mrs Frobisher tugged the strings that tied the flaps of her hat in frustration. 'Why am I defending myself to her? She's the one who came here betraying all Tean Sympathizers!'

Ben returned from clearing the boat of outsiders. He was accompanied by four men, all of whom looked as though they knew what to do with themselves in a physical tussle. Kel's estimation of his chances of fighting free dipped.

'It's the lil'chick. I remember you. Came by a couple of months back, didn't you? What you doing bringing trouble to nice people like the Frobishers?' Ben asked regretfully.

'I came because she,' Meri pointed an accusing finger at Mrs Frobisher, 'gave me a card and told me to be in touch. This is me doing so. There were no conditions attached.'

'But you obviously can't bring a Perilous here,' said Francis Frobisher calmly. Kel decided that he was probably the one who called the shots. 'We're a Tean safe haven and that means Perilous are banned. Ben?'

'Yes, Francis?'

'You know what you have to do?'

Ben scowled. 'It isn't nice, being Christmas Eve and all.'

'I'm sorry.'

'Son, you're going to have to come with me.' Ben made a move towards Kel but Meri pushed herself between them before Kel had a chance to counter.

'Big Ben, listen to me: you will not lay a finger on him. You said your purpose originally was to be a safe haven for Teans? Well then: today's your lucky day. I'm the last full blooded Tean, standing right here in front of you. He's with me, and I claim asylum for us both. So deal with that.'

12

A shocked silence greeted Meri's claim. She was running on the fuel of pure rage ever since she heard Mrs Frobisher dismiss Kel as if he were of no more account than a disposable razor. In fact, treating him exactly as most of the Perilous treated her.

'For your information, this boy, this Perilous, is the one who has kept me alive until now. His name is Kel, he's mine, so you can forget your plans to get rid of him and work out how to help us.'

'But we thought....' Mrs Frobisher shook her head in instinctive denial.

Big Ben looked to Mr Frobisher for instructions. 'Blow me down, Francis, what do you want me to do? Lil'chick is serious.'

The old man chewed on the stem of his pipe, collecting his thoughts. 'Let's take this inside. Ben, you stay with us. Keep an eye on the Perilous. Thank you, boys.' He waved off the men who had come to back up Ben. 'We'll let you know if we need you. For the moment, get rid of the spectators.'

Their argument had gathered a few interested parties

down on the walkways hoping to see the supposed thieves marched off in handcuffs, or a fight, Meri didn't think they were choosy as long as it was entertaining.

'Are you OK with going inside?' she asked Kel in a low voice.

'As long as we stick together.' He took her hand in his. 'By the way, you are awesome when you're angry.'

'Then I'd better just keep that bubbling right along then. I'm really feeling pretty scared but I'm trying to ignore it.'

'Come along if you must.' Mrs Frobisher led the way down into the main cabin of their barge home. The low ceiling was decked with orange, red and blue fabric fringes with mirror sequins, the floor scattered with big floor cushions, and walls hung with polished brass ornaments. It reminded Meri of the interior of a fairytale gipsy caravan. A black and white cat lay in regal control of the rug by the wood stove. A white parrot with a yellow tuft on its forehead hopped from leg to leg in its cage which hung from a rafter.

'Uh-oh,' whistled the bird.

'Take a seat,' their hostess said coolly.

Kel sat on the biggest cushion, pulling Meri down to share it with him. The Frobishers chose seats either side of the wood burner while Ben elected to stand at the exit, guarding the only escape if you discounted trying to squeeze out one of the portholes.

'A full blood Tean. That's a big claim for a little lady,' said Francis. 'Can you prove it?'

Meri nodded.

'Go on then,' urged Mrs Frobisher, scepticism radiating from her.

'Mabel, give her a chance.'

Meri rubbed her hands together. 'OK then. My eyesight

is much better than yours when it comes to peril for one thing. Those clothes: where do they come from?'

'Some are made by our communities around the world but a few are antique pieces mixed into the bundle that neither Mabel or I can see the pattern of without help or special lighting. We keep them together as a kind of test.'

'Check your inventory. You've a daisy print which your wife can't see. I can pick it out again for you if you like and you can test it.'

'That's proof that you have more Tean blood in you than is usual but not that you're full blood,' said Mrs Frobisher.

'Both my parents were full Tean. They were killed by a Perilous death squad.'

'So how did you escape?'

'They hid me and then I was lucky in my guardian. He made a good job of keeping my existence a secret.'

'And now? Why are you keeping company with a Perilous?' asked Francis.

'His name is Kel.'

'It doesn't matter,' murmured Kel.

'It does.' She waited until Francis was forced to concede the point otherwise the conversation was over.

'Why are you keeping company with Kel?' Francis said with a wry smile at his wife as she tutted in her corner.

'We met at school. We didn't know what we were until Kel flared out. Unfortunately it all went a bit wrong after that and his people found out about me. The fact that they think I'm full blood is another kind of proof as they've been keeping tabs on the last of us. I've been on the run and Kel has left them. Now we need your help.'

'We don't help his sort,' said Mrs Frobisher. The cat got up and leapt into her lap, circled and settled for another nap.

'You told me that you were Tean Sympathizers, set up to help people like me. Kel and I come as a package deal.'

From the shifting beside her, Meri could tell Kel was preparing to protest. 'Meri, you don't need to complicate things by asking them to factor me in. I'll be fine as long as you are safe.'

'But now you know about them, they're not going to just let you walk out, are they? So they'll have to look after you too, see that you are OK, understand that you're loyal to me.' She laughed softly. 'I was about to say that we're in this together, but that's what my annoying team leader on eco service likes saying, so I'd better not.'

'Young man, what have you to say for yourself?' asked Francis.

'Just that I would never do anything to harm Meri. I've left my people because we disagree on this point and I've no intention of going back on that decision. It's time this stupid battle between our kinds stopped.'

'There's not much of a battle left. You've killed off a whole civilization.' Francis tapped the bowl of his pipe.

'And I'm not proud of that. If she's the last, then I'm sorry, and that's all the more reason to protect her.'

'Aren't you scared of her?'

Kel turned to Meri. 'Am I afraid of you?'

She touched his cheek lightly. 'No.'

'Are you afraid of me?'

'Only that you might do something stupid to protect me.'

'I feel the same, Meri. That's where we stand, Mr Frobisher: together.'

Francis got up and opened the door to the parrot cage. Taking a peanut from his pocket he fed it to the bird.

'Uh-oh,' whistled the parrot.

'Does he say anything else?' asked Kel. 'I'm not finding that very encouraging.'

'Not when I'm in the room.' Francis gave them a shy smile and closed the cage again. 'I think he and the cat conspire behind my back. This is a lot for an old man to take in. I've got to consider the best course of action from here on. You've brushed up on the edge of something much bigger than you realize and you, young lady, really need to be taken to the centre of it. The problem is that there's no place there for your Kel.'

'Is this like a riddle?' asked Meri, wondering what he was talking about.

'I have to be careful. I just can't tell you too much without consulting the other captains. That'll take a while as we're scattered around the world.'

Ben spoke up. 'Tean Sympathizers are organized under captains, Lil'chick. Francis here is ours.'

Mrs Frobisher picked the cat off her lap and dropped it back on the rug. She shook out her skirts. 'I can't believe you're even thinking about this, Francis.'

'A full blood Tean, Mabel: that's amazing news.'

'You mean too good to be true.'

'I believe her; don't you?'

'She's just told us she can see better than us, not proved it. And even so, that isn't foolproof. We only have her word for the rest: the Perilous death squad and so on.'

'Meri, make my skin markings show.' Kel rolled up his sleeve.

Meri's immediate reaction was to be horrified by the suggestion. 'What?'

'Full bloods can do that.'

'I can also burn you to death or mess up your internal organs so, no, I won't be doing that just to convince her.'

'Please.'

'No, Kel.'

'Yes, Kel. You won't damage me. Give me just a little. If it starts to hurt, then we'll stop.'

'But I don't know how much is enough.'

'You'll know.'

'Can you really do that?' asked Francis. 'There are stories of this but I've never seen it—no living person has.'

'I'm really not comfortable trying.' Meri could see that Kel trusted her absolutely; the problem was her own self doubt. She'd held back physically with him so far, terrified she would inadvertently hurt him if she got carried away.

Kel stroked her cheek. 'Go on. Just a little. Like I do to my pottery. I just let a little flow through my fingers, a kind of letting go. When we flare out we must be doing it inside to our own skin and it doesn't harm us.'

'But Tean, remember?' Meri tapped her chest. 'A little from me might be like the idea of a little lightning strike.'

'I'll take that risk.' He picked up her limp hand and placed it on his forearm. 'Give it a go.'

Mrs Frobisher folded her arms. 'She won't because she can't. She's a fraud, Francis.'

Kel lowered his voice. 'You can't let that old bat win.'

'OK, OK, give me a second. Geez, you must be crazy to even suggest this.' Meri closed her eyes. A letting go, Kel described it. She relaxed her fingers and imagined sinking into him just a tiny amount, like resting on a feather bed.

'That's it, darling. That's nice—really warm tingle. We should've tried this before.'

Opening her eyes, she found Kel's blue ones smiling into hers. His skin was gleaming. 'Is that me doing it?'

'I think so, though now you mention it I've got a feeling I'm joining the party.' He leant forward and kissed her. 'Yep, definitely joining in.' The gleam became a blaze and Meri snatched her hand away, drawing back some of the power. She could sense a precipice over which she did not dare plunge no matter how attracted to him she felt. Her worst nightmare was to produce in Kel a burn like in the horrible photographs.

Kel, however, seemed pleased. He held up his arm defiantly, his swirls clearly visible. 'See, Mrs Frobisher. She's what she says she is.'

Meri looked down at her arm. For a second there, she thought she had seen a glimpse of swirly markings on her skin but they had faded the moment she had broken the connection. No one else had noticed as Kel's peacock display was far more impressive.

'That's a cool trick you've got there, lad,' said Big Ben. 'I've never seen the markings up close but I think I want some.'

'You're a Tean sympathizer, Ben,' muttered Mrs Frobisher. 'Have some dignity.'

'Doesn't stop me envying a Perilous, does it? That's what Lil'chick is trying to tell us.'

'So do we all now agree that Meri here is a Tean?' Francis looked over at his wife.

Mabel nodded stiffly.

'And, Meri, you'll vouch for Kel?'

'Yes, of course,' she said quickly.

'Then leave it with me. How can we get in touch with you?'

'I don't have a phone because I don't want to be tracked. You can email my guardian. You'll have to disguise it though. Pose as a musical group applying for funding—the Perilous won't have time to check all his work messages. He can pass any news on to me. We've a secure way of communicating set up.' She scribbled down Theo's contact details. 'He doesn't know the full story so be careful what you say.'

'Of course.' Francis tucked the email into his pocket. 'Expect to hear from us in a few days. If there's an emergency before then, send word to us here. I'll tell our friends that any message from either of you is to be brought to me instantly.'

Meri stood up. 'We'd better be going.'

Mrs Frobisher handed over the bag of clothes Meri had picked out for Kel and then forgotten. 'These are yours. I suppose they should be on the house.'

'You needn't—'

'Yes, I should. I'm sorry if I come over as suspicious but there have been imposters before now, you understand. They always turn out to be just a quarter or less Tean.'

Meri took the bag. 'Imposters? Why? Why does it matter how much Tean we have in us? People are just people.'

'Didn't you know? Francis, tell the child.'

The old man hooked his thumbs in his waistcoat pockets. 'Because there's a fortune waiting for a full blood claimant, as well as a whole host of people who will look to her for leadership.'

'Oh God.' Meri swayed. 'Really, it's not about that for me.'

He smiled. 'We know or you would never have shoved a Perilous in our face. But, nevertheless, it's true.'

'Kel?'

'Don't worry, Meri. We'll handle it.' Kel took the bag from her fingers. 'Thanks for these, Mrs Frobisher. I'd better be getting Meri home. She's going to need a few days too to take all this in.'

'I never thought I'd be saying this to a Perilous, but look after her,' said the lady.

'I promise.'

Big Ben stood back to let them pass and slapped Kel on the shoulder. 'I'm glad I didn't have to get rid of you, boy.'

'So am I,' agreed Kel, looking the man mountain up and down. 'I'm not sure that would've ended well for either of us.'

BACK AT THE HOSTEL, Kel waited for Meri to raise the subject of the Frobishers and the inheritance that could be hers but it seemed she preferred to cope with the new information by ignoring it. She went into distraction mode, planning their meal the next day and chatting about what they might do.

'I think there's an ice rink set up at Liverpool Street. We could go there.'

'That sounds fun.'

'Is this enough potatoes, do you think?'

'If you're thinking of feeding an army.'

'You're right.' Meri put half of them back in the fridge. 'Theo always loves his roast potatoes and Valerie can easily eat six—definitely the favourite vegetable at the Christmas table. How about your family? What's their favourite?'

'My family?' A dark cloud of remembering dumped its burden of icy rain on Kel. 'Crap, my family! I'd totally forgotten: Jenny is coming over to visit me for Christmas. With my phone switched off she must've already arrived and be wondering what's happened to me.' Kel glanced at his watch. He couldn't believe that he'd forgotten all about his sister for days. He hadn't even spared Jenny a thought. 'It's already seven. I think she was planning to get in around midday today.'

Meri quietly packed the potatoes back in the bag. 'You have to go to her.'

'She's come all the way from Amsterdam. I can't not meet up, but I don't have to spend all day with her. How about I make a quick dash over to Wimbledon? I can come back on the last train.'

'Don't you think that will make your friends suspicious?' Meri got out a single mug from the cupboard and rooted through the herbal teas for a soothing blend. 'We knew this would only work while no one was interested in your whereabouts.'

Why was this happening now? It was his fault, of course; if he'd remembered earlier, he could have put Jenny off to the New Year. 'But I can't abandon you for Christmas.'

Meri leaned against the counter, head hung. She then straightened and gave him a bright smile. 'You're not abandoning me. You're keeping me safe. I've had you for more days than I could've hoped. You go meet up with your sister, have a nice family time together.'

Kel paced from stove to back door. 'If I explain, if she's on our side...'

'Kel, do you really want to risk your relationship with your sister? She will either agree and feel torn like you do, or disagree then be conflicted about keeping your secret. Worse, she might betray you and then where will we be? Come here. Give me a hug.'

He folded Meri into his arms, wishing he could absorb her and carry her safely under his skin so they would never have to be apart. Foolish, impossible thought. 'I hate this.'

'I think I love you.'

Something beautiful bloomed inside, pushing out his ugly mood. 'Oh, Meri: I love you too. I thought it was too early to say.'

'Never too early. Do you really?'

'So much it hurts.'

'I hope it doesn't hurt to admit it?'

'Not a bit.'

'Go see your sister. Throw your friends off the scent. In the New Year we'll find a way of being together.'

'You've my number? For emergencies?'

'Yes.'

'I could write to you old style.'

'That would be sweet—as long as no one sees the envelope.'

'I won't even write your address down until I'm standing at the post box.'

'OK then.'

He tipped her chin so he could settle his lips over hers. He poured everything he felt into the kiss, his longing, his frustration, his tenderness. At first, she was a little tense in his arms—she was always so worried she'd lose control and hurt him—but then their usual magic flowed between them and she softened and moulded to him to be his perfect fit. When they broke apart, he rested his forehead on hers.

'Look after my Tean.'

Her mouth curved in a smile. 'Look after my Perilous.'

KEL WALKED out with his guitar strapped to his back, dressed in his old clothes. It was almost as if the little Christmas interlude hadn't happened, or been a dream from which he was now waking. When he considered that he had put enough distance between himself and Meri's hostel to throw off any tracking, he switched on his phone. Text messages scrolled across the screen, all variations of 'where are you?' from Jenny and a few from Ade and Lee. He noted they had only started asking at midday so he had been right to think that no one had cared that he hadn't returned to his digs the night he met up with Meri. He dealt with Jenny first.

Sorry. Phone was out of charge and I was busking in town. See you at my flat in an hour?

He wondered if he should reply to Ade and Lee but decided against it. He had said he was cutting ties with them. If he did respond then he might have to explain where he had been and he was done being answerable to them.

Jenny's reply zipped back into his inbox. *You pillock: you forgot all about me, didn't you? I've had to throw myself on Ade's mercy or be shivering on your doorstep. Some Christmas Greeting that is!*

I love you too, sister.

Kel knew he was on shaky ground. He hadn't even thought to get her a present but the shops were pulling down the shutters for the holiday. Better to be on time, he decided. He could take Jenny out as her gift.

I'm not going back to that dump you call home. Come meet me at Ade's.

I'm not welcome there.

That's not what Ade says.

I mean I don't want to go there.

Too bad. If you want to see me, you'll come and fetch me from somewhere civilized. If I go back to your area I'll probably get mugged.

You're a bodyguard, sis. You eat bad guys for breakfast.

I'm off duty.

Kel shook his head. His big sister was immovable when she got an idea lodged in her head. *OK. But we're not staying at Ade's house.*

It felt extremely unnerving to ring on the bell of the

place that he used to think of as home. The guys had dressed it up for Christmas, strings of solar lights looped through the trees and along the eaves. A drunk-looking blowup Santa lurched in his sleigh on the lawn. Rudolph with a bright red nose glowed with perky tee-total enthusiasm. The gate buzzed. Kel crunched up the gravel path, preparing what he would say when the door opened.

Swanny threw the door wide. 'So the prodigal returns.'

Kel shook his head. 'Thanks, Swanny, but I'm just here to see my sister.'

His smile dimmed. 'Come in then if it won't kill you.'

Leaving the guitar in the foyer, Kel followed Swanny into the kitchen. His mind ran a replay of the tasering incident, burning out any guilt he might have felt. His sister was sitting with Ade in the breakfast nook, heads together conspiratorially.

'Hey, Jenny, you're looking great!' Kel held out his arms to give her a hug, waiting for her to come to him. A few inches short of his height, she had a trim figure topped off with a mass of curly blonde hair. Normally that was tied up in a no nonsense bun but, considering herself off duty, it tumbled around her shoulders.

'Hey yourself, squiggle. Go on: show me.' She pulled up his sleeve.

'You'd have to get me angry first.' He brushed it back down.

'I guess that wouldn't be difficult seeing how you've gone all rebellious on us. Puberty—tough time for Perilous.' She patted his arm.

Kel didn't like the dismissal of his stance on Meri as a byproduct of teenage hormones. 'It's more than that, and you know it.'

She clapped her hands over her mouth. 'Oops: I

promised Dad not to get on your case, though you deserve a kick up the butt for being so damn stubborn.'

Kel imagined turning around and walking straight back out. He could get to Meri on the last train if he left now. 'Is this how it's going to be? I've had enough arguments about this to last a lifetime. Jenny, nice to see you. Why don't you stay here with Ade and Co? They do a good turkey. I'll see you around.'

She poked him in the chest. 'You don't have to be so dramatic. I came to see you. Ade and the guys are fine in their way—'

Ade bowed. 'Why, thank you.'

'But you're family. Let's go to the pub and celebrate.'

'Celebrate what?' asked Kel flatly. He didn't feel like there was much to cheer now he got a sense of her opinion on his stance.

'Your flare-out, of course. Tradition says the older siblings have to buy their little brothers a drink when they're promoted to the big girls and boys league.'

'If you're heading out, you'll need this.' Swanny brought her her coat, holding it out so she could slip into the sleeves.

'Thanks, Swanny.' Her smiled edged into flirtatious when dealing with Ade's chief of staff.

'See you later, Jenny. I'll get one of the lads to make up a room for you.'

Ade walked to the fridge and pulled out a couple of beers. 'There's plenty of food for tomorrow if you want to crash here tonight and join us, Kel.'

'I'm certainly staying here. Has to be said, little brother, that your place is unsanitary.' Jenny wrapped a red scarf around her neck, freeing her hair from the back.

It was probably a good idea for her to stay at Ade's as Kel only had the one miserable room and single bed but it still felt like Jenny showing to the others that she was siding against him.

'We can't all afford the Ritz, Jen. Thanks, Ade, but I don't think it's appropriate for me to spend the day here tomorrow. Jenny might like that though.'

Pausing in levering off the bottle cap, Ade scowled. 'You're not seeing her, are you?'

The kitchen went silent. There was no doubt in anyone's mind who 'her' was.

'That's none of your business.'

'It's exactly my business.'

Jenny stepped between them and laid a hand on Ade's shoulder. 'Chill, OK, Ade? Let me talk to my brother.'

Ade took a swig. 'Sorry. Yes, you're right. No point running this argument again.'

Jenny hooked her arm through Kel's. 'Come on then.'

Relieved to be out of there, Kel bent to pick up his guitar as they passed through the hallway.

'Oh, leave that old thing here, Kel. I don't want you carrying that all night. People will think we're the entertainment. You can collect it when you drop me off.'

Reluctantly, Kel left it leaning against the wall in the hallway. 'But I'm not staying.'

'Yeah, yeah. Message received. Cheer up: it's Christmas not a funeral!'

13

Kel took his sister to an old pub on the High Street, one he had visited many times for Sunday lunch with Ade and always loved for its unchanging charm. Such lost-in-the-past places were doubly popular as they helped people forget the world outside with its jerky slide into worsening climate change. With low oak beams, wreaths of evergreens and open fires, it felt a festive place to spend Christmas Eve. The main room was packed with people wearing Santa hats but he knew the owner and so, after a brief wait, was waved through to a quieter spot near the back in one of the old style booths upholstered in dark red leather. He watched his sister battle her way to the counter brandishing a twenty pound note over her head. Her killer combination of blonde hair, charm and surprising muscle shortened the wait to be served and she returned carrying two glasses of champagne. She set the drinks on the table between them.

'Cheers, Kel. Seriously, I'm really proud of you: a spiral like Dad and me. It's good to see it carrying on down the family line.'

'Thanks.'

She nudged him with her toe. 'You don't sound that happy. Don't you feel proud?'

'I suppose I do. It's just got so mixed up with the rest. You heard how it happened?'

Jenny nodded.

'She was so scared. It must've been like walking in to find Grandma had turned into a wolf.'

'You're talking about her, aren't you? The Tean girl. Yeah, it's a major cock-up all round. Dad's really worried about you.'

'I expect he is.'

'He thinks you're throwing it all away for a crush.'

'It's more complicated than that.'

'Even so, you're going this far because you've fallen for the girl and I have to ask you, without all this, how long would those feelings last normally? A few weeks? A couple of months? That's how long relationships usually last at your age.'

Jenny made it sound as though she was decades, not just a few years, older than him. 'You don't get it, do you, Jen? Even if I didn't love her, I'd still think what they are doing was well out of order—that the Perilous are wrong to hunt her.'

'The "L" word? Damn. I was hoping it hadn't got to that stage.'

He didn't return her wry smile. 'Do you think they're right? To put out a capture order on a girl who did nothing but be born a Tean? She's not threatened us, not done anything but try to live quietly away from our notice.'

'I can't believe you've already forgotten what happened to our mother. The Tean's a danger to us, Kel.'

'How? She's put hands on me and I've not been harmed.'

Jenny sipped her champagne. 'I thought you hadn't seen her since your flare-out? When did she do this?'

Annoyed at his mistake, Kel waved it off. 'That doesn't matter.'

'It does. If you know where she is, it's your duty to report it.'

'No, I resigned so I'm no longer under that obligation.'

'They won't hurt her if they catch her peacefully, you realize that?'

'So?'

'If it comes to a struggle, things might get out of hand.'

A party of Santas broke into a rendition of 'Walking in a Winter Wonderland', singing along to the digital jukebox. Kel wished they'd shut up; he was far from 'happy tonight' in his particular wonderland.

'Jenny, she's only a few inches over five feet and has no training.'

'But she's Tean. The hunters will be scared to touch her.'

'Then they should leave her the hell alone!' He fisted his hands and bent his head to rest on them. 'Really, Jenny? Is this really what we've become?'

'We've always been like this. It's you who've changed.'

'Then the rest of you need to change too, because, I swear if any of you harm her, I'll bring you all down, so help me God.'

'Calm down. I don't want to hurt her, I'm just trying to make you see that you aren't doing what's best for her if you carry on this path. If you really cared about the girl you'd make sure this ended peacefully.'

'Meaning?'

'A quiet pick up off the street, a conversation, a binding agreement that she'd not harm any Perilous, some kind of isolation from the rest of us. It would be best in fact if you did it as she wouldn't be so terrified. There'd be terms to be discussed, but I think we'd be able to find something we can all live with.'

'You do? What exactly?'

Jenny shrugged, for the first time in the conversation looking uncomfortable. 'I don't know. I'm the muscle, remember, not the politician. Dad thinks she could have a place in some kind of exile away from any Perilous.'

'Oh yeah, his idea of a cage without bars and no life to call her own. Very merciful.'

'That doesn't sound too bad. Better than spending her time on the run, always looking over her shoulder. She must feel very lonely.'

'She feels what we've made her feel, Jen. We're the problem here, not her.'

'Are you sure about that? Because from where I'm sitting, it seems as there's only one person stopping her negotiating a peace with us and that would be you.'

'If it is peace they are talking about, then I'd be all over it, but you know it's not. It's surrender. They want to send her like Napoleon to some sort of Elba. The last Tean standing.'

'Elba's better than a coffin.'

'There it is: the death threat again. And you expect her to negotiate peace?'

'Oh, Kel, it's not just about her though. I'm worried for you.' She reached out and squeezed his hand. 'How long do you think Dad and I can keep backing you on this?'

'Backing me? Did I miss the moment you said, "Hey, little brother, I really admire your respect for the human rights of an innocent girl"?'

Jenny gave a huff of disgust. 'Yes, we've been backing you, peabrain. We've been telling Osun and Ade to give you time. We've promised that your family loyalty, your loyalty to the ruling family, to being a Perilous, will reassert itself.'

'And if it doesn't? If I can't be what you want, can't think the way you approve?'

'I don't know, Kel. I'm hoping I won't have to answer that. As far as we know for sure, you've not broken any of our laws.' From Jenny's doubtful expression, however, it appeared that she guessed he had been fraternising with enemy but would prefer not to know the details. 'I don't want it to come to the point where you have to choose between us and that girl and we have to choose between you and our duty.'

'I think we both know what you'll decide if it comes to that, don't we? Merry Christmas, Jenny.' He clinked his glass ironically against hers.

RETURNING JENNY TO ADE'S, Kel walked in on a party in the clubroom, which had already spilled over into the kitchen. Ade had invited friends from school to celebrate and the music was blaring from open windows. Kel found it hard to disentangle himself from classmates who were unable to understand why he was no longer living in such prime digs. Most concluded he had to be crazy to prefer a grotty room to this mansion with only the minimum of adult supervision. He guessed Ade had put them up to it as another twist in his 'Get Kel back in the fold' campaign.

Sadie, when she could be separated from lip-lock with Lee, grilled him without a shred on subtlety as to whether he'd been in contact with Meri. Kel was aware that his old friends were listening in on his answers, standing oh so casually just at his back.

'No, she hasn't replied to my texts,' he said truthfully. He felt no need to mention that he'd spent last night sleeping beside her.

'That sucks.' The little Christmas tree baubles hanging from her earlobes bobbed in sympathy. 'She barely tells me anything when she does contact me. Just says she's OK so I suppose she is. Any idea where she's gone? She hasn't sent me her address like she promised and refuses to meet up.'

'No idea. I got the sense she wanted to get away from the area so maybe she'll never come back. Maybe she'd moved on, new friends, new crowd, you know?'

'Then I'll just have to keep on trying. I don't let friends go so easily. I know she has enemies but neither of us would do anything to endanger her, would we?'

'Leaving her alone might be what she needs from us,' cautioned Kel, wishing Lee wasn't circling sharklike just behind Sadie.

'I guess. Hey, you, come for a dance?' Sadie spun round and snagged the front of Lee's shirt.

'Yeah, baby.' Lee's eyes met Kel over Sadie's head, expression cold. Kel sent a brief thank you to Meri's lucky star that she hadn't trusted Sadie with her address. He'd have to warn her that Lee was getting close to her comp-punk friend.

Leaving the party as soon as he could wriggle out of further conversations, Kel found it was no comfort to be back in his flat. The sheets needed washing, the house arctic, the mess in the shared kitchen grown worse over the few days he'd been away as someone had had a party there too and not cleared up. Lying looking up at the ceiling, sleep eluding him, Kel struggled to keep off the slide into despair even though he could feel himself tottering on the top. Everyone in the Perilous world he cared about, the people who knew him best, were all convinced he was wrong. At the pub, Jenny had kept circling back to the fact that he was being unkind to Meri by leaving her out there as a target. Like a terrier on the scent, Jenny had scratched away at his most vulnerable spot. He wished he could contact Meri instantly to ask her opinion but there was no safe way of doing that.

'I'm going crazy. I've got to talk to her somehow,' he told the water stain on the plasterwork. Turning the light back on, he got out a piece of paper and started to write.

Dear Meri....

MERI SPENT Christmas morning going to every church service she could find locally so she could be with other people. Singing her way through favourite carols, surrounded by excited families and quieter adults who like her had come alone, she kept her spirits up by imagining Kel having a fun time with his sister, tucking in to a big meal, perhaps going skating or for a walk like she had planned for them if he had been able to stay. As long as he was enjoying himself then that made her lonely day worth it. At the last service in a flood-damaged part of Wapping, she was invited to help out at a dinner for the homeless, which was all too appropriate and at least meant she had something to fill the blank hours. Wearing a purple paper crown, she served carrots and brussels, poured custard on pudding from the hatch in the church hall, and generally tried to give the impression of someone having a good time. By the end she had half persuaded herself she was.

She got back to the hostel to find a long message from Theo. He had uploaded a video of Saddiq, Valerie and himself taken during lunch. They had talked to her as if she were there, even reading out her joke from her cracker—a touch that made her cry a little. The twist of homesickness was like a physical pain in her stomach.

In her reply, she sent a message broaching the idea of meeting up at New Year as Kel had suggested. Theo's reply was instantaneous. He must have been waiting by the computer for her to get in touch.

Absolutely brilliant idea. We'll all come so if there's any trouble we'll see them off. Are you having an OK day?

It's fine. Helped with a homeless lunch.

Well done. I've got your present waiting for you. I'll bring that too.

I haven't got round to getting you anything. What would you like?

You back home. But as I can't have that, it will be gift enough just to see you on 31st. Keep out of trouble till then.

Meri ended the conversation and opened up a browser to search up more about the Tean sympathizers, following in Kel's tracks. She'd purposely been leaving that news about an inheritance alone; but now, with nothing else to distract her, she made herself consider it. Money would be useful. It could help protect her, wrap her up in layers of security that the Perilous would find hard to penetrate. But as for the rest—the people looking to her for leadership— that was probably just Francis Frobisher getting over-enthusiastic. You could only have a leader if you had a cause and supporters. Beyond survival, she couldn't think what that would be. She was dismally ignorant about her own people. Two letters from her parents was the sum total of her knowledge.

She typed in a new search. *Where was Atlantis?*

A map came up with dots marked everywhere from the centre of the Atlantic, the Bermuda Triangle, to various locations in the Mediterranean. When she hovered over the links, the write up always included the word 'supposed' or 'rumoured'. Some of the articles cited sounded like the work of crazy amateurs with a hunch.

OK then: no one knows. So if there's an inheritance, it's not going to be land, thought Meri.

Speculation was making her head ache. She switched off the computer and turned on the crappy wall screen to watch the big film. It was last year's hit about the fires that swept through LA a decade ago. Normally, Meri admitted, you would have to hold the hero's gun to her head to get her to watch, but tonight a bit of mindless action was better than thinking. She curled up with a cup of tea and a slice of the cake she had bought to share with Kel and prepared to be entertained.

THE WEEK between Christmas and New Year passed slowly. Meri spent the time sketching and reading, going whole days without talking to anyone. The brief interlude with Kel seemed unreal, a lovely little miniature of happiness snatched from the house fire that was the rest of her life. In her mind, she would take out the moment, mentally dust off the frame and picture him standing by the window of her room, lying beside her or even just washing up at the sink. Simple, ordinary things. They had to hold her over until she could wrangle some miracle to bring them back together again.

A letter came from him in the middle of the week. It had been written on Christmas Eve and she was distressed as she read it to find he had been as miserable as she, the meeting with his sister not having gone well. He had said he was planning to see Jenny again the following day, perhaps for a walk along the Thames, but by the sound of it there was no family lunch, no games and fun as Meri had hoped. His stance had alienated him from his family. Her heart told her that they should have been together, not both feeling sad at opposite ends of London.

One paragraph in particular caught her attention:

I have to tell you, Meri, that Jenny thinks that I'm being unkind to you keeping from you making peace with the Perilous, that they'll catch you one day and it would be better for me to bring you in quietly. What do you think? My feeling is that we can't trust them but if you want to risk it, I'll stand by you. It has to be your choice. I don't want to trick you into anything, even though that is exactly what they would like me to do.

Unnerved, Meri realized that this was the first crack in his position that she was right to keep well away, even if he raised the idea only to reject it. What if they were wrong and was Jenny right? Had they thrown away a chance at negotiation?

Wanting to clear her head, she got up and walked to the windowsill to scatter a pinch of food into the goldfish bowl Zara had asked her to look after over Christmas. The two recipients arrowed to the surface, little mouths breaking the surface in the goldfish version of ravenous hunger. Did they know they were trapped? Did they know about ponds, rivers and oceans or were they content to swim in circles? Sometimes it seemed to her that she and Kel were like that, stuck swimming round and round in the fishbowl of London. There was a whole other world out there. Would going to the Perilous command to make an agreement at least allow them to swim free? But it came down to trust in the good intentions of a group who hated her. Other Teans had tried, she remembered, thinking of the mention in her father's letter of grandparents who had lost their lives on a peace mission to the Perilous.

No, Kel, you're doing the right thing, she thought, giving the fish an extra pinch. *We can't trust them to negotiate fairly.*

It wasn't pleasant, though, to think of him being put under so much pressure by his family, every action scrutinized and questioned by his old friends. It would make anyone doubt themselves.

On New Year's Eve, excitement mounting, Meri bundled up warmly in a padded black jacket she had treated herself to in the sales. It had the advantage of a fake fur trim to the hood so when that was raised her face was hidden from view. As there was some risk involved in any attempt to see Theo, she dressed for a quick getaway, running shoes and jeans, no bag. All her belongings—purse, keys and so on—were distributed in the various pockets in the jacket. She checked herself in the rust-spotted mirror in her bedroom and decided that she would blend.

Joining the queues for the river bus service, Meri stood with the others heading to Green Park for the fireworks. When the Thames flooded a few years back, the annual display was moved from the Embankment to Buckingham Palace as this was now on the new verge of the tidal waters. At the other end of the Mall, half of Trafalgar Square was submerged at high tide, the four bronze lions that surrounded Nelson's Column had their toes lapped by waves, but you could still stand on the steps of the National Gallery and watch as the fireworks went off over the rooftops. This was where she had agreed to meet Theo and friends. Plenty of other people had had the same thought, but Meri told herself this was just as well: more people meant more places to hide.

Getting off the river bus at the pontoon moored at Charing Cross, she took the chainlink walkway over the drowned station complex and up to the dry ground near St Martin's-in-the-Fields. It was easier that she was on her own, she thought, as keeping hold of anyone in this crowd would be impossible. She marvelled that some parents considered it a good idea to bring their children.

'Handcuffs might do it,' she murmured, watching one father pick up a child and carry him on his hip to stop them being separated.

Meri wormed her way through the press of bodies to reach the gallery steps. These were already occupied by parties who had come early to bag a good view but no one minded a slight girl weaving through their midst, making way without a grumble. Finally she spotted Valerie's turban hat perched like a colourful butterfly on top of the crowd. A grin filled Meri's body, not just her face, warming her down to her toes.

'Hello.' She squeezed through the last gap and bobbed up beside Theo.

'Oh thank God, Meri, you made it!' Theo hugged her to his battered black jacket. He had tears in his eyes under the bobble hat he had pulled over his fair hair. Meri could have told him that, with Valerie sporting her usual African print headgear, his attempt at being low key was wasted. 'How have you been?'

'Good thanks.'

'You look well.' He held her at arms length. 'Yes, you look good.'

'I actually quite like eco-service, would you believe it? It calls out my inner dredger.'

Theo laughed. 'Here's your present.' He handed her a slim wrapped parcel. 'Open it later.'

'Thanks—and I will.'

'Ah, sweetie!' Valerie kissed her noisily on both cheeks. 'So lovely to see you again. We missed you at Christmas.'

'Missed you guys too.'

Saddiq hugged her. 'Theo's been a miserable old goat without you around. Can't you come home?'

'Maybe one day. Thanks for, you know....' She patted her pocket that contained her Emma Boot ID.

'Anytime. It was mildly exciting breaking a minor law.' Saddiq's eyepatch twinkled as the first firework shot up into the sky. 'Here they go!'

In the distance, the clock face of Big Ben was lit up specially for the evening. Though the parliament building was abandoned, traditions died hard and the authorities went in to restore power to the clock for one night only each year. The first flurry of fireworks paused as the crowd waited, hushed, for the familiar bell to toll midnight. As the first bong echoed across flooded Westminster, a huge cheer went up and the firework display started in earnest. Meri linked arms on one side with Theo and Valerie on the other, oohing and aahing with the crowd. It felt wonderful to be in touch with the people who loved her, to be part of a group activity after a week of solitude. She hadn't drunk anything but she still felt heady like she had downed several glasses of champagne.

The display lasted for ten minutes, gunshot bangs reverberating from walls and windows, causing them to rattle. Stars mirrored in the water filling the old roads, making Westminster briefly resemble the lost city of Venice. With the layer of snow clinging to roof tiles and window ledges, the colours seemed all the brighter by contrast.

'Oh wow!' Meri said, smiling up at Theo. 'This was so worth it.'

'You don't have to rush off, do you, love?' He squeezed her arm. 'I've booked a place in a club I know not far from here. We can have a late dinner and catch up.'

'I'd like nothing better, Theo. That was an amazing display. We'll have to come every year—a new tradition.'

'It was good, wasn't it?' A young woman, blond curls caught up in a pony tail, standing on the step below, turned to speak to Meri.

Meri instinctively withdrew, pulling her hood up around her face. It had fallen down when she had been admiring the starbursts in the sky.

'Yes, lovely,' said Theo briskly. 'Excuse me.'

The woman put out a hand to him. 'I just wanted to say "hello", Mr Woolf. I understand you've been kind to my brother.'

'Your brother?' Theo pushed Meri behind him, casting a glance at Saddiq telling him to get her clear.

'Yes, Kel Douglas. I'm his sister, Jenny. He said we might find you here.'

Meri didn't wait to hear the rest. She ducked under Saddiq's arm as he moved to block the woman. Meri bolted, ramming her way past anyone in her path.

'Run, Meri!' screeched Valerie, whacking Jenny with a brightly coloured umbrella.

She had the vague sense of Theo and his friends scuffling with more people behind her but she couldn't stop to help. Half falling down the steps, she squirmed through the crowd to reach the edge of Trafalgar Square. People were already heading home, taking the side roads to the underground stations or queuing for the river buses. Her feet went out from under her as she slipped on some ice.

'Here, what's your hurry!' grumbled a man into whom she had stumbled.

She shouldered past him, making for one of the bronze lions, but then felt a tug on the back of her hood. She twisted but was trapped. Quickly, she unzipped the jacket, pulled her arms out and abandoned it to her pursuer. She was right at the water's edge now. Some of the spectators had hired boats to float along the submerged streets of Whitehall. With nowhere to go on land, Meri splashed into the water, breaking the crust of ice, hoping to make it to the nearest boat and beg a lift. The freezing water quickly rose to her waist. It was so bone-achingly cold. Desperate, Meri struck out, swimming towards a bright yellow dinghy but it never seemed to get any closer, the passengers oblivious to her as they popped corks at the moon. The current swirling around the submerged buildings swept her to the east, the yellow dinghy drawing away to the west, heading for the lights of the Admiralty Arch. She was alone in the dark water, body beginning to shut down, brain stuttering.

Two boys appeared beside her swimming strongly.

'Can we touch her?' gasped Lee.

'Grab her shirt,' said Ade.

Rousing from her stupor, Meri fought against them, flailing out with wild kicks and punches. Ade took a grip on her hair and pushed her under. She came up spluttering, mouth filled with foul water.

'Stop struggling or I'll do that again. We're trying to save you.'

'Like hell you are.' She kicked at Ade and he made good on his promise, pushing her under for longer this time. A third person joined them. He came up under her and got his arm in a chokehold around her throat.

'Give it up, Tean, or we'll drown you right here, right now,' he spat.

Having overpowered her, the three dragged Meri back to the shore. There was no sign of Theo, Valerie or Saddiq, but Kel's sister was there, holding Meri's jacket and running interference with onlookers.

'Yeah, too much to drink. Said she could swim to Big Ben. Don't worry I'll take her home and read my cousin the riot act. Going in the Thames when it's sub zero! Idiot! She could've died!'

Meri stood dripping on the river's edge, flanked by her enemies. Jenny draped the jacket around her shoulders.

'Yes, she's all right. Thanks for asking.' The crowd began to disperse. Jenny lowered her voice. 'You really shouldn't have panicked. I told Kel someone could get hurt if you weren't picked up quietly.'

Meri couldn't speak. It was like she was crumbling from inside. She looked around but couldn't see him.

A minibus drove up, Swanny at the wheel.

'Get in quickly,' he ordered. 'Ade, there's an emergency blanket behind my seat. Use it before you catch your death.'

Pushed from behind, Meri was forced into the vehicle, penned in her own seat in the middle row. Ade sat in front and shook out a foil wrap.

'I'm OK. Was only in for a minute or two. You need it, Lee?'

'I'm fine. You keep it, sir.'

'Tiber?'

'I'm OK, Ade.'

'Meri, do you want it?' He held it out to her.

She couldn't believe he dared to call her that. 'What have you done to Theo?'

He dropped his hand and let the blanket drape over his

legs. 'Nothing. Mr Woolf and his friends were stopped from following you, that's all.'

'Don't lie to me! That's not all. He'd be phoning the police right now, you'd be arrested for kidnap, so don't tell me you didn't do something to him!'

Ade shrugged. 'OK, we told him that if he involved the police that he'd never see you again. I've got some guys babysitting him. Do you believe me now?'

Turning to face the window, she stared at her reflection. 'I won't believe anything you tell me.'

'Take the blanket, Meri.'

'I'm not taking anything from you.'

'Suit yourself.' He wrapped it round his shoulders. 'OK, gang, let's head home.'

14

M eri found it ironic that they'd chosen to lock her up with the one person in the house she didn't resent. The dojo had been swiftly converted to a guest room, weapons removed of course, but they had left U-Can standing in his corner. He looked on proceedings with what Meri read as disgust. It was a smart move to put her down here: with no windows and a single door out onto a corridor, the options for escape were limited. Perhaps she hadn't misheard after all when she had mistaken it for a dungeon on her first visit?

'You can use the toilet and shower room off the laundry next door,' said Jenny, putting a stack of dry clothes on the camp bed. She left the present from Theo next to it having already frisked Meri's jacket and opened it to check the contents. 'You're free to walk around on this level but the doors leading down here will be locked, so don't waste your time trying them. When you get changed, the only place without a camera is the shower so make use of it if you want some privacy.'

Meri hung her jacket on U-Can. 'Where's your brother?'

'He wants to give you time to calm down before he sees you. It's really the best thing, bringing you in like this—you need to think about that. It would've only got worse the longer you were on the run. Kel really does care for you and, though it might not seem like it, he did what he thought was the kindest thing by handing you over tonight.'

'This is kind?'

'You're not dead, are you? That is the usual policy when it comes to Teans.'

After Jenny left, Meri was almost too exhausted to strip off her damp clothes. Only the thought of waking up still stinking of Thames mud made her go into the shower and stand under the hot jets. She let them pummel her back, washing dirt and tears down the drain. Finally, the water started running cool so she dried off and put on the t-shirt and drawstring pyjama trousers Jenny had found her. They were far too big. Rolling up the bottoms, she walked barefoot back to her prison. She stared at the black camera in the middle of the ceiling, red light winking. After the grief she had felt in the shower, fury roared in like an express train. No way would she be able to sleep knowing they were watching. She wasn't sure if she believed Jenny about Kel but how else had they found out about her secret meeting with Theo? Her guardian would never have said anything. It didn't add up—unless she believed Kel had changed his mind and decided to let them bring her in. If he had, she wasn't sure she would ever get past his betrayal.

She paced the room, trying to make sense of her swift change of fortune. One minute she'd been marvelling at fireworks, the next fighting for her life. Had Kel done that to her?

God, had he?

She wasn't giving up on him, not until she had proof, and she certainly wasn't going to start the new year despairing of her chance of escape. An opportunity surely had to come if she were patient? Moping was not the answer.

Snatching up the present, she ripped off the paper. A gold chain with a crystal droplet fell into her hand. Holding it up to the light, it cast a rainbow on the floor—all the colours of the spectrum only she could see.

'Oh, Theo.' He always knew what she would like, how to make her feel special. She had to get out not only for her sake but to check her foster dad was safe.

Meri put on the necklace and then prowled her cell, examining every corner. As her futile attempt to escape had shown, she was well behind on self-defence techniques. If she'd managed to land one good kick or punch she might've made it to a boat and not be in this situation.

She picked up the droid's manual which had been left on a shelf. 'OK, U-Can: let's see what you can teach me.' Pressing the red button, she walked the droid out of his corner. 'I'm gonna imagine you're one of those lot upstairs. Get ready to rumble.'

ADE BROUGHT Meri breakfast in the morning. He was accompanied by Lee and Swanny who looked far less comfortable in her presence than the boss. Swanny had his fingers resting on the trigger of a taser clipped to his belt.

A pleasant morning wake up call then, she thought with grim humour.

'I've been told you haven't slept.' Ade put the tray on the

weights bench. Meri didn't move from her hiding place in the corner behind U-Can. She'd worked out that it was the only spot in the room that meant that the camera couldn't see her clearly.

'You can force me in here but you can't force me to sleep.' Muscles ached after her long work out with the droid, her knuckles skinned.

'True, but you'll need to be rested for the trial.'

'What trial?'

'I promised Kel we'd give you one. I guess trial's the wrong word—more like a hearing.'

'No, I think trial was probably the right word for what you've got in mind. You're not really interested in hearing anything, are you?'

'It'll be in a couple of days when our leader can get here. He wants to decide your case in person.'

'And I suppose he's a qualified judge and you're going to give me legal representation?'

'He's not a judge, Meri. He's our king.'

'I don't have a king.'

'King of the Perilous. His word is law around here.'

'So not a real court of law then. I think the word you're searching for this time is kangaroo—as in kangaroo court. I don't recognize that you have any right or any power over me.'

Ade's foot was tapping in irritation. Point to her. 'We know that, but it's irrelevant. The concession to give you a hearing isn't for you—Tean rights aren't high on our agenda —but for those among us who want to see that we're playing fair.'

'Like Kel.'

'Yeah, like him.'

'Why isn't he bringing me breakfast? I've made it for him often enough.'

Ade exchanged a glance with Swanny. Interesting: there were some things they didn't know.

'He's had to go out this morning,' said Swanny.

'Of course he has. Or he's not staying with you at all and you're lying about him knowing about me being here, trying to break me down.'

Ade shook his head. 'Eat your breakfast and get some sleep.'

'I think I can make my own decisions, thank you.'

'Meri, don't do anything stupid like not eating just to spite us. None of us want you to suffer.'

She thumped the back of her head against the wall. 'You actually believe that don't you, Ade? Just get out. You've made this a prison, but it's my prison now so I get to say what visitors come through that door. I don't want to see any of you again.'

'You're hardly in the position to call the shots,' muttered Lee.

Meri shot out of her corner and advanced, hand stretched out, pointing at him. 'No?'

'Get away from me!' Lee moved into a fighting stance, arm raised to block any touch from her.

Meri stopped in the centre of the room and covered her face with both hands, shoulders shaking with a mixture of laughter and sobs. 'You're actually scared of me. Wow, I didn't get it, did I? This is all about the fact that you hate that you're terrified; it's not about me being a Tean at all.' She tested the theory by taking a step towards Swanny. He too flinched back. 'OK, I won't touch any of you. Just do me the favour of staying the hell out of my way.' Grabbing a blanket off the bed, she stalked back to her corner and curled up behind the droid.

'Fine, Meri. We'll leave you alone for now. Eat your breakfast. Please.' Ade ushered the others out then shut the door behind him.

KEL WONDERED where everyone was when he returned to school a few days into the New Year. No Ade, no Lee. Normally, he would welcome the break from having their eyes on him in every lesson they shared, but to find both of them away just didn't feel right.

In Art, he made his way across the classroom to Sadie. She'd started on a new project, a canvas splashed with angry reds and blacks like a massacre of crows.

'Hi, Sadie. How was New Year?'

She grimaced. 'Total systems crash. You?'

'Quiet. Made some money babysitting for some people in my place.'

'At least you did something. I just sat at home watching TV with my parents. Saw the fireworks at Buckingham Palace—looked amazing but I was stuck inside. Can't believe I was so lame as to let Lee spoil my night.'

Kel had been hoping she'd mention her boyfriend and here was the opening he'd wished for. 'What did he do?'

'Stood me up at the last moment, didn't he, the prick.'

'Did he say why?'

'No, nothing. Just that he had some business to deal with. Who has business on New Year's Eve for microchip's sake?'

A horrible suspicion wormed its way into Kel's mind. 'You didn't tell him what you did for Meri, did you?'

His heart sank. She was looking away, trying to appear innocent. 'Sorry, that doesn't compute.'

'Look, Sadie, I lied to you about seeing Meri because we were at Ade's. I have been with her, for a couple of days actually last week. We ran into each other in town. She told me you set up secure comms to Theo.'

'So what if I did? It's not illegal, well not completely, just a little into the grey area of Homeland Security's dos and don'ts on encryption.'

'I'm not criticising you. That was kind of you and really important to her. But I need to know if you told Lee.'

'Why would it matter?'

'Because Meri would've told you she had enemies.'

'Yeah, she did.'

'What she didn't mention, I'm guessing, is that they are much closer to home than she let on.'

'You mean that comp virus Lee was hacking me for information all this time? That's why he hasn't returned my calls and texts, the sodding unnecessary system update of a fecking boyfriend!' A few more crows died in horrible splashes of red.

He had to give her top marks for her cursing. 'So you told him?'

'Yeah, and I even showed him how to do it! I was boasting, Gates forgive me. Wanted to impress him.'

'I'm sure you impressed him.'

'I want to kill him! Take a fecking hammer to his hard drive.' Sadie kicked over her chair. 'What can I do? Can we warn Meri?'

Miss Hardcastle bustled over and pointed to the chair. 'This isn't the kind of behaviour I expect in the classroom, Sadie.'

'I feel sick!' Sadie rushed from the room, palm clamped in front of her mouth.

'Oh, well, in that case.' Mrs Hardcastle put her hands on her hips.

Kel picked up the chair. 'I'll go check she's OK.'

'She's probably in a bathroom. I can send another girl to find her.'

'It's fine. I'll sort it out.'

Grabbing his bag as well as Sadie's, Kel strode out into the corridor. He found Sadie alternating between hyperventilating and kicking the pot belonging to the school olive tree, centrepiece in the mindfulness garden.

'Here.' He put her satchel down on the wall.

'I can't believe I was so stupid! Such an analogue brain!'

'If it's any consolation, I imagine Lee does like you. If he has a type, you're it. But it's just that he also worked out you were a way to find Meri. I guess he got clued in to that by our conversation on Christmas Eve. You realize he was listening?'

'Can we get to her before he does?'

Kel sat on the wall, rubbing a sprig of rosemary between his fingers as he pieced the sequence of events together. Lee stood Sadie up on New Year's Eve. Meri's plans, on Kel's suggestion, had been to meet up with Theo in the crowds watching the fireworks. He wished he hadn't proposed it as it made her vulnerable. If Lee had moved quickly, he could've got into the messages between them. But had there been time?

'We need to talk to Theo. He'll know what's going on. Can you make his comms safe again?'

'Yeah, I can change the code. I can make any microchip-sucking hacker feel like his balls have been fried by my firewalls by the time I've finished putting up defences.'

'OK, you stay here and do that. I'll go round to Theo's flat and see if he's OK. Text me when it's safe to use the email again.'

'I'll go to the cyber cafe then and do it now.' Sadie hugged her bag to her chest. 'I've messed up, haven't I, Kel?'

Yes, probably. 'Sadie, there's no point feeling guilty about an honest mistake. Let's get this sorted. One last thing: can you send a message to a man called Big Ben: he owns an internet cafe over at St Katharine's Dock?'

'Sure. Nothing easier. What do you want me to say?'

'Tell him that things have taken a colourful turn for the worse and that Meri might need a quick way out of London. We'll be in touch.'

KEL ARRIVED outside Theo's flat and rang the bell. No answer. It was possible of course that he was at work. Not able to leave it at that, Kel rang the bell for downstairs. The intercom buzzed.

'To whom am I speaking?'

'Oh, hello. I'm a friend of Meri. I was wondering if you've seen Theo?'

'Come on in, dear boy, come on in.'

The door buzzed and Kel entered the familiar hallway. A door at the back opened and a man with sparse white hair, dressed in a navy silk dressing gown and black slippers, appeared in the entrance.

'Forgive my state of deshabille. Sloppy habits of the retired,' he boomed in his ripe tones.

Kel remembered Meri once mentioning the former opera singer who owned the house and had kept the flat downstairs. 'Mr Kingsley?'

'That's right. Have you heard of me?' His old face was wreathed now in a delighted smile.

'From Meri.'

'Oh.' The light dimmed a little.

'She said you were an amazing tenor in your time.'

His expression brightened. 'That is so sweet of her. She was kind enough to listen to a few of my recordings from my prime. Come on back if you don't mind a little mess.'

'A little' was an understatement. Mr Kingsley's flat was stuffed with musical memorabilia starting in the 1970s and coming right up to date: framed posters, old vinyl records, tapes, video cassettes, CDs and DVDs as well as the antique machinery required to play them. Kel squeezed his way along the packed corridor and into the sitting room with French windows leading out to the pretty snow-covered garden at the rear. A King Charles spaniel sat curled up on a red velvet cushion on the sofa. She raised her head with the merest hint of interest before settling down to the more important business of sleeping. A record player softly poured out a delicious soprano duet from some opera Kel thought he should probably recognize if only from its use in advertising but admitting that was not going to make friends here.

'So you're after Theo?' asked Mr Kingsley, moving a stack of music so Kel could sit next to the dog.

'That's right. Have you seen him?'

'Not since New Year's Eve. He went out with Valerie and Saddiq but I didn't hear them come back. They normally knock on my door and we share a wee dram in the small hours, but not this year. To tell you the truth, I was a little hurt but now I'm starting to worry.'

'Have you tried calling him?'

'Of course. Theo would never leave his flat this long

without asking me to water his plants. He loves his herbs. I could only think of one explanation. I thought that perhaps he'd gone on the spur of the moment to see Meri, try for a reconciliation. It broke his heart when she upped and left so suddenly.'

'She didn't leave by choice.'

Mr Kingsley sat down in his armchair by the record player. 'No, I suppose she didn't. It's not like her to worry him like that. Do you think I should report his disappearance to the police?'

'I don't know, sir.' Kel sat forward, hands clasped between his knees. 'I'm going to try some other people I know, see if they have some answers. If I don't come back, or if Theo doesn't return by the end of tomorrow, maybe you should give the police a ring?' Kel decided his loyalty to the Perilous didn't go so far as to protect them when they had overstepped to interfere with good people like Theo and his friends.

'I believe you might be right. And who are you again, young man?'

'I don't think I introduced myself. I'm Kel Douglas. I'm Meri's boyfriend.'

'I'm so pleased she has a young man of her own. She's such a lovely girl. Well, thank you for calling round. Charlotte and I were going a little mad trying to work out what to do.' The dog looked up at the mention of her name then settled back with a grumble. 'Even *Duettino Sull'aria* isn't helping and *The Marriage of Figaro* has never failed us before.'

'I'd better be going. I'm sorry if you're worried.'

'Not your fault, dear boy.'

Kel wasn't so sure of that. He feared that his brief

appearance at the Christmas party might have started the firing pistol for this new round of disasters.

THERE WERE AN UNUSUALLY large number of cars parked in the drive and on the street outside Ade's house. The drunk Santa had been removed, though the strings of lights remained, suggesting that the inhabitants were on their best behaviour. Kel didn't bother pressing the gate buzzer but tapped in his old code. Good: they hadn't yet got round to changing it. Not sure exactly what he was facing, he walked quickly down the path as if he had every right to be there and used his old key to get in. The foyer was empty but he could hear voices in the club-room. Had they brought Theo here? Were they trying to force him to tell them where Meri could be found? Determined to get Theo out if he was indeed in there, Kel slipped inside.

And into his nightmare.

The place was packed, standing room only at the back, windows misting up. Most of the furniture had been cleared apart from a table at the far end under the wall screen at which sat Osun, Kel's father, Swanny and Ade. Jenny stood to one side behind Ade's cousin from Amsterdam, the member of the royal family she usually guarded. In fact, from a quick scan of the room, almost all the Perilous royals were present, something that rarely happened outside the annual reunion. On her own in the middle of all this sat Meri. Tiber and Lee flanked her, with tasers drawn and every indication in their expression that they were prepared to use them if she made a wrong move.

Kel was too late, way behind the game. They'd got to her already.

'We've heard from the witnesses.' Osun appeared to be

winding up the case for the prosecution. 'This young woman does show the characteristics of a Tean; and her family history, such as we've been able to piece together, suggests she's the girl who disappeared in the attack at Mount Vernon. That ties up that loose end. Are we agreed? Please raise your hands if you believe she's Tean.'

Every single hand apart from Kel's and Meri's went up.

'Then we progress to the main item on our agenda and that is what to do with her. Meredith Marlowe, do you have anything you wish to say at this point?'

Meri ignored him, staring over his head at the blank screen, fingering a crystal on a chain. It sent rainbows across the room, flickering over faces. Kel shifted along the wall to catch a glimpse of her expression and then saw that behind her stood U-Can, sneering at the proceedings. So she had brought a friend with her after all.

'Meri, now would be a good time to stop the "not listening" act and speak up in your own defence,' said Ade.

She folded her arms, slumping in the chair as if the proceedings bored her. 'There's no point. My legal adviser,' she waved at U-Can, 'will speak on my behalf. The only thing I want to know is what have you done with Kel?'

'Nothing.'

'Then where is he?'

Kel shouldered his way through the onlookers. 'I'm right here.'

'Kelvin, don't approach the prisoner!' warned his father.

'Just try stopping me.' Shoving Lee out of his way, Kel reached Meri and hugged her tightly, determined no one was going to separate them again. 'What are you doing here, darling?'

Her nonchalant act vanished and she gave a single choked sob before controlling herself. She pressed her face against his chest. 'God, I don't know. One minute I was enjoying New Year, the next the crazy gang were kidnapping me. They told me you set me up.'

'Did you believe them?'

'Only for about thirty seconds.'

'Kel, move away from her!' barked his father.

Kel ignored him and shrugged off Lee's attempt to haul him away from Meri by the back of his jacket. 'I didn't know anything about this. Lee got to Sadie.' He glared a warning at Tiber, who had raised his taser. 'Put that down. We're not attacking anyone, are we?'

'Is she OK?' asked Meri, pretending to be oblivious to the consternation around them.

'Just kicking herself. She didn't know she was betraying you. I went looking for Theo.'

'He's not home? Oh, well, that changes things, doesn't it?' Meri lifted her face and turned on Osun and Ade. 'Yes, I have something to say. What have you done with my guardian and his friends?'

Ade stood up. 'They're being kept at a safe location until such time as we reach an agreement with you.'

'You've taken hostages?' Kel was sincerely shocked by that move. 'Who authorized that?'

'I did,' said his father. 'I gave permission to do so in the interests of making this capture run as smoothly as possible. None of us want anyone hurt.'

'I can think of quite a few people I want hurt right now,' murmured Meri.

'Right with you there, darling.'

'Move away from her, Kelvin. You're not helping,' said Rill.

A sickening sensation churned in his gut, part disillusionment with his father, part helpless fury. 'No, Dad, I'm not moving. You seem to have neglected to provide her with any representation so if it's OK with Meri, I'll stand for her.' He stroked the back of her head. 'Is that OK?'

'Oh yes.'

'Right then, let's get this over with.' Kel stood so that she had her back against his front, both facing the table of judges. His mind was working fast to find an angle that would convince them to let her go. He only had one argument he could think of instantly and that was as likely to piss them off as persuade them. Still... 'The Perilous law says that Teans have to be destroyed because they're dangerous to us, correct?'

'No one is talking about destroying her,' said Osun.

'Some of you are thinking it but that's not my point. She's not dangerous and I can prove it.' Kel whipped off his sweater and t-shirt. Spinning a surprised Meri around, he clamped her palms to her chest. 'OK, Meri, do your thing.'

Every Perilous in the room took a shocked breath as he broke one of their most instinctive taboos: skin to skin contact with a Tean.

'Kel, as much as I like you with your top off, this is hardly the place.' Typically, Meri tried to protect him by making it a joke. 'You'd better cover up, Ace.'

'Kel, have you lost your mind!' Jenny took several paces towards him, intending to pull her little brother to safety.

'Stay back, Jenny. If she does hurt me, then I deserve it for stupidity, but I hoped you knew by now that I'm not stupid.'

'This isn't going to prove anything,' said Ade.

'Yeah it will.' Kel smiled down into Meri's green eyes. 'You all may be hacked off with me but I'm guessing that most of you don't want me to be burned to death. I've just handed Meri here the equivalent of a loaded gun. She could use the threat of hurting me to walk out of here with me as her hostage. Seems fair as you've taken three to use against her.'

'We don't know that she has the knowledge of how to use her power to kill you,' said Rill. 'You're bluffing.'

'I'm not and she could. Better than that: she's got it under control and can make my markings appear without harming me. Go on, darling, show them. Make me flare.'

'You sure?' She sank her teeth into her lip.

'They want a show; let's give it to them.'

15

Meri couldn't believe Kel was doing this. The reckless wonderful boy had managed to wrong foot the others and still make the invitation intimate. In fact, she'd felt the whole atmosphere shift the moment she'd seen him, like her own personal thunderstorm crackling and clearing the oppressive heat building up in the room. His courage could only be answered by her own.

'OK, brace yourself.' She pressed her hands flat against his chest, not closing her eyes this time but keeping them locked on the nearest markings so she could judge this to perfection. As ever when she touched him, she was terrified of harming him, afraid of the passion that could so easily flow freely between them, flooding him with too much power. At least with a hostile audience, she felt in less danger this time of forgetting herself. Pushing a little of her power into him, the lines where she was touching lit up first, then spread through the network under his skin.

Several onlookers screamed and Kel's sister cried out: 'Stop her! She's killing him.'

Kel responded by rubbing Meri's shoulder blades. 'No, she's not, Jen. She's showing you how beautiful a Perilous and a Tean can be together. This is how we were always meant to be from the beginning.'

One by one the spirals emerged more brightly on his skin like a chain of beacons taking its signal to burn from the last one in the line.

'That's probably enough,' said Meri. She'd taken it a little further than she had in the barge. It was tricky to keep back her power, like tipping water from a heavy can, so much more wanting to gush out.

'That's good, darling. Hold it there a second.' He stood there, blazing proudly before her judges. 'You can all see I'm not fighting, and I'm certainly not making love in front of you lot, but she's able to bring my markings alive without hurting me. Teans have an amazing gift to give us. As Meri's just showing us all, it doesn't have to be a threat.'

'And if she loses control, if she loses her temper, what then?' asked Kel's father.

'Then I do this.' Meri lifted her hands and stepped back. Kel's markings slowly faded. 'I don't know where you all got the idea I was some kind of murderous bitch out to fry you all.'

'Ah. That is the central point of this hearing, Miss Marlowe. We got that notion from your parents.' Kel's dad stood up. 'If I may, your majesty?'

Osun nodded. 'Go ahead, commander.'

The mood shifted. Kel pulled his top down quickly over his head. 'No, Dad, don't.'

Meri could sense something really bad was about to happen, something that snuffed out her glimmer of hope that their demonstration had swung things her way. 'What's he doing? Kel, what's going on?'

Using his hands as blinkers, Kel tried to turn her face towards him and away from his father. 'Don't watch this, Meri. You don't need to see this.'

She shook him off. 'See what?'

The screen flickered on to a grainy shot of a sunny day some fourteen years ago according to the date/time stamp.

'I was there, you see,' explained Rill. 'So was Kel's mother.' Behind him a fight took place on a riverbank. A man and a woman threw a bundle about the size of a small child into the water then turned to repel their attackers. Each person they touched collapsed in agony, writhing on the ground as their markings burned and smoked. She could feel Kel shudder as one woman went down. Though the footage was poor quality, the pain was all too apparent. Two armed guards appeared. 'That's me—the one on the left. We took out the Teans but not before they killed five of ours, Kel's mother included.' Guns were fired and the couple were both hit, the man twice. Hand flailing to hold hand, they staggered away and over the edge, into the water. They didn't resurface.

Meri felt sick, drained of everything but horror. She had never imagined, never allowed herself to think what those final moments were like. 'You killed my parents.'

'Yes. In self-defence.'

'Don't lie—not to me. You murdered them. I was there. I know what happened. We were just eating ice cream, having a day out, but you chased us—parents carrying a four-year-old child—you hunted us down like exterminators going after rats.' She was shaking so hard she thought she might collapse.

'Meri, please.' Kel tried to hug her but she was too stiff with pain to allow herself to seek comfort. 'Why did you show her that? She didn't have to see.'

'She did, Kelvin. She needs to understand what she represents to us.' Kel's father was relentless, just as he had been that day.

Meri gave a sobbing laugh. 'Why am I here? What can I possibly have to say to you? You think I care now what my parents' murderers think of me? Did you bring me here just so I could agree to my own execution, meaning you could all feel exonerated?'

'Not execution,' corrected Rill. 'A kind of house arrest was what we had in mind.'

She dismissed him. She wanted nothing to do with her parents' murderer. 'Kel, did you know your father was there —that he shot my parents?' she asked. 'That my mum killed your mother?'

'Yes, I did.'

She felt like she was tottering on the edge of a precipice. 'Why didn't you tell me?'

Kel looked desperate, eyes holding great oceans of pain to match hers. 'I don't know. I guess I was afraid what you would think of me.'

'You should've told me.'

'I'm so sorry.'

'Do you agree with your father? Do you think I should agree to house arrest?' *Please say no.*

'Absolutely not.'

'OK, OK.' With his support, Meri felt she could breathe again. 'Then there's at least one decent Perilous left. Commander Douglas, I'm not walking into your prison. I've done nothing to deserve that, whereas you—I can't believe I'm having to say this—you killed my entire family. If there's any justice here and if anyone gets locked away, it should be you.'

'You won't accept house arrest?' asked Rill.

'No.' Beside her, Kel sucked in a breath.

'So you're forcing us to more extreme measures?' Rill looked to their so-called King Osun who was sitting grim-faced beside him.

'I'm not forcing you to anything. You are choosing your own path. Me, I'm walking out. I've broken no law of this land and I don't recognize your court. What you do to stop me is on your conscience.'

Osun cleared his throat. 'And what about your guardian? Don't you care what happens to him and his friends.'

Meri's voice cracked a little. 'Don't you dare—don't you dare act as if it's my fault what you do. Of course I care but I can't stop you. I'm trusting that your hatred only goes as far as a Tean, not three ordinary people who don't even know what this is about.'

'If you cooperate, then they have nothing to fear.'

'If I cooperate I might as well be dead and none of them would forgive me for that.'

Ade rubbed his forehead wearily. 'Meri—'

'Meredith.' She was damned if she was going to let Ade use her nickname. He had no right to that now.

Ade gave a humourless smile. 'Miss Marlowe then, if we're getting so formal. Please, you have to think about Kel. You are forcing him to choose between his family and you by taking this stance.'

'He's wrong, Meri. This isn't about me,' said Kel.

'If you enter into an agreement with us, you'll still be able to see him—we can sort something out.'

That was cruel: holding out the one thing that could tempt her to compromise. Meri looked round the room, not a friendly face in sight bar the one beside her. 'I need to think. Give us a moment, will you? I need to talk to Kel.' She waited until Lee and Tiber moved a little further away before pulling Kel's head so his ear was at the level of her mouth. 'How do we get out of this?'

'I'm relieved you're not insulting me by considering sacrificing yourself on my behalf.' Kel caressed her cheek and shook his head, giving the onlookers the impression they were arguing about what to do. 'Weak points in the room, the windows and the door at the far end. All exit to rear garden. Remember, the people standing behind members of Ade's family are bodyguards, trained like me, so we have to avoid them. And we have to make sure Tiber and Lee don't get a clear shot with the tasers.'

'Understood.' She nestled into his chest. 'I guess that window is much closer. Throw my chair through it and we can jump.'

'Then run straight to the far lefthand corner past the tennis court. There's an old shed there. I'll boost you onto the roof and we can get over the wall.'

'And then?'

'Run like the wind.'

She lifted her head and cradled his face in her hands. 'What are our chances?'

'Fair.'

'That means appalling, doesn't it?'

'Cynic.'

'Yeah, that's me.' Smiling despite the situation, Meri could feel her old self reasserting its presence after the shock of the footage showing her parents' execution.

'It's a plan.' Kel frowned, gaze searching the room for inspiration. 'But first we're going to need one heck of a distraction.'

'I've got that covered.' She surreptitiously took the remote for U-Can out of her pocket. 'I had time on my hands so I read the manual and made some adjustments. Me big red button; you chair, OK?'

He kissed her. 'Oh yeah, baby.'

They stepped apart, grinning like reckless fools. God, she loved him so much.

'So, have you agreed?' asked Ade. 'You'll go into house arrest for Kel's sake?'

'Kel and I always agree as we want what's best for the other.' Meri moved to the far side of U-Can as Kel edged behind her chair. 'After careful consideration, our decision is this: we're going into...freestyle!' Pressing the remote, Meri ducked. U-Can began to spin and starfish in quick succession, whirling through the room in unpredictable circles.

'What the—!' exclaimed Ade as people began diving out of the way.

Kel heaved the chair through the window and jumped after it, Meri a fraction of second behind him. He cleared like a champion hurdler while she stumbled and went down on her hands, cutting her palms on shattered glass. Even so, she was up and running before she even registered the pain. Taking cover in the bushes at the rear of the garden, she found Kel crouched to give her a lift. Using his hand as a stirrup she let him boost her up on the shed roof. Tarred roof ground against her cuts but she bit her cheek and held out a hand to help Kel. No need: he managed to spring and grab the edge of the roof, hauling himself up by his own muscle power.

'Go!' he gasped.

Meri slid down the other side of the apex and carried on over the ivy covered wall. Her ankles felt the shock as she hit the ground. They had emerged into an alley that gave access to the backs of the mansions for garden services and rubbish collectors.

'This way.' Kel grabbed her wrist, mindful not to press her cuts. 'The Common.'

That was a good idea: so much cover, so many exit points. Even if every Perilous from that room was searching for them, they still had a chance of escape. They ran down the alley, cut over the next street and took the first passageway that led towards the Common.

Kel suddenly threw himself down, dragging her with him, using the cover of a holly bush. Two cars streaked by.

'Up!' Kel pulled her to her feet and they started running again across the frozen ground. Thanks to the popularity of this area with joggers and dog walkers, their footprints were lost among many, leaving behind no easy way to track them through the churned snow. This time they didn't stop until they were far into the Common and in a thickly wooded area.

'OK, breather,' said Kel.

Meri rested her hands on her knees, bent over, panting. 'I really shouldn't have cut P.E. for so many years.'

'Hands?' Kel checked her cuts. 'We need to get to a chemist. Get something for those.'

'Let's get away first. You have a plan?'

'Kind of making it up as I go along but I'm thinking we should keep to open ground. If we head north-west, we can go through Richmond Park to the Thames. I don't think anyone will expect us to go that way. We can get to the river and take a water bus downstream—that's going to be the most difficult part as they'll be watching public transport.'

'Is your phone on?'

'Shit.' He dug it out of his pocket and was about to turn it off but Meri stopped him.

'It's too late. Leave it on and wait a moment.' Meri looked for possibilities, dismissing the mother pushing a baby along in a pram. Not fair to involve them. Turning the other way, she saw that they were on the verge of a golf course, a wide strip had been cleared of snow to allow the really keen golfers to practice. A man was having trouble getting his ball out of the rough, his bag of clubs standing a little way off. Taking the phone off Kel she sauntered over and dropped it into the top.

'Get away from my clubs!' barked the man, hurrying over to save his prized bag.

Meri held up empty hands. 'Keep your hair on—just looking.'

'Well don't. Scram. This course isn't open to the public.'

'Excuse me for breathing.' With a flounce, Meri turned her back and walked into the trees. The golfer headed off in the opposite direction, dragging his trolley behind him like an unwilling dog on a short lead.

'Good thought,' said Kel, 'except neither of us has a phone now.'

Meri imagined what would happen when the Perilous converged on the man on the fairway or back at the club house. With a temper like that, the golfer would probably call the police and his lawyers if anyone tried to empty his bag. She just hoped it would tie up Ade and the others for precious minutes. 'Too risky to keep a mobile. The moment you switch it on someone can track you. Let's get away from here before they work out what we did.'

Kel helped her over the fence surrounding the golf course. 'It feels very 1980s to have no phone.' Kel took off his jacket and draped it over her shoulders.

She huddled down, grateful for the extra warmth. She'd escaped in the clothes they'd lent her, baggy tracksuit trousers and hoodie: not enough layers for a freezing January. 'Welcome to how our grandparents used to live.'

'Weird.' He danced on the spot to keep warm. 'How will we know which way to go without the map app?'

'I guess we'll have to be radical and look at the sign-posts.' She tried to hand him back his coat but he refused.

'I'll only keep it for a little while until you get cold,' she said.

'I won't get cold. I'm buzzing with adrenaline.'

Walking swiftly rather than running, they kept going north-west on the Common, cautiously crossed a main road on an overhead walkway, and entered Richmond Park through one of the ornate black gates with the royal crown. The first things Meri noticed inside the park was the tent city of homeless people stretched down an old avenue of oak trees. People were warming themselves around braziers and cooking over open fires. A Salvation Army van was handing out blankets.

'Why don't you get one of those?' suggested Meri.

Kel joined the queue and snagged a brown checked rug that, with a quick stab of a penknife borrowed off one of the tent dwellers, he put over his head like poncho.

'I don't want to speak too soon, but I can't see anyone following us,' said Meri. 'Do you think it'd be OK if I stopped for a moment at the shower block and washed my hands?'

'I think we can risk that.' Kel pulled up the hood to the sweater she was wearing. 'But you need to understand that the Perilous have connections in law enforcement. They'll be getting the CCTV feed and any drone coverage so we've still got to move quickly.'

'Got it. Just a quick wash then.'

Meri felt much better having cleaned the dirt from the cuts. They had stopped bleeding so they couldn't be very deep. If anything, her ankles hurt more from the jolt of her bad landing off the wall. If getting out of tight spots was going to become a habit, she'd have to put serious work into her escape techniques.

When she came out, Kel had a cup of soup waiting for her, also thanks to the Salvation Army. For himself, he'd got a woolly hat from somewhere which he wore pulled down over his ears. He looked very adorable like that but this probably wasn't the right moment to mention it.

'When I get somewhere safe, I'll have to send the Sally Army a donation,' said Meri, taking a cautious sip of the vegetable broth. 'OK, Ace, where next?'

'What's with the ace?' he asked, drinking from his own paper cup.

'Well, I figured it fitted as you were my ace in the hole back there at Ade's house. I don't think I could've sprung myself out of that room.'

'Not even with U-Can?'

'I'd've given it a go, but I think I wouldn't have got as far as the window.'

He smiled. 'Not even with freestyle?'

'Pretty cool, wasn't it? You really should read the manual, Kel.'

'I promise you, next time I will.'

They started walking further into the park, no longer feeling the desperate hurry to flee. The more casual they looked the less attention they would attract.

Now she had time, Meri let the confusing whirl of impressions from the trial land like a flock of starlings coming to roost for the evening. 'I'm sorry about your family. I didn't want you to have to choose between us.'

'You had it right, Meri: it's not you forcing me to do so; it's them with their stubbornly old-fashioned view of the world.'

'They might come round one day.'

'Maybe, maybe not. The ball is in their court, isn't it? I'm sorry about, well, you know, what my father did.'

Meri threw her empty cup into a recycling bin. 'I'm not sure what I think about that yet but I know it's not your fault.'

'Still, it's a horrible connection: my father, your father. And your mother, my mother.'

'Let's shelve it for now and work out how to make it out of London alive.'

He put an arm around her shoulders. 'Sadie will've sent a message to Big Ben by now. I asked her to do so because I was thinking the barge people were your best bet for getting out of London.'

'Yours too. You can't stay here now either.'

'The Tean sympathizers didn't seem so keen on helping me. If it's a deal breaker, you have to go alone.'

'Uh-uh, no way. Together or not at all.'

Kel was avoiding her eyes. 'We'll see. Let's get to them first. Have you got any money?'

'No, nothing. They took my stuff including my ID when they caught me. Emma Boot is no more.'

'So they know who you were pretending to be and can track you in the eco-service. That means the hostel is no longer safe.'

Meri sighed. 'Yes, I guess so. I made good friends there.'

'I'm sorry.'

She slipped her arm around his waist. 'You don't need to keep saying that. I know you are. I'm not so much sorry myself as monumentally pissed off.'

'Me too now you come to mention it.'

'They won't hurt Theo will they?'

'With you out of the picture? I'd say not. They only took

him as leverage. If you're no longer here then it's a useless lever and they'll free him. I've got the downstairs guy cued to phone the police tomorrow if not.'

'Mr Kingsley? That's sweet of him.'

'He'll follow through, I'm sure.'

'I can't imagine Theo and friends making very cooperative hostages.' Meri tried to persuade herself they'd be fine. 'They'll get out one way or another.'

Meri was beginning to feel tired. The adrenaline of escape had passed and her body was beginning to crash. 'I'm sorry to be a wimp but can we have a rest? Once we leave the park, it might be easier to travel across the city after dark.'

'You're no wimp. It's a good idea. It's two now so it'll be dark in a couple of hours. Let's look for a spot where we can keep warm and see if anyone is approaching.' He turned a slow circle. 'What do you feel about that clump of trees over there?'

'The one near the deer? Fine by me.'

'Clear ground around it. Once the deer get used to us they'll react to any newcomers and give us warning. If the Perilous bring dogs, it will confuse the scent.'

'Dogs? Crap. I hadn't considered that.'

'Yeah well, you've never been the quarry in a manhunt before, have you?'

'Actually, that's the story of my life, Kel. It's just never had a chapter involving bloodhounds.'

They crossed the open grassland between them and the trees. The deer lifted their heads and ran a short way, but not putting much effort into it. Once Kel and Meri were settled by the foot of a fallen tree, the herd drifted back, heads lowered for the more important business of nosing out grass from under the snow.

'It's pretty here,' said Meri, sitting with her back to Kel's chest. They were sharing the warmth of poncho and coat. 'You could imagine Henry the Eighth and his courtiers ride over the hill there on a deer hunt, feathers in caps and velvet cloaks flapping.'

'That's if you ignore the vapour trails from the planes headed for Heathrow and the roar of the traffic.'

She squeezed his knee. 'Imagination, Kel. You blank those things out.'

'I think the deer prefer things as they are now. Protected, not chased to their death.'

'I know how they feel.'

He kissed the rim of her ear in sympathy, then stiffened. 'Keep still, darling.'

Obligingly, Meri froze. A black dot had appeared over-head. Not a bird of prey but a police surveillance drone doing a sweep of the park. 'Good job this poncho is brown.'

'I don't think it can spot us unless it's got infrared. Even then, the deer are our friends as the drone might just think we are part of the herd hunkered down here.'

It buzzed twice overhead before carrying on towards the west.

'Should we move?' asked Meri.

'I think your idea of doing the next stage after dark is a good one.'

'And if the drone spotted us?'

'I don't think it did but I'll keep watch. We'll have plenty of warning of anyone approaching. You have a rest—sleep if you can.'

And oddly enough, she did. Burrowed into the circle made by Kel's arms around her, she felt safe enough to let go and sleep more soundly than she had managed whilst stuck down in Ade's basement.

It seemed only five minutes had passed when Kel shook her gently awake.

'Sorry, darling, but we'd better get moving if we don't want to climb the gates. They close them at dusk.'

She yawned and stretched. 'Any sign of the drone?' The deer now moved like ghosts of themselves across the greying field.

'No, it's been very peaceful. Apart from your snoring, of course.'

'I don't snore—do I?'

'You kind of whiffle and mutter.'

'Great.'

'It's sweet.'

'I'm glad you think so.' She got up and turned to pull Kel to his feet.

'I think my legs have gone dead. I didn't dare move and wake Sleeping Beauty.' He shook them vigorously.

'Thank you for letting me rest. I hadn't been sleeping well since I was caught. They kept a camera on me twenty four seven.'

Moving quickly now, they made it to the gates as the park warden was closing them.

'Cut that a bit fine, didn't you?' the lady asked, padlocking the exit.

'Are we the last?' asked Kel.

'I should certainly hope so. Just turned away a bunch of people looking for a lost dog—very insistent they had to go in, they were. I told them that they'd have to come back tomorrow. Rules are rules.'

That didn't sound good.

'Oh? Did you see which way they went?'

'Have you seen their dog then?'

'Might've. I think it got through the boundary along

there.' Kel pointed to the east. 'Probably making its own way home.'

'That's usually the case: dogs have more sense than their owners. Still, if you've a mind to be helpful, the people went towards Richmond town centre. If you hurry you'll be able to catch up with them. There was a woman and two young men of about your age. She was wearing a red coat, but I don't remember how the others were dressed.'

'Thanks. We'll go and look for them.'

Once they were out of earshot, Kel said: 'My sister has a red coat.'

'Yeah, I remember. She was wearing it at New Year.'

'It might not be her.'

'But it might.'

'They'll have to spread themselves quite thinly to search all the areas we might've reached by now. And stopping for a rest has probably upset their calculations.'

'You mean they might think we are further on than we are?'

'Exactly.'

'So what do we do?'

'Jenny knows I usually travel on the Underground. I think they'll go there first, maybe even leave someone to watch the station. We should try the river bus.'

'Right. And where do we catch that?'

'By the bridge.'

Making their way through suburban streets rather than taking the more direct route along the main roads, they reached Richmond bridge without incident. The houses on the far side were dark, abandoned to the frequent flooding on this bend of the north bank. An impromptu settlement of houseboats had sprung up in what used to be the back gardens of the terraced streets. On the south bank a busy river bus stop flourished, this time of day at the height of its business of ferrying school children home and returning workers from the city downstream.

Kel rubbed at the back of his neck, uneasy. 'I don't know what's triggering them, but my instincts are going crazy. I think we should watch for a while, see if there is anyone on lookout.'

'Bus shelter?'

They took cover in the shelter for the road bus service, balancing on the revolving perches put in there in place of proper seats to deter the homeless. Being without a home herself, that struck Meri as an unnecessary cruelty. What harm would it do to give someone a bed off the ground for the night? She and Kel might need one later.

The line of uniformed children spooled like maroon thread onto the bobbin, embarking on the boat going upstream. The boat tooted that it was departing and engines revved. Once that had cleared, they had a better view of the stubby water bus pier. A few people were queuing for the boat that would take them into the city centre, the service that Kel and Meri would catch if judged safe.

'It looks OK. There's no one I recognize,' said Kel.

'I don't know if your nerves are affecting me, but now I'm not sure,' admitted Meri. 'Can we go a bit closer?'

'Let's go singly, me first, then you. If anyone is watching, they'll be looking hardest at couples.' He dug in his pocket. 'Here's some money for your fare.'

'Thanks. Be careful.'

Kel sauntered towards the ticket office. The attendant, a smiley woman with short grey hair, was standing outside chatting with her regulars. Kel struck up a conversation as he bought a ticket. Fingers cold, he dropped a couple of coins as he tried to give her the exact change and they both reached down to get them. That was when Meri saw the ticket attendant's arm above the wrist.

Don't panic. Play it cool, she told herself.

Jogging up to Kel, Meri tapped him on the shoulder, trying to keep out of view of the woman. 'Hey, Bernard, you forgot your dental appointment, you dope.'

'What? Oh, yeah.'

'Mum sent me to catch up with you. You'll have to take a later service.'

'Right, OK. See you later.' Kel pocketed the ticket and followed Meri off the wooden planks of the pier to the pavement. 'What was that about?'

'She's one of you.' Meri kept walking, hood pulled forward as far as it would go. 'Not sure which, maybe a leaf, but definitely Perilous markings above the wrist.'

Kel swore. 'Do you think she was on the lookout for us?'

'I don't know. She didn't seem to recognize you, her markings weren't flaring. You would know your procedures better than me.'

'There's an alert process that gets rolled out by text but she might not have checked that if she's been at work all afternoon. Still, someone might think to get in touch and ask her if she's seen us if we appear to have shaken them.'

'We can't go back there.'

'No, too risky.'

In agreement, they carried on over the bridge. The water bus that they had intended to catch pulled up at the pier and then beetled off down the river. No point regretting such an easy exit, thought Meri. Nothing about running from the Perilous was destined to be easy.

Reaching the north bank, Meri's eye was caught by the encampment of houseboats. 'I wonder....'

'You wonder what?'

'Francis Frobisher said the river people were often Tean Sympathizers. Let's look for signs of peril.'

Kel smiled at the pun. 'That's us: go looking for danger. But seeing peril is your deal, Meri, rather than mine. I'll watch your back.'

They turned off the main road and into the improvised marina. Where the road dipped below river level, wooden boards had been laid together to make a snaking pathway, narrow and in places slippy with silt. Homemade signs announced they were entering the Boat People's Community of Cambridge Gardens. Venture on at own risk. The sign ended with a stick man dropping into the river with a splash.

'Not exactly encouraging visitors, are they?' muttered Meri. Rounding one large rusty iron boat, an ancient coal barge by the looks of it, she found what she had been searching for: a Thames pleasure craft converted into a houseboat, peril-coloured stained glass in the windows. If there had been more light, she guessed that the bunting stretching from stem to stern was the same colour but for now it flapped a dull grey in the darkness. 'I think this is it: the Tean sympathizers headquarters in this community.'

Kel didn't waste time asking if she was sure. 'You'd best go first. Experience suggests they won't take kindly to me.'

Meri approached the gangway unclear of the protocol of making a call on a boat. 'Hello? Anyone home?'

A radio burbled inside, local news reporting an altercation at the golf club on Wimbledon Common. The DJ was cracking a joke about a man who had been arrested for taking a swipe with a nine iron at a foreign visitor in a misunderstanding about a set of clubs.

'Try again,' urged Kel.

Meri got a little bolder, going up the gangway and

tapping on the folding doors that led into the main cabin of the houseboat. The radio shut off and after a longish pause an elderly lady appeared in the doorway, dressed in a flowered overall and suede slippers, hair like a scanty serving of white candy-floss.

'No, thank you,' she said smartly, shutting the door again.

Meri rapped again, determined not to be turned away without a proper conversation. 'Please, we don't want to sell you anything. Tea and Sympathy: does this mean anything to you?'

The woman cracked the door open and peeked out. 'Who are you? What do you want?'

'We need help. I can see peril in your stained glass.'

The woman sucked in a breath. 'Show me your arm.'

Meri obligingly bared her forearm. 'Can we come in? The Perilous are chasing us and we need to get to the Frobishers down at St Katherine's dock. They can vouch for us.'

Reluctantly the woman stepped back and opened the door the whole way. 'Come in then. Who's the other one?'

'My boyfriend. Please, let me explain inside.'

Meri felt a huge sense of relief once she was between four walls again. Kel followed but remained standing by the exit, uncertain of his welcome. Meri hated that he never felt at ease with her kind, but there were more urgent matters to sort out right now.

The houseboat had many windows, showing its origin as a floating restaurant taking tourists on pleasure cruises from Richmond to Windsor. Tables and chairs had long since been removed and the cabin converted to a comfortable sitting room decked out in white and blue. A seagull painted on a bleached board hung over the entrance, giving the vessel its name: Gull's Nest.

'What are you called, lass, and what's Tea and Sympathy got to do with you?' asked the old lady. She pointed to a window seat, inviting Meri to sit down. 'I don't recognize you from the meetings.'

'I'm Meredith Marlowe. He's Kel Douglas. Do you know how to get in touch with the Frobishers? It would be quickest to ask them, or Big Ben. Just tell them you have Meri and Kel here and we need help.'

'Don't hold with phones.' The woman pulled some yellow curtains over the windows on the land side of the boat. 'Arm of the state, they are, pinning us all like beetles to specimen cards. Francis writes to me if he needs my opinion on something.'

'Are you the captain of this settlement then?' asked Kel.

'You know about that, do you? Yes, I am. Mary Magellan, though everyone round here calls me Ma.'

'Has Francis written to you recently?' asked Meri.

The lady went to a pile of unopened post on a ledge in her little kitchenette. 'Been away at my daughter's for a few days. Haven't got to this yet.' She leafed through. 'Why, yes he has.' With painfully slow ceremony, she opened the envelope with a knife, put on her glasses and read the contents. 'Oh my goodness: it's marked urgent.' Her gaze went first to Meri then with more doubt to Kel. 'Is this about you? The last Tean and her unsuitable choice of friend?'

'I don't know about unsuitable but will you help us?'

Mary nodded and tucked the letter in the pocket of her overall. 'Of course. It's what we all swear we'll do when we join the movement.' She tottered over to Meri and touched her hair reverently like she had never met anyone so precious before. 'I fell in love with a full-blooded Tean once when I was about your age. Never forgot him. He was a dashing young man, quite turned my head. Would've married him in a trice if he'd've had me but he wanted a girl with more Tean in her than me. I'm only an eighth.'

'He sounds a fool to me,' said Kel gallantly.

Mary shot him a grin. 'I can see why you fell for this one, Meredith Marlowe, even if he is one of them. So, what's all this about you being chased?'

Meri quickly filled Mary in on the events of the past few days, starting with her capture at New Year.

'They've put a watch on all the transport links?' asked Mary.

'By now, yes,' said Kel. 'They don't know where we're going but there's a high risk they'll know we've not yet left the area. The woman at the river bus might remember us if they get round to asking her.'

'Then we need to get you away as quietly as possible. Give me a moment. I'll get one of the younger ones to get a boat ready. You'll need your own transport and one of my grandsons moonlights as a river taxi driver—don't tell the taxman.'

'His secret is safe with us,' promised Meri.

'And I'll ask my son-in-law to call Big Ben. They know each other from a little smuggling operation in which they both have a share.'

Meri smiled at Kel. 'We've fallen among a bunch of pirates, haven't we?'

'Free traders,' corrected Mary. 'That goes back in my family far longer than even the Tean inheritance. Wait here a moment. And young man, for heaven's sake, sit down. I'm not going to hurt you.' She changed slippers for ankle boots and left the cabin.

Obeying the captain's orders, Kel sat next to Meri. 'I was rather more concerned that she would think I'd hurt her.'

'Don't worry about that. Ma Magellan strikes me as pretty indestructible. How old do you reckon she is?'

'Ninety at least. Her grandson might well be a pirate pensioner already.'

'I'm hoping he's more of a capable young Jack Sparrow sort.'

'Doesn't Jack's boat sink in every film they make?'

Meri wrinkled her brow. 'Not in part sixteen if I remember rightly. Theo loves those films.' Her expression crumpled as worry returned to her.

Kel hugged her to him. 'Don't worry: Theo'll be all right.'

'I hope so. I'm trusting a lot in your people being decent at the bottom of everything.'

For a person possibly in their tenth decade, Ma Magellan proved capable of moving quickly once she had made up her mind. She returned with her son-in-law and grandson, both raised as river men used to hard work and with the muscles to prove it. The older one was already talking on a phone.

'There they are,' Ma Magellan said without preamble, gesturing to Meri and Kel.

'Thanks, Ma.' The man held out the handset. 'Big Ben wants a word.'

Meri took the phone.

'Lil'chick?'

'Yes, Big Ben.'

'Your boy got word to us that you were in trouble so we've had time to get an evacuation organized. You get your-self to the landing stage at north end of Tower Bridge and we'll be waiting for you. Got a way out of England for you.'

'Tower Bridge?' Meri directed the question to the grandson who gave a thumbs-up. 'Yes, we can do that.'

'Thing is, it's for one person only, Lil'chick. Not the Perilous.'

'Then no deal.'

'Francis said you'd say that, but you have to understand that Kel won't be safe where you're going.'

'He's not safe here either since he sided with me. We're a package deal; I made that clear from the start.'

'We're not trying to be difficult; it's just that there are those who won't be convinced he's good news.'

'Ben? Package. Deal.'

He sighed. 'OK, Lil'chick. I had to try. See you at the bridge.'

Meri handed the phone back to Mary's son-in-law.

'Everything OK?' asked Kel.

'Nothing we can't handle together,' she said firmly.

'But he said....'

Meri put her finger to his lips. 'It doesn't matter. You've got to trust me. I'll keep you safe from my guys just as you did for me with yours.'

16

Kel had his doubts about the boat Ma Magellan called a river taxi. Its electric motor ran smooth and quiet, cabin lit with very low lighting: a smuggling vessel if ever there was one. Still, if it made the skipper happy to call it a taxi, then who were they to argue? The features that made it good for illegal operations also meant it was perfect for a getaway vehicle.

Sonny Magellan, a dark curly-haired man of few words, sat at the controls with his eyes narrowed at the river, concentrating on avoiding the many obstacles just under the surface.

'Tide's turning,' he said.

Meri hovered by his shoulder. 'Is that good?'

'Depends if the hunt is ahead or behind.'

Familiar landmarks of Westminster passed and they reached the heart of the city. The Thames was busy with river police patrols, water buses and private craft. Kel kept out of sight as much as possible, using a borrowed pair of binoculars to scan the shore.

'Ah.' Sonny took their speed down a knot or two.

'What?'

'Looks like the police are doing a spot search under London Bridge.'

Kel turned his binoculars ahead. Floodlights had been rigged in the centre arch and all craft were being funnelled towards the police checkpoint.

'They sometimes check for unlicensed water buses and taxis,' Sonny explained.

'Like you.'

'Yep. Like me. Though I usually get warning from a friend on the force. He gives me the heads-up to keep off the river.'

Kel focused on the nearest police boat. 'I think I can see Swanny on board. This isn't a coincidence. It looks like he's got friends in the force too.'

'Swanny? One of yours?'

'Yes. But, believe me, he will do anything to stop her.'

Sonny gave a brisk nod. 'Right then, I'll take us over to the south bank. A shallow bottomed vessel like mine can get between some of those buildings right into old Southwark. I can drop you there and you can get to Tower Bridge on foot.' Sonny pointed to the next bridge just after the one where the police were stationed. The two towers were lit up like a cathedral stretched across the waters: a tantalising glimpse of the last gateway before they escaped the city.

'Sounds like the best option. Meri?' asked Kel.

'Not like we have a lot of choice. Let's try it.'

Crouched out of sight as best she could, Meri held on to the side of the boat as it surged in a U-turn. Sonny took an inlet between high buildings and nudged the boat into the warren of flooded streets beyond.

'Good job the tide is high. Wouldn't be possible other-wise,' said Kel, coming to crouch beside her. He placed the binoculars in her lap in case she wanted a look.

'Old Stoney Street,' said Sonny. 'There's a back run here used by smugglers to what used to be Borough Market.'

'Handy.'

'Yeah. I can cut across the inlet where London Bridge station used to be and drop you at the pontoon leading to Tower Bridge. You'll have to make your own way from there as I can't get under that.'

Over on their right, the skyscraping spike of the Shard jutted into the night, dark now as the occupancy in this part of flooded south London had sunk as the tidal waters rose. It looked a little like a rotten tooth thanks to the blackening of the unwashed windows. As they gazed up, a military heli-copter appeared from right behind, heading for them. Searchlights danced underneath, crisscrossing the ground.

'I think they're on to us.' Meri shuddered. 'Someone must've seen us leave the river.'

Kel swallowed his dismay. Panic was no use now. 'We're almost there. Across the bridge and we're with reinforce-ments. Meri, trust me: we can do this. Sonny?'

'Yeah, yeah, I see it. Hold on. Gonna have to take a few chances.' Sonny shoved the throttle forward, picking up speed. He wove around the half-submerged street furniture —lampposts and signboards advertising products long since gone out of fashion. A hundred yards behind them, two speedboats roared into the shallow lagoon that had been the railway tracks. He swore. 'They're coming in hot. Get ready to disembark!'

Kel clutched Meri's hand, guiding her over to the side, putting himself between her and their pursuers. A sharp crack sounded from the rear and the motorboat's wind-screen shattered.

'They've guns!' yelped Meri. She hadn't really under-stood until this moment that they were serious about killing her if they couldn't capture her.

'Really? Never've guessed,' said Sonny. 'Fecking Perilous. Slowing in five....four...three...two...one...Go!'

Kel jumped onto the pontoon and reached back to give Meri a hand. 'Thanks, Sonny!'

'Take good care of each other!' With a wild grin, Sonny spun the boat in a circle, switched on some floodlights of his own, and drove straight at their pursuers, dazzling the pilots. One boat swerved and crashed into a signboard, turning over in a spectacular roll. Definitely reckless pirate stock, thought Kel, hoping their skipper didn't pay a high price for helping them. Kel didn't have time to see if there were any survivors from the wreck as the other craft was almost at the pontoon, several Perilous readying to jump the gap. He chased after Meri who hadn't looked back. He caught up with her as she kept sprinting towards the towers. Sirens sounded behind them as police cars raced along the pontoon some way off to the south.

'More friends...of Swanny's?' she panted as he drew level.

'Let's not stop and ask.'

The incline increased as they reached the old road surface.

'Got a stitch.' Meri clamped her hand to her side, but she didn't slow.

More lights came on, spotlighting them as they fled towards the north bank. Then Kel noticed the road was sloping even more than it had before.

'Meri, they're lifting the bridge!' That hadn't been done for years. The Victorian mechanism was judged too delicate to put through the strain of lifting the road as it once had to allow tall ships to pass under.

Meri put on a burst of speed. He felt so proud of her: she was really digging deep. 'Who's doing it? Friend...or foe?' she panted.

'No idea. But if we don't get across we'll be stuck.'

On the far side they could see a party advancing to meet them, a big man at their head.

'That's Ben!' said Meri.

'Lil'chick, you gotta fly quickly!' bellowed Ben. 'We're cutting them off!'

So it was the river people lifting the bridge! That was a good strategy, but only as long as they got the timing right. The crack in the roadway had widened to half a metre. They were almost there.

Then shots rang out behind them. Meri stumbled and fell.

'You're hit?' Kel dragged her up. He could see her left calf was bleeding.

'Bloody hell, that hurts.' She sucked in a pained breath. 'I think it just grazed me.'

'Can you walk?'

'Is there a choice?'

'Keep going. I'll hold them off.' Pushing her towards Ben, Kel spun round to face the Perilous. He was relying on the fact that they didn't want to kill him. At least, that was the hope. As long as he could stop them getting a clear shot, Meri should be able to get over.

'Remember...' gasped Meri, limping on. 'I'm not leaving without you.'

She would do what she had to do, Big Ben would make sure of that, thought Kel. 'Come and get me, you fecking cowards!'

The car from which the shot had come screeched to a halt, blocking the entry to the bridge. His father, Jenny and Ade emerged from the rear doors. Of course they had to be there for this, thought Kel grimly. Striding forward, his father raised his gun and aimed just past his son's head.

'Get out of the way, Kel.'

He spread his arms wide, making himself as big a target as he could. 'If you want to shoot an unarmed girl, then you'll have to do it through me, Dad.'

Not waiting for her brother to get clear, Jenny crouched, took aim and fired off two shots, Ade beside her took a single one, both trying to avoid him. Horror filled Kel that he might not have done enough to spoil their aim, but when he glanced over his shoulder, he saw that none had found their target. Meri had leapt the gap and disappeared into a huddle of people, shielded by Ben and his mates, leaving just the trail of blood from her earlier injury behind.

'Going to gun down a whole group of innocent people?' Kel asked bitterly.

'Who are those men?' asked Rill, lowering his weapon.

'Friends.'

'Of yours?'

'What does it matter?'

The bridge was still rising, making it hard to keep his feet.

'Kel!' called Meri. 'Come on! It has to be now!'

Rill holstered his gun. Even he wasn't prepared to fire into a crowd with so little chance of hitting his intended target. The Perilous could bend the law but not totally flout it. 'The Tean's right. You've got to choose before it's too late. Us or the people who killed your mother?'

Kel risked a look behind him. He could barely see Meri but he knew she was watching. She would be all right whatever happened, her new friends would make sure of that.

'Don't go, Kel. Stay with us,' pleaded Jenny. 'We're your family.'

'Kel, we can sort it out,' said Ade. 'Whatever you've done, you're still one of us.'

Meeting his father's eyes last of the three, Kel wanted to howl, punch something, do anything to relieve the tearing pain he felt. This was his final chance to go home with them.

But his choice was clear.

'I'm not one of you, not anymore.' Turning, Kel sprinted up the slope. His mind chipped in unhelpfully that it would be one pathetic failed exit if he got to the top and found the gap too wide. He'd jump anyway, he'd already decided that.

The split had reached three metres, not too far if he hadn't to battle against an incline. Pushing hard, he leapt, arching his back to carry himself forward. Big Ben was waiting on the other side, hands outstretched.

'Kel!' He didn't know if that was Jenny or Meri he could hear screaming.

His fingers missed Ben's hand by a whisker but he just managed to catch the edge of the road surface. He banged into the underside of the bridge and would've lost his grip if Ben hadn't dived and caught hold of his wrists. Using his considerable strength, Ben hauled Kel up onto the top.

Kel lay on his back, heart pounding. Rolling over he saw his father, Ade and Jenny watching from the other side, his sister pale with fear at the near miss. Seeing him safe, one by one they turned their back and walked away.

No regrets, Kel promised himself.

'Get a move on, lad, if you're coming. It won't take that lot long to get to the other side if they're determined to keep on chasing.' Ben set Kel on his feet and helped him along until they reached Meri.

'I could kill you for leaving it to the last moment!' Meri broke free of the men surrounding her and launched herself at Kel, hugging him and hitting his chest at the same time.

'That would rather defeat the object of me surviving.' He embraced her, careful of her injury. Someone had already bound it with a white bandage so it could keep for now.

'No time for that,' Ben broke in, interrupting their kiss before it got started. 'This way.' Swinging Meri up into his arms, he led them at a jog to the northern end of the bridge and down a flight of damp steps to a motor launch. 'Get on board.'

'How will you stop them catching us on the river?' asked Kel.

'Look over there.' Ben pointed to the string of barges that had emerged from their mooring spot at St Katharine's dock and now blockaded the Thames east of Tower Bridge. A sign rigged between the masts declared that they were running an impromptu winter fair. Londoners crowded on board, enjoying the live music, cheap food and drink the Tean Sympathizers were providing. 'I can't see anyone ramming those in full view of the public.'

Meri tucked herself close to Kel. 'And where are we going?'

'The captain's brought the yacht up from Gravesend. We are going on a little sea voyage.' Ben patted Meri's shoulder gently. 'Mabel was a doctor before she married Francis and joined the Sympathizers. She'll treat your injury.'

As they travelled on downstream, a huge white yacht

appeared around the next bend of the river, the kind of vessel billionaires used to party on board in Monte Carlo back at the beginning of the century. Sleek lines with solar panels and wind turbines on the topmost roof, it cut through the water coming directly towards them.

'Wow, who does that belong to?' asked Meri. She laced her fingers with Kel's.

Big Ben chuckled. 'You.'

'What?'

'If you're the last full-blooded Tean. That's part of your inheritance.'

'You're kidding? I can't believe it! I've no idea how to sail something like that. Does it come with a crew?'

'Of volunteers.' Ben gestured to the men who had come with him to the bridge and were now surrounding them on the launch, watching for pursuit. 'These are your crew.'

They looked a capable set but Kel wasn't keen on Meri sailing off into the unknown with anyone. 'And where exactly are we going?'

Big Ben grimaced. 'I suppose you'll have to know eventually. Remember that I warned you not to, won't you, Kel? The course is set for Atlantis.'

'Now you are joking.' Meri backed into Kel for support. 'Atlantis was destroyed.'

'Says who?'

'Well, legend for one.'

Ben grinned, gold tooth glinting in the lights of the waiting yacht. 'Then you're in for a bit of a shock, aren't you, Lil'chick? One full-blooded Tean, one Perilous: the islanders are just going to love that. I can't wait to find out how they take it.'

The implications of taking Kel to such a place struck

Meri hard. She turned to Kel. 'It's not too late. We can go ashore. Do this another way.'

Kel framed her face in his hands. 'It's your inheritance— your future. You should claim it.'

'Our future, Kel. We'll go together.'

'If you're determined, then you can take me into the arena, just as long as I have my Tean gladiator who reads the manuals with me.'

'Always.'

The motor launch drew up alongside the yacht. Taking care with her injury, Ben carried Meri on his back up the rope ladder to the deck of the yacht, Kel just behind them. The vessel had four decks so they had to go up another three sets of stairs to reach the control room. Like something out of NASA, it held a bewildering number of screens and switches. Francis Frobisher waited for them at what Kel took to be the wheel. His wife stood beside him, arms folded, no more friendly than she had been on last meeting.

'All clear?' the captain asked Big Ben.

'Got away by the skin of our teeth but yes.'

'Right. Good to have you both onboard. Has Ben told you the plan?'

Meri nodded. 'Yes, but not where Atlantis is exactly.'

'You realize it will be dangerous for you both? I could take you somewhere else, France maybe, and you could both disappear.'

'And do what? Live how? Always in fear, always on the run?' Meri shook her head. 'I don't want my life to be like that anymore. Kel agrees.'

Francis flashed his wife a quick grin as if Meri's reply had pleased him. Mrs Frobisher rolled her eyes at her husband. 'So which course shall I set, Meri? France, or the place we call our ancestral home: Atlantis?'

Meri looked up at Kel. He gave her a nod. 'Take us to Atlantis.'

'I hoped you'd say that.' With a flourish, Francis gave the order for the engines to be started. 'I've always wanted an excuse to go.'

'You mean you've never been?' asked Kel.

Francis shook his head. 'No, far too dangerous.' He patted the console. 'I hope you like your yacht. The island leaders sent it to fetch you once they heard of your existence. I thought it might come in useful when I got your message earlier.'

'It's very impressive,' then she added in an undertone for Kel, 'but not exactly me.'

Ken helped Meri onto a high stool while Mrs Frobisher fetched a medical kit. They gazed out the window of the control room, keeping out of the way of the busy crew setting sail under the stars. London disappeared behind them, leaving just a smudge of light on the horizon.

'I hope you're ready for an adventure?' Meri asked.

'The adventure started when I first saw you.' Kel ran his hands over her shoulders, urging her to relax. They were safe—well, almost. There was a lot still to do: Theo to save, Meri to make secure, their future to settle, but for the moment they had reached a place where the Perilous could not get to her and he could briefly drop his guard.

She turned her head to look up at him. 'It's been a roller-coaster, but I'm pleased you're here with me now. It's going to be OK.'

She couldn't promise him that—and it wouldn't be her fault if things went wrong. 'I wouldn't get off the ride even if I could. I say we should sit in the front carriage and make the most of it.'

She smiled. 'Like sitting at the front of the bus?'

'Exactly.' He bent down, brushing her hair away from her eyes. 'So we're a Perilous-Tean couple—the first in history.'

Meri stroked his face. 'It's time the world moved on. I think we're up to that challenge.'

ABOUT THE AUTHOR

Joss Stirling is the author of the best-selling *Savants* series. She was awarded the Romantic Novel of the Year Award in 2015 for *Struck*, the first YA book to win this prestigious prize.

A former British diplomat and Oxfam policy adviser, she now lives in Oxford.

For more information, please visit
www.jossstirling.co.uk

ALSO BY JOSS STIRLING

Savants series

Finding Sky

Stealing Phoenix

Seeking Crystal

Misty Falls

Angel Dares

Summer Shadows

Struck series

Struck

Stung

Shaken

Scorched

Printed in Great Britain
by Amazon